Danger's Last Resort

by

Joanna Sheen

Victoria Farm Press Ltd.

This edition published 2015 by Victoria Farm Press Ltd,
Stokeinteignhead, Devon TQ12 4QH
www.victoriafarmpress.co.uk
ISBN 978-0-9926844-6-4

Printed and bound in Great Britain by:
Maslands Printers Ltd of Tiverton, Devon.

Set in Minion Pro.

I have to dedicate this story to my Mother – Diana Hatherly – I know it is just the kind of story she likes reading. Love you x

Acknowledgements

A big thank you to everyone that has helped and supported
me with the book – to all the beta readers, Richard, Pippa, Emily,
Penny, Jo and Kate. Thank you all and a big thank you to Sue,
the editor, you helped so much thank you!

Also to Andy and the team at Maslands,
you are superstars and I am so grateful!

Other books co-written by Joanna Sheen with Julia Wherrell
A Sticky End (Swaddlecombe Mysteries Book 1)
A Violet Death (Swaddlecombe Mysteries Book 2)
A Fowl Murder (Swaddlecombe Mysteries Book 3)

Chapter 1

"Smarmy weasel, greedy, grubby, stupid old man, I hate you, your hotel *and* your job." Rose smacked her hand against the steering wheel, then winced when it hurt. She had worked hours and hours of unpaid overtime since taking the job as junior manager at the Castle Hotel, and still he asked for more. She would give anything for a new job, a new boss and – with any luck – a better pay packet at the end of the month!

Rose indicated left and turned into the driveway of her parents' home. The little lodge lay in the shadow of a manor house, the grounds of which had been a second home to her throughout her childhood.

She slammed the solid oak back door with rather too much force. Her mother sat hunched over the table, and jumped as the noise reverberated around the kitchen. "Since when did temper tantrums work for you or anybody, young lady?" Pearl's usually immaculate dark brown curls were flattened, and her eyes puffy.

"What's wrong Mum?"

"Dorothy had a heart attack in the early hours of this morning and she passed away." Pearl sobbed as the final words came out. "She was such a lady and I just loved working for her up at the manor." Tears fell onto her flowered apron as she fished into the front pocket for a handkerchief.

Rose joined her at the table, her vision suddenly blurry. "She was getting on, but wasn't that old by today's standards, surely? I'll miss her desperately." She gazed out of the kitchen window at the garden she had spent many happy childhood years exploring and enjoying.

They sat in silence. Rose took her mother's hand and held it tightly. "Dorothy was like an extra aunty to me. I remember long cosy evenings sitting by her fire – she told wonderful stories and taught me so much. I'm sure I got my dream of travel from her; she'd been everywhere, and described the places and people brilliantly."

Pearl bit her lip in an effort to stop crying. "Running the house was never just a job, it felt like being there for a family member and best friend. Ted never minded taking her around between taxi jobs, either – she was always so sweet and grateful. He'll miss her too."

"Put the kettle on. I'm sure you've had loads of tea, but an extra one never hurt." Pearl was famous for her endless cups of tea: a cure-all for everything. The doorbell chimed as Rose reached into the fridge for some milk. "I'll get it."

A grey-haired gentleman in a smart suit stood at the door. His face was as grey as his hair, and he was obviously troubled. "Good afternoon. Rose, I presume?" Rose nodded, wiped her eyes and tucked a stray strand of long blonde hair back behind her ears.

"John McKay, Dorothy Wilson's solicitor. I wonder if I could have a moment – and perhaps your parents are home?"

"Why of course, do come in. I've only just heard; you must forgive us if we're a bit quiet."

"I too am terribly sad; Dorothy was a life-long friend as well as a client. My wife and I will miss her greatly."

They walked through the small but immaculate hallway to the kitchen. Pearl was startled at the sight of a stranger in her home. "Mum, this is John McKay, Dorothy's solicitor – he wants to talk to us. When will Dad be home?"

"Not for a while, he had a job taking him up to Exeter airport, and with it being rush hour and all that... How do you do, Mr McKay?"

"Delighted to meet you Mrs Hill."

"Oh – please call me Pearl."

"Tea or coffee Mr McKay? Milk, sugar?" Rose busied herself pouring water onto teabags in mugs. "Tea, no sugar, would be perfect thanks." John McKay placed a worn leather briefcase on the small kitchen table and pulled out a chair. Rose found herself sniffing again, and apologised.

"Please, believe me, my wife is in the same state; it's such a sad loss. Dorothy was very fond of you all. She would talk about you, Rose, with such pride – as if you were her own granddaughter – and Pearl – she told my wife that she simply couldn't cope without you."

Pearl bent over her tea and a large tear dropped into the chintzy mug. "Sorry, I was trying to help." He smiled weakly, feeling a little awkward.

"It helps knowing she was as fond of us as we were of her," replied Pearl. "I remember Rose's graduation: Dorothy sat next to me and squeezed my hand when they called out 'Rose Hill'. She was as proud of Rose as we were."

This last comment had Rose grabbing a tissue from the sideboard as her tears began to flow freely. It had been a wonderful day when she graduated from Southampton with a degree in Business Studies. Seeing her parents and Dorothy in the crowd, looking proud, had made her feel so happy.

"Lovely though this tea is, I must tell you why I'm here. Dorothy considered her funeral quite extensively, especially recently, and she has left full instructions about the hymns, prayers and order of service. She has also decreed that she wants the will to be read out to all parties involved, immediately after the funeral instead of a wake."

"That seems sad, I could've done a special spread for her." Pearl blew her nose loudly and frowned. Cooking for other people had been her life-long mission. Her family were very aware that she often equated happiness with food, clean plates and treats.

"I think she had a motive for her instructions. Dorothy rather fancied herself as a stage director and wanted a little bit of drama, which – knowing her relatives – there's bound to be!"

"If there's no food to organise, how will we be involved? We're allowed to come to the funeral, please, it means a lot to us?" Rose felt quite panicked at the thought of being excluded from saying goodbye to someone she had loved deeply.

"She has specifically requested that you and several other friends attend the reading of the will together with the family. That alone should cause a little scene or two, but my wife Kathleen will be there and will sit with you."

"Oh!" cried Pearl and Rose in unison. They frowned at each other. Mother and daughter both had dark blue eyes and high cheekbones, but that was where the similarity ended. Rose was a natural bubbly blonde with enviably long legs and a fabulous figure. Pearl at sixty-one was the perfect advertisement for a cuddly mother figure, her dark brown curls arranged in the same style that she had worn for some thirty years or more.

"I'll drop off the details of the venue and date of the funeral in the next couple of days. I would also be very grateful, Pearl, if you could make sure the house is clean and tidy for the next incumbent. I would hate anyone to make a comment about the cleanliness. I have removed the contents of her safe and other bits that might be 'borrowed' by her nephews and nieces."

"Of course, I'd hate it not to be perfect – I remember some of her family, very clearly." Pearl's already grim expression turned just a little darker at the memory.

* * * * *

Ted Hill put a comforting arm around his wife and daughter as they walked down the path away from the cemetery. The trio made a sad sight; they all wore the traditional black and Pearl had chosen a large black hat that she favoured for such occasions.

"I feel empty inside," Rose sniffed quietly.

"I know dear, us too," said Pearl.

They climbed into Ted's taxi, his office, his pride and joy and his way of keeping a roof over their heads. Cars had always been his passion, and when they'd saved enough for the deposit on a suitably reliable model he had been determined to make a go of being a taxi service. He specialised in airport runs but just as happily took elderly ladies to the library or shops, and was always the perfect gentleman.

"I wish we didn't have to go to this will reading," said Pearl. "I feel out of place and it all seems old fashioned and rather melodramatic."

"We already have the best legacy, my dear, the memories we have of her laughing, our times together and the great advice she gave our family over the years."

Rose bit her lip and concentrated on the upholstery, trying to stem the flow of tears. "Don't start me off again Dad. It hurts so much that I can't share problems with her or discuss life in general any more."

"You'll have to make do with us, girl!" he replied with a wry laugh, revealing a remarkable set of white teeth. For a moment he seemed younger than his sixty-five years. His hair had the odd strand of grey but – as is often the case with men – it only served to make him look more distinguished as opposed to older!

"I'm sorry – I didn't mean… you know what I meant." Rose smiled at her parents. She was aware how lucky she was to be part of such a strong and loving family unit. She had been told many times what a longed-for baby she had been, arriving after Ted and Pearl had given up hope.

They pulled up outside the solicitor's offices and Ted parked in a space reserved for visitors near the main door. As they were about to get out there was an irritated knocking on the driver's window.

"I say my man, could you move your car? We have an important meeting here and you may not realise it but this is a space specifically reserved for clients, if you would." With this the man marched off and climbed into his Mercedes, revving the engine impatiently.

Ted's mouth opened and shut like a fish, and it was Pearl that broke the silence. "I think it would be better to park further away. Today shouldn't be an arguing day." He opened his mouth to disagree, but the look on Pearl's face silenced him.

They carefully reversed and the Mercedes whooshed past. It just missed them as a Range Rover nearly beat it to the spot, the woman driver hooting fiercely. She wound down her window and screamed abuse at the driver of the Mercedes. Pearl and Rose ducked down in their seats as Ted drove to the nearby public car park.

Rose's giggle broke the silence. "You know who they were, don't you?"

"I do indeed," replied Pearl, "Dorothy's dear and loving family." She too couldn't hold back a splutter of laughter. "Come on – let's get this over with."

As they entered the reception area a loud argument was in

full swing. It seemed the Mercedes and Range Rover drivers were equally unhappy about their parking combat.

"Ladies and gentlemen! Attention, please LADIES AND GENTLEMEN!" John McKay was standing at the bottom of the staircase. "If you would follow me we have a room reserved upstairs."

"If I get a parking ticket I'm sending it to you Seth – you could see I was there before you and you deliberately blocked me, shameful behaviour."

"Amelia, despite your best beliefs, the world does not revolve around you and your children and no: you were not there first. Some little oik had taken the spot and I had to clear the way."

"Seth, dear." A tall slim woman standing next to Seth nudged him firmly and nodded in the direction of Ted and his family.

"Bloody Nora, John old chap – what the hell is this? Are you selling tickets to Aunty's flippin' will reading, couldn't resist making an extra buck or two?"

"Ladies and gentlemen, all of you…" John emphasised the word 'all', and shot a smile at Pearl. "If you could cease hostilities for five minutes and decamp to the meeting room?"

They all trailed up the stairs, Seth and his wife taking a very firm first place in the procession. Ted, Pearl and Rose held back, and followed Bert Cullum, the gardener. They sat down and were soon joined by a silver-haired lady with a beautiful smile. "I'm Kathleen McKay, we can all sit together!"

Rose felt annoyed at these rude people, but also a little overawed by the whole process. Everyone sat down and John McKay stood at the front, an assistant seated beside him.

"Good afternoon ladies and gentlemen. My apologies for this meeting; it was not my idea but that of Dorothy Wilson, the deceased. Perhaps you'll allow a little patience for the whims of an elderly lady."

"Nutter towards the end, never knew what day of the week it was." Seth looked bored. Rose had to bite back a reply that Dorothy had indeed known every day of the week, but since her nephew had got the day wrong when he last visited on the scrounge and had interrupted Dorothy's plans, possibly he was the nutter – but she said nothing.

"Just check that everyone is here please, Sophie," John McKay nodded at his assistant as he sat down.

"Yes sir," she replied, holding up a sheet of paper. "If I call your name perhaps you could raise your hand?"

"Oh for heaven's sake – what a ridiculous pantomime! Proof surely the woman was demented." Range Rover Amelia flicked her expensively bleached hair and looked as though she was being made to attend an event in the worst possible taste.

The young assistant calmly read the instructions (perhaps Dorothy's solicitors were enjoying the performance?). "At the reading of my will I would request the following people in attendance: Seth Wilson my nephew and his dear devoted wife Serena, assuming they're both still together of course."

A ripple of astonishment passed round the group. "That is just the last straw." Seth stood up and made to leave until his wife took hold of his elbow and muttered, "Quiet Seth, just shut it." He sat down and raised his hand half-heartedly.

"My niece Amelia and her husband Neil, preferably without the dreaded Tarquin and Sandiego or John will have the worst job being heard above the ruckus."

"How rude," muttered Amelia, raising her hand. Her husband remained silent as always.

"My gardener Bert and my dear neighbours and friends Ted, Pearl and of course little Rose. Finally my dearest friends John and

Kathleen McKay." All those mentioned raised their hands except John, who probably felt his attendance was taken as read.

John stood up again and cleared his throat. "Dorothy has asked that I read her will in full, just as she wrote it, and she wishes you all to remain seated until I have finished. Should there be any arguments or disagreements, she left a second will to be brought into play, under which her entire estate is to be left to the RSPCA."

All those present gazed at each other, some horrified, others smiling. Kathleen had to raise a hand over her mouth to prevent a giggle escaping. Rose felt grateful that she was sitting with them. John pushed his glasses further up his nose and looked around expectantly to see if there were any comments. You could have heard a pin drop.

"I, Dorothy Wilson, being of sound mind – despite my family's opinions – and good health for one of my age will distribute my estate as follows:

"To my brother's son Seth Wilson, I leave the family estate agency business. I assume Seth will have been expecting this and in all fairness his father put a tremendous amount of effort into it before he passed on. Whether it'll continue to flourish under Seth's guidance remains to be seen but perhaps if he chooses to listen to his wife Serena, who talks a tremendous amount of sense on a good day, it may stand a chance. I would suggest that Serena remains on the board but will leave that to Seth's discretion."

Seth sat ramrod straight as this was being announced and was obviously pleased with his catch. He cast a supercilious glance around the room. "I'm the eldest nephew, it was pretty cut and dried." Amelia seemed a little disappointed but Neil, her husband, remained silent.

"My jewellery I leave to be split amicably between Serena and Amelia, and I would hope they can come to some agreement. I have taken one valueless piece out of the collection and left it with further instructions for John.

"To my sister's daughter Amelia Wilson-Lawrence, I leave the manor house here in Devon and the three letting properties in Portsmouth, to do with as she sees fit. Neil I assume as an accountant can give her good advice; whether she'll listen to it is another matter. I also leave Tarquin and Sandiego Wilson-Lawrence, my great nephew and niece, a college fund of £100,000 each in the event they attend university. Should they choose to skip such mundane pastimes, the fund reverts to the RSPCA."

Amelia started smiling as the bequest was read out but her expression went from delight as she inherited the family's massive house to indignation as the proviso on the children's college fund was announced. "That's ridiculous – poor Tarquin really finds it hard to sit still and read – university may just not be right for him!" Neil placed a restraining hand on her arm and she stopped speaking.

"Bert Cullum, my dear friend and excellent gardener, I'm very grateful for your help and loyalty and I'll rest easy knowing I pass the garden down to Amelia in perfect health. Whether Mrs Wilson-Lawrence chooses to retain your services I cannot dictate, but she would be a fool not to. In recognition of your hard work, I leave the sum of £20,000 on the proviso that at least some of it is spent on visiting your son and family in Australia and buying your wife a proper engagement ring, which has long been a dream of yours.

"Ted, dear Ted, you have always refused any payment for your taxi services taking me here, there and everywhere and you have been a loyal friend, to you I leave the sum of £80,000."

At this point the relatively peaceful gathering was split by a furious "I say, that's not on, ridiculous waste of our money" from Seth as he shot to his feet, his face bright red.

"Do you have a problem, Mr Wilson?" enquired John. Seth's wife whacked his arm and dragged him down into his seat while hissing at him to shut up, no doubt in panic about the potential loss of their inheritance.

John coughed before continuing. "Now where was I, yes Ted… I leave you the sum of £80,000 which I hope you'll spend not on a family expense, but follow your dream and get down to that Jaguar garage and buy the car we spent many happy journeys discussing, please: for me?"

John looked up – as did the entire group – as two large tears rolled down Ted's cheeks. Kathleen leaned over and took his hand.

"My Pearl, now what should I leave you, when in all honesty you have been the best friend and supporter anyone could want?" At this point Seth once again looked fit to burst with indignation and muttered under his breath, interrupted only by surreptitious kicks from his wife.

John gave them a pointed look and received murderous glares in return. "Pearl: I felt the most enjoyable legacy for you would be my collection of designer handbags. We giggled often about my guilty pleasure and you took great care of them, always thinking you would never have such treasures yourself. I no longer have need of them, so I leave you all the contents of my wardrobe and trunks…"

Now it was Amelia's turn to stand and exclaim. "That is completely out of order! Aunty knew I always wanted those, we discussed it often. They're worth thousands, it's not right for them to be left to a cleaning woman!" Rose wondered how Dorothy and Amelia could have discussed anything 'often' as Amelia had visited rarely, but kept that thought to herself.

"If you would sit down, Mrs Wilson-Lawrence." This time it was her husband Neil's job to pull her back into her seat. "… the contents of my wardrobe and closets. I'm fully aware of the value on the secondhand market of some of my designer pieces, both clothing and handbags. I want you to derive the maximum from your inheritance, Pearl, and so I have asked John to make a full inventory of my cupboards as at his last visit, to ensure other members of the family don't steal items to which they're not entitled."

Pearl suppressed a smile, not just from the thrill she would get from owning such exotic treats, but also at Amelia's obvious discomfort as she attempted to push her handbag under the chair with her feet. John looked at Amelia and raised an eyebrow, but she feigned indifference.

"Right, surely that's it with all the ridiculous oddments." Seth stood up and John glared at him even more ferociously. "I made it quite plain, sir, that you were required to remain seated until I had finished and no, there is a little more."

Rose thought how kind it was of Dorothy to understand everyone's dream and how happy her parents would be with their gifts. Her thoughts were interrupted by a dig in the ribs from Kathleen at the mention of her name.

"Rose, my little Rose," John was continuing, "you have been the granddaughter I never had, we shared a special connection and I have followed your life closely and loved being part of it. I hope I might have been able to help solve some problems when you came to me and you certainly gave me a reason to feel life was wonderful on many occasions. To you I leave a special part of my life, my beloved Summer House on the island of Barbados. As I haven't visited the property for a while, I'm not sure of the state of repair and so I'll leave a fund to help with any changes, should you want to stay there. It will also cover a plane ticket for you to see it and make your decisions. I would also point you towards an excellent carpenter named Soli Wilkes should you need shutters fixing or more."

"Probably a ridiculous little hut that's falling to pieces if my experience of Barbados is anything to go by. Aunt Dorothy was obsessed, spent far too much time on holiday over there doing nothing useful," Seth muttered at Selena and she nodded. "To be honest there was little I liked about Barbados, the southern corner where we stayed was adequate but really much of the island was substandard."

Amelia turned and whispered to Neil, "What are the property values on Barbados anyway?"

"Very low and falling from my scant knowledge," he replied quietly. "The father got the best lump there, nothing for us to lose sleep over."

"So that concludes the bulk of the will," continued John. "There are some legacies to local churches and other charitable donations. The remaining funds include a small holiday allowance for myself and my wife for which we're very grateful, bills, commitments and of course any remaining taxes."

There was a pause, then several conversations started at once.

"It was obvious that the family firm was to be mine, darn lot of work gone into that over the years."

"Indeed dear, but not by you possibly," Serena smiled and Seth looked mutinous. "I feel sure we'll expand and continue healthily over the next few years with some sensible input. I feel comforted that Dorothy suggested I remain on the board, an excellent idea. Come along, I want to sort my share of the jewellery before that ghastly Amelia gets her hands on it."

"So will we rent those properties or sell, Neil?" asked Amelia. "We really don't want to lose all that money in some awful property slump, the big house will need a fair amount of upkeep. Should we keep a gardener? I guess so, I hate gardening myself and you are never home." As was the norm, Neil just nodded while Amelia continued her one-sided conversation. "Perfectly horrible of Aunty to threaten our two angels with poverty unless they go to university, we'll have to try and argue that one."

"Yes my dear," replied Neil.

Rose's only communication was to say "Wow" to her mother.

John McKay raised his voice over the hubbub, "Thank you everyone for your time. I'll be in touch over the coming weeks and months to organise the legacies as there will be probate and taxes to sort out. Could I just ask Rose and her family to stay behind to speak to me?"

The belligerent family members left, grumping and groaning about how little they had achieved from this meeting (despite having been bestowed millions), while Bert just sat twisting his cap between his hands, shaking his head in wonder. Ted had stopped mumbling 'flaming Nora' under his breath for a few minutes, and Pearl's smile was huge and could barely be measured.

Rose wasn't sure how she felt: what a brilliant yet possibly frightening gift. She had been to Europe and once on a long-haul flight to New York when she and a group of girlfriends had bagged a budget shopping weekend deal in the paper. What could she do with a house in Barbados, what state would it be in, and how do you cope with property far away?

"Come over and sit down," said John pulling out a chair. "I'll go and organise some teas and coffees with the girls," offered his wife.

"Marvellous Kathleen, I could do with a cuppa!" John looked at the Hills. "So I'm guessing there were some happy surprises amongst those bequests for you?"

"I'd have been over the moon with the tiniest of tokens from her," said Pearl. "Material goods will never replace the companionship I have lost, or fill the gap in my life without having her to look after. I have to be honest and say I'd rather clean the

14

local school or some other place than work for Amelia and her family when they move in!"

"Dorothy wished you all the greatest happiness that she could bestow and she hoped she had got her plans right."

"Whether I can bring myself to buy a Jag with all that money I really can't say." Ted shook his head as he spoke.

"It'll take me a while to sort and release funds, let's wait and see how events unfold."

Rose summoned up her courage and took the plunge. "Mr McKay, I do feel overwhelmed being left this house in Barbados. I'm sure Dorothy meant well but how will I administer it or visit? My funds are going to be limited for a long while yet. I've finished the post-grad management course now, but I'm still very junior at work and the wages are quite small, complete rubbish really for what they get me to do."

"Please call me John; we may have quite a few opportunities to get to know each other better in the not-too-distant future. The first item I wanted to talk to you about was the fund that Dorothy and I organised to help with your project. It's in two parts: I can advance funds almost immediately to get things underway. This involves flight and accommodation for us to do a site visit, and should more be needed there is a larger trust fund available."

"Oh sweetie, what fun, you can have a holiday in Barbados and get some sunshine and smiles. I'm sure Mr McKay will be a good tour guide!" Pearl hugged her daughter.

"My wife will also be travelling with us. We were lucky enough to get the legacy of holiday trips to Barbados for several years, and Kathleen would love to come too."

"I could add some of my funds from the car," Ted added looking at Pearl, "if you want to go too?"

"No, let's take everything slowly. Mr McKay and his wife will look after Rose for this trip. It sounds as though there might be some official bits and pieces to sort out, and we don't want to get in the way."

"Probably a wise move, there may be plenty more opportunities. Now Rose, when do you think it might be convenient for you to take a few weeks' holiday from work?"

"I haven't a clue! Could you bear with me – I guess I could ring and ask what the situation is?"

John nodded. "Perhaps you would care to use a telephone in my office? I wouldn't mind a chat with your parents for a few moments."

As if on autopilot Rose walked into his office, where the assistant handed her a phone. Behind her she could hear her parents and John talking in low tones. She sat in a leather-studded chair beside the partner's desk and dialled the main reception office of the Castle Hotel, where she was the junior manager.

"Yes I know it's inconvenient Mr Fenton, yes… I know I'm not usually allowed two weeks' holiday at this time of year, yes sir, but it's important to me and I'd do my best to make up for it upon my return." Rose could imagine his dirty fingernails raking through his greasy black hair as he sat with his feet up on a cluttered desk.

"No sir, I couldn't wait another two or three months before taking the holiday." Rose felt a tidal wave beginning to rise up inside her. They had treated her appallingly; she'd worked hundreds of hours of unpaid overtime, and had been dog-tired for months.

"No I'm sorry sir, if that's the case I'll have to tender my notice, obviously I'll work the month to help you find a replacement."

She moved the phone away from her ear in response to a shrill cacophony of swear words. When it ended with "We'll forward your pay to date and P45", she replied, "Thank you sir," in a quiet voice.

What on earth have I done, she wondered?

Chapter 2

"Damn rude, that's what I say it is, ruddy solicitor!" Ted paced up and down while Pearl sat at the kitchen table with her hands curled around a mug of coffee.

Rose stood by the toaster waiting for it to pop up. She was dressed comfortably for a long journey, in jogging bottoms, flip-flops and T-shirt, with a sweatshirt tied around her waist in case she got cold during the flight. Her curly blonde hair was tied back with a favourite scarf and carefully chosen, easy-care clothes filled the rucksack on the floor by the table. Rose had experience of several flights (albeit mainly to Europe), but always with the cheaper airlines where checking in a suitcase was extra cost and a nuisance as you had to wait for hours beside an ever-circling luggage carousel at your destination.

"Dad, he wasn't being rude; he explained that the car collecting me came with the price of my ticket and he didn't want to cost you the petrol to get me to the airport. Now come and drink your coffee. Toast?"

Ted sat down grudgingly and nodded to signal that he did indeed want toast. There was a firm knock at the front door. He leapt up from the table, obviously intent on criticising whichever innocent taxi firm had been given preference over his own services. However, Rose beat him to it. "I'll get it – drink your coffee Dad."

Stood on the doorstep was a uniformed chauffeur, and as Rose peered past him she saw a black stretch limousine parked outside the front gate. "Transport for a Miss Rose Hill?" The chauffeur raised his eyebrows.

"I erm... yes, that's me, one moment." Rose couldn't quite decide what to make of a limo arriving; it seemed a huge extravagance, and surely cost as much as the plane ticket. As it was all out of her hands, she shrugged and called to her parents. "Dad, Mum, the taxi, I mean... umm... car is here."

Ted marched out of the kitchen, probably assuming it was a substandard taxi firm and feeling the need to check the vehicle. He stopped next to Rose when he saw the chauffeur.

"Perhaps I could start loading the luggage, Madam?" The chauffeur peered around the hallway, no doubt expecting piles of suitcases. Pearl emerged from the kitchen, holding her daughter's rucksack, and laughed. "Oh dear Rose, you're going to be a bit of a disappointment. Here you are!" She handed over Rose's rucksack and the chauffeur's eyebrows progressed further up his forehead. Pearl hugged her daughter and they both giggled.

"Have fun darling," Pearl squeezed Rose tightly. "Ring me or email whenever you can, we'll be longing for news." Ted hugged her too, both parents suddenly looking suspiciously dewy-eyed.

Rose was sad to be leaving them behind, but it was only for a week or two; and she felt excited, if somewhat anxious, about what might lie ahead. "Bye both and I'll keep you posted. I'd say check my Facebook posts and you'd see loads of pictures, but I guess you'll forget how to!"

Suddenly a loud and furious honking emanated from the driveway. The chauffeur and Rose turned round to see where the noise was coming from. Dorothy's niece Amelia sat in her Range Rover, face twisted in an expression of rage. Tarquin, her youngest child, was contorting himself out of the back window in an effort to see the limo in all its glory, and would have fallen out of the car had he gone much further. Sandiego his sister was pulling at his legs, demanding to be able to see.

The chauffeur turned to Rose. "Would it be convenient to leave now, Madam?" Rose grinned. "Yes of course, but no hurry." The chauffeur's professional countenance cracked and he nodded in understanding. He placed Rose's rucksack in the limo as though it were a designer suitcase and slowly walked over to the Range Rover.

"My apologies Madam, we'll be proceeding shortly. I'm sorry to cause you any inconvenience but due to the length of my vehicle I would ask if you could reverse your car out of the driveway, thus ensuring our departure with greater speed."

Rose couldn't hear exactly what Amelia replied but, judging from the changing colour of her face, she wasn't happy. "Bye Mum, bye Dad – sorry to dash but I wouldn't want the Wicked Witch of the West to get any greener!"

Both her parents laughed and waved as the chauffeur held open the door for her and she climbed into the limo. He opened the glass panel between them and politely enquired, with a slight smile, "A friend of yours Madam?" Rose giggled and decided she was going to love this new adventure.

"We'll be meeting up with Mr and Mrs McKay at Gatwick," he continued. "There's a choice of beverages in the fridge to your right and a small selection of snacks, including some excellent chocolate muffins that I personally recommend." He winked at her and closed the glass panel.

Rose was disappointed, as she would love to have chatted with him to make the journey go faster. But maybe it wasn't the done thing to talk to a chauffeur. She turned her attention to the snack cupboard, and the selection did indeed look fantastic. The drinks fridge was mainly filled with champagne which she had already decided to avoid for the flight. Not champagne specifically, but articles about long-haul flights always say avoid alcohol and she intended to do that. There was, however, a delicious-looking mango smoothie which she couldn't resist. She sat back in the seat with her smoothie and chocolate muffin and couldn't have felt more like a superstar if she had tried.

The glass panel was slid open again. "Excuse me Madam, I was checking you had woken up?" Rose blinked and realised she had been fast asleep. "Oh I'm sorry, I must have dozed off!"

"That's fine by me, shows you trust my driving! We're approaching the terminal at Gatwick, thought I should check on you."

Rose blinked, feeling sleepy and confused. Had she really slept for almost the whole journey? This was probably the only chance she would ever have to travel in a limousine and she had slept through most of it. Hastily she cleared away the empty bottle and swept away some crumbs, and tightened the scarf around her hair.

The car swept up to a small cordoned-off area beside Departures. Standing waiting were John and Kathleen McKay, which sent a warm feeling of confidence through her. It was nice to have two people to travel with.

The chauffeur opened the door and took her rucksack. "Shall I check this in for you, Madam?"

"No, I'll carry it on, thank you – and thank you for a smooth journey." Rose shook his hand and panicked about whether she should be giving him a tip, but saw John move forward and press a note into the chauffeur's hand.

Kathleen came over and gave her a hug, "Morning Rose, did you have fun in the limo?"

"Oh, the chocolate muffin was delicious and the smoothie out of this world!"

John and Kathleen exchanged a smile. "I'm glad you enjoyed yourself, let's get this check-in nonsense started and we could have an early lunch or a snack, maybe in the lounge?"

Rose was not listening. Being on a plane was always a treat for her, and she was getting excited. Her mother had offered to make her some sandwiches but she had a feeling food wasn't allowed through security, and no water bottle either (as she had found to her cost when she had gone to Italy with her friends last summer).

She lifted the rucksack onto her back and walked through the automatic doors towards the check-in desks. She was thrilled they were travelling with Virgin Atlantic: she'd heard they had brilliant films and, although she had a book with her, she could never read for long on a flight.

They approached the Economy check-in desks and the queue was long, but Rose shrugged it off as the normal part of taking a flight. Suddenly John darted off to the Upper Class area where a smiling uniformed lady welcomed him through. He turned and waved at Rose to hurry and join them. She hung back as queue jumping wasn't her 'thing', and they had plenty of time to catch the flight.

John was waving more urgently at her now and so she stepped forward towards the Upper Class area. A thirty-something young woman took her arm and held her back.

"Sorry love," she said in a slightly condescending voice, "that's First Class, to save you the embarrassment." The young woman moved past her and entered the cordoned-off area between her and John and Kathleen. She felt nervous; she didn't have a ticket, let alone an Upper Class or First Class one, she'd just been following John.

"She's with me." John took Rose's arm, shepherding her past

the 'helpful' young woman who now gave Rose a pitying glance, judging her on her accompanying an elderly man.

"John why are we in this area? I don't mind joining a queue, honestly!"

"Rose forgive me: I was following Dorothy's instructions. She didn't want you to know you were travelling First Class – she hoped it would be an exciting surprise for you. I see now that it might have been better to let you enjoy your surprise a day or two before you travelled!"

"First class – how exciting – and how sweet of Dorothy. I'm sorry – I never thought it might be important to dress appropriately… goodness… how embarrassing!"

"Not one bit Rose! Hold your head up high: you deserve your seat as much as all the others. Now come on, let's get checked in – do you want to check your rucksack in or take it as hand luggage?"

"To be honest I'd rather have it in the cabin with me. I've got my hairbrush, my dollars, and everything personal, I'd rather keep it with me if that's OK."

"Not a problem, let's get through security and get to the lounge – they do great food there!"

The ever-smiling young woman behind the desk processed their tickets quickly. It seemed John and Kathleen's cases had already been sent through, and before she knew it they were heading to the escalators. "Here's your ticket in case we get separated." They turned left to the separate fast-track security section.

Rose was smiling and shaking her head in disbelief when they came out at the other end in a matter of minutes. "That's a bit different, great to whizz straight through! I could get used to this Upper Class bit – what a treat. It's a shame I can't give Dorothy a hug to say thank you."

Entering the Virgin Atlantic Clubhouse was another eye-opener for Rose. There was a great view of the runway as well as a good-sized spa section, dining tables with menus, and comfy chairs. She was in seventh heaven.

"How hungry are you? Champagne? Cup of coffee? It's all complimentary Rose, have anything you fancy... Kathleen dear, champagne?"

"Go on," Kathleen replied with a smile. "I daren't have too many but it's such a special start to a holiday for me. You may have been to Barbados often, John, but it's a first for me!" She turned to Rose. "John accompanied Dorothy on trips for many years. If I didn't know differently I could accuse her of being the other woman!" She squeezed John's arm, and it was obvious they had a great relationship.

"Come on – let's have a bite to eat – and Rose, do ask at the spa if you want any of the treatments they offer, probably more your sort of thing than mine – I enjoy the view and the cappuccinos!" Rose felt it was like having a father to accompany her, although it was a bit strange having a holiday with such new 'friends'.

They sat at one of the small tables and had champagne (Kathleen) and coffees for Rose and John. Rose decided to have a wander round; the spa looked interesting, but would she have time for a treatment? As she returned to the table she overheard John and Kathleen's conversation.

"Step by step Kathleen, she's a strong young woman, but this would be a daunting discovery for the strongest of people. Dorothy felt she would be more than capable and I trust Dorothy's judgement implicitly."

"But John, she's still young, wouldn't it have been better to warn her, let her think about it, maybe bring her parents?"

"Blame Dorothy, not me." John looked up, noticed Rose nearby and flashed a glance at Kathleen to end the conversation.

"You found the cookie plate?"

"I most certainly did," replied Rose, wondering what he was covering up.

The flight was announced and Rose grabbed her rucksack. They headed towards Gate 19 and yet again were wafted past the queue and through the Upper Class line in moments. Shortly afterwards they announced boarding and another constantly smiling crewmember was soon showing Rose to her seat.

High on excitement, Rose pushed her rucksack into her own overhead locker: no pushing and shoving bags in competition with other passengers! The seat was a small cubicle, with a comfy-looking chair and a large footstool. She fished in the pockets beside her and found a duty free magazine, details of all the films (oh my goodness!) and a menu. A menu? Look at all the choices – she could get used to this! She flipped through the duty free offers but decided she would get presents for her parents on the island or on the return journey.

The next two or three hours seemed to waft past: a delicious meal, constant attention and a film she had been wanting to see for ages. Checking the screen she saw they were less than halfway through their eight-hour-plus flight, which felt a bit boring. Sitting still wasn't her favourite pastime!

She remembered that it was important to walk around during a flight, and with lots of space here in first class that wasn't a problem. She got up and stretched her legs, giving Kathleen a wave as she walked past. At the back of the cabin was a cocktail bar, which felt a bit surreal – as though they weren't on an aircraft at all.

Sitting at the bar was the young woman who had tried to direct her away from Upper Class when they were checking in. She gave an apologetic shrug when she saw Rose. "Sorry, love, interfering where I shouldn't as ever! I'm Cheryl, wanna come join me for drinkies?"

Rose hesitated. Cheryl had obviously been having 'drinkies' from the airport lounge onwards and she seemed more than a little tipsy, but hey, meeting new people was always interesting. "Sure, I'm Rose." She held out her hand.

Cheryl straightened up, "Watcha having, loadsa tequila on tap here, champagne, wharreva you want."

A crewmember popped up unobtrusively and asked Rose for her choice. "A sparkling water with lime or lemon for me – Perrier? If not club soda would be fine." She climbed up on one of the bar stools and swivelled it a bit; she wanted to remember this experience! Dorothy was a real fairy godmother for giving her such a special trip. "So, are you headed to Barbados on holiday too?" she asked.

Cheryl shook her head. "Nah, work for me but hey! What's not to love about work like this?" She took another gulp of champagne and continued. "Guess we might be kindred spirits, saw you and your bloke. I'm joining my boss Eric on the island, not exactly a portrait but no dog's dinner either. Older blokes have that added extra don't they, money! So what if we have to sleep with 'em to get the perks."

Cheryl lifted her glass as though to make a toast, and took a sip. Rose felt increasingly uncomfortable and didn't want to discuss her trip at all. "What exactly do you do?" she asked.

"Personal assistant – and damn good one at that, I might add! Eric's a hard taskmaster but we get results we do. Property deals, developments, marinas that kinda stuff."

"Oh that sounds interesting," Rose lied, thinking it sounded boring and remembering her manager at the hotel. She felt that bosses were often vastly overrated.

"Nothing gets past my Eric," continued Cheryl. "Slightest chance of a deal and he's there, complete sniffer dog. Managed to get a sweet deal last month, local guy desperate for money, got him to flog his granny's house for a quarter of what the land was worth – sucker! The world is full of suckers."

Rose now felt more than uncomfortable and wanted out of the conversation, but wasn't sure how to escape politely. In the nick of time she felt a hand on her shoulder and turned to see John behind her, shaking his head and pulling a face. Rose shrugged: she couldn't quite get his message.

"Missed you in your seat Rose, you coming back anytime soon?" said John. Rose felt confused, and then John inclined his head towards Cheryl. Rose understood he was rescuing her.

"Ah the lovebirds are at it." Cheryl sipped her champagne and waved goodbye as Rose slipped off the bar stool and walked back towards John and Kathleen's seats. John explained. "I heard what she was saying as I passed the bar. Believe me you do not want to spend a moment of your trip with her, nasty piece of work – as is, I suspect, her boss."

"That sounds as though you have met them before?"

"I believe I have by reputation, Rose. Not people you would ever want to get involved with."

"Her boss did sound unpleasant. Thank you for rescuing me."

Rose relaxed into her seat and lay back for a while with her feet up. There had to be some old TV programmes she could catch up with, or a film from the huge list she could choose from.

At long last the pilot announced over the intercom that they were beginning their descent into Barbados and gave them a weather update, which sounded perfect to Rose. It may have been inappropriate to dress in a T-shirt and flip-flops to travel Upper Class, but it would be refreshingly cool now that the temperature was on the rise.

Once the engines were switched off, Rose took her rucksack

from the overhead locker and filed in behind John and Kathleen as the passengers disembarked. As she walked out onto the stairs she was enveloped in a warmth that made her smile. She was surprised that they had to descend stairs and walk across the tarmac; she had envisaged a much more sophisticated airport for such a glamorous island.

Once through immigration and the McKays' luggage collected, John turned to her. "There should be someone waiting to collect us if all has gone to plan and we're on time."

"It is exciting," Kathleen was taking her cardigan off, "feeling that warm breeze and knowing it'll be the same tomorrow and the next day. I love home, but a bit more sunshine wouldn't go amiss!"

"I may look quite calm but I'm bouncing off the walls inside," replied Rose. "This is unbelievable – I have to keep pinching myself!"

They scanned the line of people meeting travellers and saw a sign saying 'John McKay'; all obviously had gone to plan. A steel band played outside the exit door of Arrivals and the warm, vibrant music served to intensify the unfamiliar yet friendly feeling of the island.

The driver smiled widely at John, his white teeth sparkling in the bright sunlight. He was over six feet tall and, judging from his physique, kept fit. His shirt was wonderful but extremely bright, featuring parrots and jungle life in brilliant rainbow neon colours. "Welcome back John, long time no see, the island missed you."

"Hello Ian, I missed you too. Let me introduce my wife, Kathleen," at which Ian shook Kathleen's hand enthusiastically. "And this is Dorothy's friend and protégé Rose Hill, she was especially fond of her."

Ian studied Rose critically. "Loving Miss Dorothy as we did, I believe you must indeed be a precious person." He pumped Rose's hand enthusiastically. "I have had the privilege of knowing Miss Dorothy all my life and a lovelier lady didn't exist on God's good earth. Now let's get out of this sunshine and into the car. I may be Barbadian but I'm not keen on the heat myself."

Rose loved Ian's open friendliness and felt herself relaxing into holiday mode. They climbed into a plain but serviceable black saloon car. Ian turned the air conditioning up and there was a collective sigh of pleasure as they cooled down.

John leant forward to talk to Ian. "Do you need to get back right now or could I ask for a slight detour round the island, to give Rose and Kathleen a feel of Barbados?"

"Nothing would please me more! There have to be some perks about your father being your boss and the garden can surely wait – maybe I offer a prayer that those weeds stop growing today."

John turned back to the women. "Ian is Edmund's son and Edmund was the main gardener for Dorothy. They became friends and she joined his family for Christmas one year. He still does the gardening, but Ian helps with most of the heavy work now."

Rose felt nonplussed. If must be a really big garden if it needed large amounts of manpower – but maybe they worked in other gardens too, and Dorothy had been one of many customers. Much as she loved flowers, her knowledge of plants and gardening was zero. Her father had kept their lawn under control and her mother was a dab hand with houseplants, but apart from that they could hardly be described as a green-fingered family!

Ian drove along roads bordered by beautiful trees and plants. He mentioned all the horticultural names, most of which went over Rose's head, but she remembered bougainvillea, bright colourful trails of hot pink and coral flowing over gates and through trees. She thought she recognised a bright red plant from some flowers her mother often had around Christmas, but didn't say anything as she was bound to be wrong. They turned a corner and there was a garden that was obviously much loved and tended and Ian pointed out a huge bush, virtually a tree, and said it was a poinsettia.

"I wondered if that's what it was. My mother has small plants in the house at Christmas but nothing in this league."

"It's a beautiful plant, and one of my favourites. We're lucky with the weather here, we get plenty rain and plenty sun, the perfect recipe for God's beauty, eh?"

As they drove over the crest of the hill the most breathtaking vista appeared with waves crashing onto rocks and a pure turquoise-blue sea sparkling in the sunshine. Kathleen pressed her nose to the window. "Oh my goodness! That is postcard perfect – John, do you have your camera?"

"Packed in the boot I'm afraid, but we'll have plenty of chances to take pictures in the days ahead."

Every few yards Ian would point out a house and give a short history, or talk about a church. There seemed to be some rivalry between the churches, with numerous denominations and sizes, and Ian was obviously proud of his Anglican upbringing.

They passed an old cigarette factory (where again Ian supplied much information), signs to a plantation, Gun Hill, and many different bays. Rose felt quite overwhelmed and was looking forward to taking some tours while she stayed with many interesting places to see. Ian explained too how most of the tourist activity took place on the western side of the island, on the Caribbean Sea, but the eastern side of the island was on the Atlantic Ocean and much greyer and less tourist-friendly.

"I do hope I might be able to ask you for hints and tips on places to see in the next week Ian. I think you must be a mini local encyclopaedia – it'll be fun exploring the island."

"Always Rose, you only have to ask."

Rose gasped in wonder as they approached the most beautiful display of bougainvillea. It resembled an Impressionist painting; the colours were wide ranging and the whole effect was stunning. As she stared at the glorious blooms, a small sign came into view: 'Summer House 2 miles'. She turned to John, and noticed Kathleen looking at them both. "There's a sign?" she said, puzzled.

"Yes, I… err… step by step Dorothy and I agreed…"

John's words trailed away and a much larger sign appeared – somewhat weathered and in need of repair, but a large sign nevertheless – proclaiming 'The Summer House, Five Star Accommodation'.

Rose stared at John uncomprehendingly. "The Summer House? I assumed it was a sweet little beach bungalow… this is Dorothy's Summer House?" They swung up a driveway and there before them was an enormous creamy-white colonial style building, with verandas running around each side and a wind-torn British flag flying at half-mast.

"Rose – this is the property Dorothy left you."

Chapter 3

Rose got out of the car. Her legs felt unsteady and a combination of shock and tiredness after the long flight was catching up with her even though they had all managed some sleep on the plane.

"I don't know what to say! This is all too much to take in."

"I fear yet again this is proof that Dorothy's idea of a fun surprise was all a bit too much, and I should have followed my instincts. However she was worried that you might say an outright 'no' and not even come over and see Barbados – that was the main reason for her plan. Bear with me, Rose; I'll try to scrap any more of Dorothy's carefully planned surprises. We'll sit down shortly and I'll explain it all."

Ian had taken all the McKays' suitcases out of the car, but no one appeared to come and help them. "Allow me." Ian grabbed two cases and took them into reception. Rose shouldered her rucksack and picked up the small third case, while John led the way in through the heavy studded oak door. Ian waved goodbye as he deposited the cases, and shook his finger at John when he went for his wallet.

The reception area had once been expensively decorated. An array of British coats of arms lined one wall and a suit of armour stood nearby. Surrounding these items were framed pictures of early twentieth-century Barbados, with scenes of Edwardian couples playing croquet on the lawn or enjoying a game of tennis. Times had changed and, it seemed, the fortunes of the hotel too. There was a side table that had seen better days. A pile of disorganised leaflets lay on it, some still in the original bundles in which they had been delivered.

Rose noticed many signs that the staff were unmotivated, and cleanliness was far from a priority. There was a noticeboard with advertisements for events in the hotel and for last Christmas's festivities, and an Easter egg hunt had 'Cancelled' written across it.

Rose followed John and Kathleen over to the reception desk, where a young woman with a nosering and highly decorated nails sat, looking bored. She didn't leap to her feet as they approached. Her dress was tightly fitted and showed far more cleavage than Rose (and no doubt Kathleen) deemed acceptable in a professional environment.

"Good afternoon young lady," said John, in a voice that Rose could tell was not happy. She and Kathleen exchanged glances. "You wantin' a room?" came the response.

"That would seem a good guess, young lady. Now Miss Hill has been specifically booked into Room 5, I believe."

"Doubt it," replied the receptionist. According to her staff badge her name was Summer, but her personality clearly didn't reflect the name her parents had chosen for her.

"I beg your pardon… err… 'Summer.'" John peered at her badge. "Why would the booking not have been made?"

"Oh s'been made all right, right pain having to clean that one out after all this time, some B-list celebrity I bet, but she ain't due till tomorrow nah, can't have been Room 5."

"Perhaps you have my booking? I usually have Room 4."

Summer sighed as though she was being ultimately long-suffering in even conversing with him, and flicked on the computer. How she used the keyboard was beyond Rose's imagination.

Summer's nails were so long it was a miracle she could perform even the simplest task.

Summer looked up from the computer and shrugged. "Same for your room Mister, no booking till tomorrow, no can do."

"What date do you have for the booking, Summer?" Rose knew John's voice was going below freezing now. Had Summer been more alert she might have seen the danger coming.

"Says it here, clear as day, Wednesday 23rd, no can do." Summer checked beside her computer keyboard and Rose noticed an open paperback book. Perhaps that was why she hadn't been paying enough attention to the arrival of three new guests.

John's face was quite a picture now. Had he been born a dragon, he would most definitely have been breathing fire. Kathleen touched his arm, muttering, "Blood pressure John? Let me?"

John nodded, and Kathleen pressed forward. "Now look young lady, before we have to ask for the manager, when did you last change the date on your calendar?" She nodded her head towards the calendar, updated daily by pulling off the top sheet. Currently it sat looking somewhat sad and announcing yesterday's date.

Summer reached for the calendar and Rose spotted a flicker of unease in the girl's eyes. "Because young lady, today is Wednesday 23rd and I feel your greeting for the new owner of the hotel has been beyond abysmal. Now call your manager please… immediately!" Kathleen clapped her hands as if to encourage a young toddler.

Fear now showed in Summer's face and she stuttered as she realised her mistake. "Oh I'm sorry, I… I can't call the manager as he went, told me it was tomorrow you were arriving and that we shouldn't, I mean that we needn't worry, it would all be ready on time. He's out at an appointment currently, I'm sure he'll be back soon." She was trying to cover for him. Now fully alert – if not completely panicked – she started clicking away at the keyboard.

"Room 4 should be ready by now I reckon, as the maids have completed their rounds today. Let me check on Room 5: it was a slightly larger project seeing as the previous owner hadn't been here for a while."

Summer turned away from them, dialled an internal number and they heard a muffled conversation, which despite being muted conveyed abject panic. "All is good, Room 5 is ready and waiting, you could all head up there while they finish Room 4, there was a delay apparently."

"That'll be fine."

Summer passed over a form to Kathleen. "Sign here Miss Hill, purely formalities." Kathleen gave the form back, then indicated Rose. "Probably better to get the real Miss Hill to sign it."

Rose watched Summer's face go from discomfort to disapproval and then finally disbelief as she gazed at Rose's clothing and rucksack. "Could I see your passport please?"

Rose could see her holding back the form until she had checked her passport and compared the photo with the real thing. As it was recently renewed the picture was particularly accurate, so Summer shrugged and Rose signed the form.

"I'm guessing the lift is functional?" asked John.

"Course – fifth floor. I'll ring once they get to your room, but sign this meanwhile."

Rose had to turn away. Had she been a member of the public she would have been shocked rigid, but as this was her area of expertise it jarred even more having to deal with such an appalling member of staff. Summer handed Rose a key that had a dirty fob on it proclaiming '5'.

"No help with luggage I guess?" asked John

"Nah I can't leave the desk, too busy with guests." Summer was looking intently at her nails.

Kathleen snorted and took the smallest suitcase. Rose firmly grabbed the largest case and glared at John to deter him from stopping her, and John took the middle-sized one. As they waited for the lift, John looked from Rose to Kathleen. "Not a word, OK, not one. Let's get into the room for some privacy and we can have a discussion."

The key did indeed unlock Room 5, a greasy residue coming off the fob as John turned the key. The room was huge and, ignoring the tired furnishings, Rose's eyes flew straight to the panoramic view from the massive windows. The bay stretched for miles and a combination of turquoise water and clean yellow sand was enough to seduce anybody.

"Oh that view is genuinely to die for! I hope I can capture it on my camera to show Mum and Dad: that is beyond wonderful." Rose turned to John and Kathleen. "What a shame that such a beautiful hotel should have such terrible management."

"Indeed," sighed John, "it broke Dorothy's heart but there was nothing she could do. As the hospital appointments became more and more frequent she daren't fly over here, and frankly she felt she wasn't strong enough to cope if she did. Dorothy spent many happy years here and left it to you as it was truly part of her heart, and she could only leave it to someone she loved."

Rose felt tears welling up. She had loved Dorothy in return, and many memories would stay with her for the rest of her life.

"Is there is a kettle, tea-making things?" asked Kathleen. She pulled open a few drawers, and a door of the wardrobe, and sure enough, found a tray with somewhat dog-eared ingredients for that uniquely British solution to almost every problem. "Come on – tea will make us all feel better."

"We could ring down for some fresh milk?"

Rose giggled, "Now how likely do we think that is! I'll have black, you two can do the fake milk."

"No, I'm going to take my life in my hands and go down to the kitchen and ask. You two have a natter without me, you have a great deal to discuss." With that Kathleen picked up her handbag (did she plan to pay for the milk, or was it maybe a comfortable prop?) and marched out of the door.

"You have a truly lovely wife, John."

"No need to tell me: I've known how blessed I am for many years. Nearly forty years we've been married, and she's a gem." Rose felt happy for them but experienced a wave of self-pity. Why the 'right man' had been conspicuously absent in her life she had no clue.

"Let's sit and I'll try and make a better job of explaining everything to you. I'm sorry Dorothy's plans backfired somewhat, but we'll follow my plans for a while!"

"I feel totally overwhelmed to be honest – it's been difficult to understand what's happening."

"Yes – and I can see now how wrong we were, but let me fill you in."

They settled comfortably on the sofa and a chair in the far corner of the suite. Rose curled her feet up into the voluminous armchair, hoping she wouldn't struggle to stay awake; the time difference and the long journey were starting to affect her.

"I could ramble for hours about Dorothy's life and adventures, but that's for another day. I met Dorothy when I was a junior, newly qualified solicitor and she came to the office frequently when she was buying this place and there were various other business issues."

"But why Barbados?" interrupted Rose.

John shrugged. "She came here on holiday with her parents and fell in love, both I suspect with a young man on the island and also with this place. Shortly afterwards her parents were killed in a car accident and she became a wealthy young woman. But she always had a strong head for business and a clear eye for a bargain. She lived over here for some years and built this place up into a real international hotspot. Celebrities from all walks of life came here from Princess Margaret to Eric Clapton, Richard Branson to politicians and all sorts."

"It seems strange; we had no idea about Dorothy's life."

John nodded. "She was flying high; every project Dorothy touched turned to gold. The first twenty years she owned this place she rarely came back to the UK, and then it changed. She would never tell me what or why, but she became disenchanted and spent more months at home next door to you. I know for a fact she loved spending hours with you and watching you grow."

"It's making me smile hearing all this. It was definitely due to huge encouragement from Dorothy that I did a business degree and the hospitality management courses. Maybe she wanted me to follow in her footsteps?"

"She wrote this version of the will quite a few years ago now, probably when you first went to university. Yes, she had her plans."

"I can see why she didn't go a bundle on her nephews and nieces," laughed Rose.

"Poor Dorothy was conflicted. Given half a chance she would have written them out of her will altogether, but she loved her brother and sister and knew how much they would have been hurt to know their offspring had disappointed badly. This was her compromise, and they will probably never realise they got the mouse's share of the will rather than the lion's." John smiled at his analogy.

Rose frowned. "Sorry, but I'm confused – surely the manor house is worth millions? So why would this be the lion's share?"

John pursed his lips together and nodded, as if mulling over what to say. "This is where I have to start digressing from Dorothy's plans, but she trusted me and I feel we have had enough evidence that the plans thus far have been stressful for you…" John hesitated; ever the good solicitor, it obviously pained him to digress from a client's wishes.

"This hotel alone, Rose, is worth several million pounds for the ground it stands on. Dorothy left quite a lot more in trust. That was intended for funding this trip over and, if necessary, bringing your parents over to help you make up your mind about what to do."

"I feel a bit queasy now you've told me all that to be honest. I expected it to be a tiny, tatty shack."

"Well that was the point – I wanted to throw off the dogs and keep them from contesting the will, holding up what needs to be done here."

Rose was puzzled. "Needs to be done?"

"There's a deadline approaching. A property company has put in an offer for the land and it expires this week. As the new owner you would have to decide what your response is going to be."

Rose rubbed her temples and gazed at the floor. "I have to decide this week whether to sell or not?"

"Indeed."

"Several million?"

"Indeed."

"I can't… No, I have no idea, I can't even think straight for a while."

Kathleen bustled back into the room, clutching a large jug of milk with a victorious grin on her face. "Success my love?"

"Did you doubt me?" Having put the jug on the coffee table between them, she opened her bag with a grand gesture and brought out two wrapped packets of biscuits, a box of tea bags and some packets of sugar. "See? Everything is possible if you find the right young lady."

"Surely not Summer on the front desk?"

"I should say not! I gathered gossip too: apparently she's the manager's daughter and got the job despite missing some important qualities." Kathleen was smiling and had obviously enjoyed her adventure downstairs. "No, I met a young girl called Yvonne who seems to be the only one who knows what's what and she has the most wonderful work ethic, remind me to tell you more. She was lovely and apparently there's no chance of food here but a food van that parks a short walk away does great burgers made from today's catch of flying fish... and what did she say... oh yes! Try the banana ketchup!"

Pleased with her information Kathleen pottered about making fresh tea and passing the biscuits. Rose sipped the hot tea and tried to think. This was all impossible to take in. One minute she was a struggling junior manager, and now she owned property worth millions.

"You said a decision was required this week, so how many days do I have?"

"If I remember correctly it was due on Friday which means you have just over twenty-four hours." John looked grave.

"Could you try and change the date – could it be put off for say a week or two? I feel overwhelmed and truly unqualified to have any thoughts or make decisions on the fly."

John nodded and took his mobile out of his pocket, "Let me see what I can do." He slid open the doors to the balcony and wandered out of earshot.

A few moments later he returned, leaving the doors open. "I managed to speak to the company but apparently the man concerned flies off the island on Friday afternoon and their hands are tied."

Rose felt a mixture of panic and excitement. This was all so huge it was hard to keep cool and calm.

The room phone rang, and John answered. "Fine, there'll be someone to help us with our luggage? No? We'll have to come to reception for the key. Right." Kathleen grinned at him and it developed into a giggle. "No problem Summer, thank you for all your help."

John put the phone down and they all laughed. "See the funny side," said Kathleen. "Life is too short for Summer to upset us and it's a perfect day outside. We must go for a wander down the beach."

Having helped them get their suitcases into the charming Room 4, Rose went back to her enormous suite and had a good look around. The two rooms were huge, and although rather dated were in good condition. This, she assumed, was because Dorothy had only visited intermittently over the past twenty years. Why, she wondered, had Dorothy loved her life here for so long and then lost her enthusiasm? She checked the wardrobes and found more space than she could ever fill, let alone just with holiday clothes. She hung up the T-shirts and shorts and dumped her rucksack on the floor.

The king-sized bed, with a heavy chintz canopy and drapes, dominated the bedroom area. The bedside tables were rococo in style with gold filigree and cherubs; more cherubs held up the canopy and were repeated in lamp bases throughout the suite. Rose's eyes kept straying to the view from the windows, utterly magical and impossible not to love.

The bathroom was elaborate, not to her personal taste as there were more gold cherubs on the light brackets and an ornate gold mirror, but impressive nevertheless. The gold tissue box that matched the mirror made her smile; it was a bit over the top, Hollywood style. The shower however had a nice strong jet and she revelled in relaxing and letting the water pound on her back. She was only too aware how few clothes she had packed, but she had been expecting a very different holiday. The hotel laundry facilities would be a waste of time so she quickly rinsed out the bits she had been wearing on the plane and changed into clean clothes.

The phone rang and she picked it up hesitantly. "Hello?"

"John here, shall we meet in reception in say ten minutes?"

"Sure, can't wait to explore!"

Summer was sitting at the reception desk, looking more alert, as Rose came out of the lift. John and Kathleen were in the comfortable armchairs, again outdated, but in keeping with the faded gentility of the hotel. "All set?" John looked up.

"Absolutely, I had a shower and I'm raring to go now, quite refreshed and awake."

"Well speak for yourself dear, us oldies are going to need an early night!"

They headed out of reception and followed hand-painted signs 'To the beach', noticing that despite all the neglect and grubbiness inside the hotel, the gardens were truly stunning and beautifully kept. As they approached a particularly beautiful bed full of ginger lilies, Rose noticed a man bent over, weeding.

John stepped forward. "Edmund, hello, have you got a moment?" The man in question straightened up when he saw John and rubbed the base of his spine. "Back doesn't get any better John! How nice to see you on our beautiful island."

"I'm sure it doesn't, but your family is doing an excellent job here in the garden, you should be so proud!"

"Oh the good Lord does as much in the garden as ever we do. I explain to the weeds that they're in the wrong place and encourage everything else!" Edmund, despite his grizzled hair and stiff back, was a good-looking man and had a beautiful smile.

"Edmund, can I introduce someone to you?"

41

Edmund tilted his head to one side. "But surely this is the beautiful young girl that I have seen pictures of, your childhood sweetheart I believe?"

John smiled at Kathleen's blushes. "Edmund! You are an outrageous old flirt." Edmund didn't look too worried by the description and transferred his glance to Rose. "Yes, and this is another young lady I'd like you to meet. Edmund – this is Rose Hill, a real friend to Dorothy and now the owner of the hotel."

For a moment Edmund's eyes clouded over. "We were all sad to hear Miss Dorothy had passed away. Heaven is a better place for an angel than this everyday world." He bowed his head for a moment. "Aha! Rose! It took this old man a moment but of course, little Rose that played a sheep in the nativity play, and learned to play the recorder which Miss Dorothy loved when you played to her."

"That was years ago! How do you know those things?"

Edmund took her hand. "You brought a lot of fun and love into Miss Dorothy's life, and anyone that made her love and laugh is a good friend of mine. Please let me offer any help you might ever need."

John was smiling at both of them. "Edmund and Dorothy were both passionate about the garden and Edmund was such a good friend, we felt lucky to have his loyalty and friendship."

Rose felt there might be more to the story, but saw that Edmund was a sweetheart and obviously a great gardener. At least that was one area where the hotel was world class.

"We're off to the beach Edmund, but you and I must have a rum sometime, yes?"

"Would be my privilege John." With that Edmund returned his attentions to the weeding and they moved on towards the beach. As they neared the perimeter of the grounds Rose heard loud music, heavy bass notes and thumping drums. It wasn't unbearable, but loud to be sure. Whichever house it was coming from it didn't seem to worry about the neighbours.

John and Kathleen looked at each other in horror, and Rose could see they felt uneasy. "What's the noise?" Rose asked.

"I can guess where it's coming from, but I'm not liking the answer," said John grimly.

They moved on a few paces, the music becoming louder, until a bungalow came into view. The grounds around it were shabby; many of the plants dead and litter spoiling what should have been an idyllic little house. "Is this on hotel grounds?" asked Rose.

"Oh very much so. It was intended to be the owner's accommodation, but recently the manager has moved in."

Rose thought it was odd that the manager of the hotel should allow his bungalow to get into such a state of disrepair, even if it was merely a home that came with the job. She jumped as two young ladies ran past them. Long-legged beauties but with such miniscule bikinis on they were all but naked. Kathleen looked shocked.

Rose, being younger and more broad-minded, laughed. "Oh don't worry you two! I assume Summer is having some college friends over while her Dad is away. She did say that the manager wasn't available, didn't she?"

John looked down at the ground and seemed ill at ease. "I think perhaps you two should continue to the beach while I deal with this."

"No John, we'll come too," insisted Kathleen.

The trio advanced over the thick exotic grass that seemed to pass as a lawn throughout the grounds. Music was blaring out of every open window and there were more young women dancing outside the house. "Well!" said Kathleen as she spotted that some were topless. As they stood there, unsure how to sort this out, a late-middle-aged man came out wearing tight Speedo trunks that left absolutely nothing to the imagination. As they were combined with an overhanging beer belly even Rose had to swallow hard and avert her eyes.

The man noticed them standing there and yelled over, "Geroffa my property, I'll get the law on you, private I said." It didn't take a mastermind to tell he was extremely drunk.

John seemed lost for words and was frozen to the spot, so Rose took matters into her own hands. "I understand this is the manager's accommodation, sir, and I suppose that you are a guest at his daughter's party. I would make the point that you are not acting in an age-appropriate manner and, I'm guessing, taking a risk that the manager could return at any moment."

Kathleen looked impressed at her speech. John appeared to be about to speak when the man shouted at Rose. "You wanna come join us? Nice breasts girl for your age."

This jolted John out of his semi-trance. "McGuyver! You are a disgrace and if it were within my remit you would be fired this minute. I'm taking these ladies for a walk along the beach, and when we return I want to see you in reception fully dressed and ready to speak to the new owner of the hotel."

"Ah get lost you withered old goat! You've got two ladies to play with, although why you want the old dear I can't guess – each to their own, I suppose – the young one is a nice handful or two."

At that point Summer raced past them towards her father. She shook him and shouted, "Dad, Dad! Pull yourself together – this is the new owner of the hotel."

McGuyver peered at his daughter through red-rimmed eyes, and it took a while for the information to filter through. Summer went inside and the music stopped. Rose was shocked. It was interesting that she felt angry both on Dorothy's behalf as she had trusted this man, but also for herself. She realised she felt a spark of pride in ownership.

Summer came out of the house and walked up to Rose. "My apologies, Miss Hill, I think my Dad, well he must be ill, this is out of character." She started shooing all the half-naked girls into the house. "I'll deal with this, leave it with me." She marched up to her father and slapped him hard round the head, making him reel. Then she went into the house and the shouting started as she dispatched the party-goers.

"Let's go for a nice long walk and let the sea air blow those sights and sounds out of our heads," said Kathleen.

As they crossed the soft sandy strip between the gardens and the beach the view changed from spectacular to miraculous. Rose took a deep breath, gazed at the blue, blue sea and immediately fell in love.

Chapter 4

Rose barely slept that night. Everything that happened the previous day had been completely overwhelming, from the First Class flight and arriving in Barbados right through to finding out about the hotel and the gross hotel manager. She lay awake, her mind sifting through all the information, trying to make sense of the new developments.

She drew back the curtains. Although it was only six o'clock she knew she wouldn't get any more sleep, so decided to go for a walk on the beach. The sight of the bay that had met her eyes on arrival at the hotel yesterday was breathtaking, and had worked its magic on her.

Grabbing a pair of flip-flops she made her way through a completely deserted reception (now there's a surprise) and raced towards the beach. There was no sound from the manager's bungalow and she kept her distance. Flip-flops in hand she ran as fast as she could towards the waves. Running felt exhilarating, and the gentle paddle she had planned would be such a special way to start what promised to be a heavy day.

As she raced towards the sea, a jogger came from nowhere and crossed her path. Rose stumbled and fell onto the sand.

"Jesus! I'm terribly sorry!"

"Wow – that hurt!" Rose struggled to get to her feet. One knee was grazed, but she was mainly winded and shocked. She had assumed she would be running alone on private property, and she felt her anger rising. "What the hell are you doing on this stretch of beach anyway?"

"Being here, living my life, apologies for breathing." The young man raked his fingers through tousled brown hair, his tan betraying long days spent in the sun.

"This is private property. You have no right to be here – and anyway you should look where you are going."

"Wrong on two counts, lady." He looked irritated, and a red tinge suffused his cheeks. "Firstly there is no such thing as a private beach on Barbados, they're all government owned – sorry, no flashy guest privileges. Secondly I suspect it was *you* who wasn't looking where she was going. I'd already started slowing down – you were running – good style by the way – straight for the waves."

Rose stared at him, annoyed at his critique and ruffled by the whole encounter. "Apologies, I had been led to believe the hotel owned the beach – but no way had you started slowing down. You were too busy listening to your headphones to focus on anything else."

"Please, can we start again? I hate to quarrel with someone so beautiful before we've even been introduced. I'm Shane, Shane Gregson, and I'm currently living on Barbados trying to earn an honest crust so I can revel in the sandy beaches and go for early morning jogs!"

Rose hesitated, not sure whether to be charmed or to walk away from the whole incident, but weakened as Shane smiled at her. "I'm Rose, Rose Hill, I'm sort of here just for the next week or so."

"I assume you are on holiday here with some gorgeous husband – no, worse – don't tell me this is your honeymoon?"

"No I'm here with…" At that point John came down onto the beach and called to her. Shane's eyes widened in confusion. He looked at John, then back at Rose.

"John, we have to stop meeting like this!" She was laughing loudly now. "Sorry Shane – but that's not the first time in the last few days people have got the wrong end of the stick. Here comes Kathleen, his wife. Shane Gregson: this is John McKay, my solicitor and family friend."

An amused Shane held out his hand. "Good to meet you sir! Rose and I bumped into each other, literally I guess."

"Shane, this is Kathleen, John's wife." Again Shane shook hands.

"I have plenty of plasters and antiseptic wipes if you need them for that graze, dear?" Kathleen was looking down at Rose's leg. "No it's fine, only a scratch. I'm guessing you two couldn't sleep either?"

"John got up to find out what the deal was on breakfast, but he couldn't find anyone to ask so we thought we would enjoy the beach and if needs be check out a local café."

"The best breakfast place," Shane butted in, "has to be Angel's Bar – it sounds strange but it's a bar at night and a café by day and the breakfast is brilliant. I go there every morning."

"I think that sounds really different," said Kathleen. "Why don't you young people go there and report back later? John and I only want a quick bite, and I'm sure John has to get back for work-related stuff… don't you dear?"

John winced as she nudged him, but his frown lifted as he understood what she was getting at and he nodded enthusiastically. "Yes, work, important phone call, can't wait, breakfast will have to. We're planning to potter about today to recover from yesterday Rose. Feel free to entertain yourself or join us if you get… bored."

Rose giggled to herself. They were a dear couple and it was sweet to see how they were trying to push her and Shane together for the day; presumably any young man was good news in Kathleen's book. That wasn't going to happen, she was sure, but it was a sweet gesture on their part.

"So you up for it Rose… breakfast? It's on me, my way of saying sorry?" Shane looked hopefully at her. John and Kathleen shared a glance, and waved as they wandered off. Rose didn't have to think too hard; it would be fun to relax for an hour or two. "Why not? I'm here to enjoy myself, it would be good to start by doing that."

"Can you walk, the bar isn't far?"

"I'm not hurt – I was just surprised and none too pleased, I guess."

They walked slowly down the beach towards a weathered shack. As they came closer she could see a large and rather tattered sign proclaiming that it was Angel's Bar. A big and beautiful lady greeted Shane enthusiastically and Rose marvelled at the intricacy of her hairstyle, cornrows twisted into a wonderful creation at the back of her head.

"Shane my skinny boy, you come to let Aunty Flo feed you up, can't have you getting any thinner, it's not healthy!"

"Thank you Flo! Yes, I'd love your usual breakfast – and the same for my friend Rose here." Shane indicated Rose by way of introduction. Flo narrowed her eyes and nodded. "I see your friend needs quite a few of Aunty Flo's breakfasts. It's not good to be that small girl, we gonna have to work on you."

Rose wondered what the breakfast might be and decided on balance the most likely thing would be a full fry-up, typical greasy spoon fare. It wasn't a meal she indulged in too often, but she did feel very hungry this morning. They sat at a large table set for four with a beautiful view of the ocean.

"Flo is a sweetheart and has a massive following of gentleman callers, but we aren't quite sure if they love her for herself or her cooking."

"I assume it's a British sort of fry-up?"

"Along those lines I suppose, but with a Barbadian twist."

In a matter of moments Flo was back with tall glasses of orange juice. As Rose took a sip, she realised it was a mixture, probably mango, pineapple and orange. Coffee arrived in a stylish metal coffee can alongside a large jug of milk.

"I love this juice, but if I finish all this and the coffee, I won't have room for the bacon and egg." Shane tilted his head to one side. "You winding me up? Wait till it arrives."

Flo, followed by a young girl with beautiful brown eyes and a fabulous figure, arrived laden with plates of food. "Here you are Shane. I keep sayin' – if you don't eat all my food, you never going to get big and strong enough to marry my Angel here." Angel dipped her head shyly, peeping at Shane from under her fringe. Rose was quietly amused at his flushed embarrassment.

Flo leaned over them and started filling the table (which could never have seated four: finding room for this breakfast for two was going to be a challenge). Shane stood up and manoeuvred the plates to fit in the extras that Angel carried.

"For the new lady, we have ham and eggs, our very best Barbados flying fish caught this morning. These are plantains, corned beef hash with peppers and onions and some of Flo's potato balls. Angel has brought you the very best bakes on the island, her speciality – you see why men are crying out to marry her! – crispy dough balls with spices and brown sugar and cane syrup and finally my favourite, rainbow banana bread. Enjoy!" Bestowing a massive smile on them both she shooed Angel away from the table with a muttered, "I tole you so, you too slow…"

Rose sat open-mouthed, momentarily panic stricken. "Tell me – this is a special feast and she's playing a trick on me?"

"She has rounded the selection up more than usual but no, this is pretty much a typical Flo special."

"You eat all of this every morning?"

"Not a chance; and besides, if I did clear all the plates she would be mortally offended. Part of Flo's mission in life is to feed men far more than they're able to eat. I suspect if I did have the appetite to clear this lot I would be in real danger of having to marry her!"

"Where do I start?" Rose gazed over the array of food. The flying fish was in a thin crispy batter, the dough balls in syrup sparkled in the sun: any one of the dishes on offer would be wonderful, but *all* of them?

"I suggest you try a small bit of each, then if we ever came here again, you'd be able to order..." Shane stopped suddenly. "Sorry – I mean you might not want to, or might come with someone else, or..."

"Perhaps the flying fish and plantains, it sounds different and delicious." Rose helped herself to a small piece of fish and a spoonful of plantains and watched with amusement as Shane piled his plate with large amounts of ham and eggs, hash and potato balls, but slowed down once he noticed Rose watching him. "I've been up for a couple of hours... jogging uses a lot of calories!"

"The plantains are delicious – they remind me of savoury bananas – and this fish is wonderful."

"Hello – what did you think plantains were? They're bananas but not as we know them and yes, the fish here is mega fresh, but I rarely get past the ham and eggs. Am-a-z-i-n..." He stopped, as the enormous mouthful of ham he had taken didn't allow for polite speech. Once she had finished her fish, he suggested she try both the dough balls with syrup and Angel's cake. The banana cake was a gorgeous marbled mixture of lurid pink, emerald green and chocolate. Angel was obviously a fan of bright colours, even in her cooking.

"I'm totally stuffed," sighed Rose. "I may never eat again."

"Oh I'm sure you will."

A piercing whistle came from the other side of the bar. "I guess you are about to meet some of my friends," said Shane, still working his way through the dough balls.

"You little bugger Shane, trust you to sneak a girl past us and not share!" A tall and very handsome young man, who reminded Rose of a young Sean Connery, bounded over to the table and kissed her hand. "Charmed m'lady," and Rose caught her breath for a brief second. She stared at him, her mouth slightly open. He removed his sunglasses (which must have totally obscured his ability to see when indoors), saw her properly for the first time, and immediately tensed.

Shane stood and made the introductions, "Jamie, this is Rose; Rose this is Jamie and our friends Tilly, Jane and Greta. We all met while we were travelling and then gravitated to Barbados and enjoy hanging out together."

At that moment the palpable tension between Jamie and Rose struck the others in the group. "Is there something I don't know here, guys?" asked Shane. Jamie seemed a bit stuck for words so Rose began. "I err, we, that is… Jamie and I met at university."

"Yes," nodded Jamie, "met, met at university."

Shane and the others waited for more details but as none were forthcoming he shrugged and started dragging another table over to make a huge seating arrangement that might suit ten. "Usual for Jamie and the others please Flo!"

All Shane's friends were welcoming and seemed fun, and Rose felt it was impossible to walk out at this point. She had been wondering if she could spend the day with Shane, but that was out of the question now.

Shane checked his watch. "Damn, excuse me Rose and all of you, I promised I'd get more rum and supplies to the Blue Parrot before nine. I'm never going to make it and Hernando is going to go crazy, I've got to run. Jamie, you lot, working today or pizza?"

"Nah, no work today, whole day of luxury, you got lunch free?" Jamie glanced at the girls, who all nodded. "Sure, nothing after this delivery until this evening, assuming he doesn't fire me on the spot for being late with it! Pizza?" Shane put a few notes on the table.

"Great," Jamie turned to Rose. "You got to rush, or do you want to stay and finish your breakfast with us?"

"I should be going really," said Rose. Looking agitated, Jamie turned to look at her. "I have loads I want to say, could I have your mobile number?"

"Lame Jamie, lame." Tilly passed Rose a pen from her handbag. Quickly Rose scribbled her number on a paper napkin and handed it to Jamie. "Perhaps we'll talk more when we next meet."

Tilly moved closer to Rose. "Seriously, please will you stay? It's great to meet new people and any friend of Shane or Jamie's is a friend of ours. I've known Jamie for quite a while now – have you kept in touch since university?"

"Err, not really, we haven't seen each other for seven years," replied Rose. "Bit of a misunderstanding when we parted."

"OK, just nice to know where things stand." Tilly looked thoughtful as she replaced the pen in her bag. "More dough balls? Come on – do stay!"

"Only if you don't make me eat another thing. I'm totally stuffed – I may not manage anything else for a week!"

Flo, approaching the group, overheard her. "You child need to come here more often, you have the appetite of a mouse – we need to get you eating properly before you go home!" Flo added more plates to the tables and the seemingly endless array of dishes, all laden with food, made Rose feel even fuller.

Tilly smiled. "Flo's determined that all women reach her size as soon as possible! How Angel stays so slim is beyond me."

"Me too," replied Rose.

"So where you staying?" asked Jamie.

"She already gave you her phone number, Casanova!" laughed Greta.

Rose smiled. "No it's fine, I'm at The Summer House." She was surprised by the reaction around her when she mentioned the hotel. "Have I said something wrong?"

"No, just that I had a bad experience there and 'one for all, all for one' – that sort of thing – it turned us against the place." Jamie moved the ham on his plate to one side to make room for some fish.

"I only arrived yesterday, I haven't spent more than a few hours there yet. No chance to find out what it's like really."

"You probably won't want to if you meet the manager," Jamie glared darkly. "That man is the pits, complete git, the way he treats the staff is disgusting."

"What happened?" asked Rose, thinking that she had already decided the man was horrible.

"Long story. When I first came here I applied for a junior manager's job there, but immediately took a dislike to the man. He was offering way less than minimum wage and told me I would be paid in cash, no questions asked. That's not unheard of, but it all seemed a bit dodgy. I was desperate for work and some money, even if it was low wages. I felt it would be good to get some experience in the hotel and it included bed and board so I thought I might as well give it a try."

"So you took the job?"

"Sure. It started going wrong from the beginning; the kitchens were dirty and way below health and safety standards. When I tried to complain to the manager he yelled at me and found me some particularly nasty task to sort out." Jamie had managed to clear his plate and was still going, Rose could only watch and marvel. "One night the receptionist, Summer – who just happened to be the manager's daughter – came onto me big time and she definitely wasn't my type. Anyway I didn't really want to mix business with pleasure so I refused very politely."

"I bet that didn't go down too well."

"True," said Tilly.

"Next morning Summer appeared in reception with a black eye and told her Dad that I had beaten her and tried to rape her. Her father called the police and I had the devil's own job making them believe I was with Shane that evening. Luckily one of the guys from the police station is a mate of Shane's and he happened to be in the bar with us, so perfect alibi. We were playing cards till the small hours and I went home with Shane and slept at his place. Scary though, and of course her Dad sacked me on the spot, despite the fact the girl had lied."

Jamie seemed angry and the girls had gone quiet. Rose felt sad that Jamie had been unfairly treated and found herself disliking Summer even more than she did already. "I'm glad you had a friend to back you up. It must have been very intimidating."

Tilly leant over. "Shane's been a great mate to all of us too, and it's over a year now we've all been travelling together. Tell you what, have you got any plans for lunch today?"

"What – apart from not eating because I haven't recovered from Flo's breakfast?"

"Oh fresh air, sea breezes, you'll be hungry again!" insisted Tilly. "Come join us at LBW's for lunch? Jamie and I often go there…" Tilly tailed off and Rose thought she was beginning to spot some not-so-subtle hints.

"LBW's?"

"It's a pizza place, in fact the *best* pizza place! LBW's is because

Larry the owner is a cricket fanatic, cricket terminology… leg before wicket… and they also happen to be his initials – clever name, huh!"

As Barbados had a great cricketing history Rose had expected to see plenty of signs of enthusiasm for the sport around the island. She hesitated. "I'd love to. I have some exploring to do this morning but maybe, say one or one-thirty, I'll see you there? I really must be going now though." She seized the opportunity to take her leave. Whether agreeing to a lunch that included Jamie was sensible or not she really couldn't decide, but there it was – she had.

Rose wandered back along the beach and gazed at the sea, marvelling at the colour that always seemed unreal in postcards sent by friends on holiday in exotic places. It truly was turquoise and the serenity and the beauty took her breath away, filling her with a sense of calm happiness that she hadn't felt in ages.

Seeing Jamie again was interesting, but it brought back all the hurt. The discomfort in her stomach didn't just come from overeating at breakfast. She wasn't going to let him imagine that they would be able to take up their relationship where they left off; it couldn't happen after such a long gap. She was a different person from the girl he had abandoned. Even though in some ways she had well and truly moved on, she still felt angry and the hurt was always lingering at the back of her mind. She had cried for weeks, blaming herself for having caused the break-up somehow. But anyway, Tilly seemed quite proprietorial – maybe she was worrying unnecessarily.

Walking into reception, Rose spotted Summer with her feet up on the desk. A combination of the urge to slap her for hurting Jamie and irritation at the apparent non-acceptance of the fact that she was owner of the hotel meant she gave the girl one of the nastiest glares she could summon. Summer either had the hide of a rhino (probably) or didn't care, as she shrugged and slowly lowered her feet to the ground.

Rose considered talking to her, then decided she needed to be better armed and that nothing was going to spoil her first full day on Barbados. She returned to her room and donned a comfortable pair of shoes. She also grabbed a bikini and towel in case she came to a beach on her exploration and fancied a swim.

Back in reception she wondered which way to go, but was damned if she was going to even speak to Summer, far less ask her advice. She stood at the door and looked down the drive. Which direction to choose? Either way would lead to somewhere beautiful, so she chose left and set off.

She wandered down the road, past the beautiful flowers decorating the roadside. The sun shone down, brightening her mood and tempting her to sing, but she resisted. When a vehicle slowed behind her and hooted merrily she hopped out of the way, hoping she wasn't about to be mown down. She turned to see Ian in the black taxi that had picked them up from the airport.

He slowed to a halt beside her and wound down his window. "Good morning Miss Rose Hill, and how are you this wonderful day?"

"I'm fine thank you Ian. I was unsure where to explore – I'm just enjoying the flowers and the sunshine for now."

"Good job I came along! Would you care to join one of Ian's famous tours of the island? I have a couple of hours free before I have another airport run."

"How kind, that would be wonderful!"

Rose climbed into the passenger seat and thought again how lovely most of the people she had met in Barbados were. There seemed to be a kindly spirit around (even if some were not so lovely, but maybe that was the same the world over).

"I'll start at the beginning. Our island has eleven parishes, all given saints' names –apart from Christchurch, one of the biggest parishes on the south coast. We're in the parish of St James right about now which is where our dear Miss Dorothy's Summer House is situated, and indeed where many of the nice beaches and hotels are set. This side of the island is much more interesting to the tourist than the other side, as here we're touching the Caribbean Sea, whereas the other side is the much greyer Atlantic. I love our blue sea and sky, one of the Lord's best creations."

Rose agreed with him. She settled down to listen to his wonderfully lilting voice and take in the vast local knowledge he had to share. Ian took her past special beaches, told her about the rum factory at Mount Gay as they passed by, talked about the ancestors of his island and some of the plantation houses that were part of the history of the island's sugar industry. She could have listened to him for hours; he was a natural tour guide and seemed to be a special person.

"I love hearing you talk about your island – you make it all fascinating."

"I love to talk, I do, and it has been a complete pleasure to accompany you this morning. However, I have to think about work for a while so where should I drop you off – back at the hotel?"

"Ian, I'm sorry, forgive me for not realising! Where is LBW's pizza place? I'm meeting some new friends there for lunch."

"Oh – an island connoisseur already! LBW's is the best pizza place in the Caribbean and not too far from here, a completely convenient stopping-off place. I may even take some of his wondrous creations for my lunch on the way to the airport, a fortuitous choice indeed."

Ian drew up outside a brightly coloured restaurant, the walls adorned with surfboards decorated with lobsters and LBW flags, and happy, chatting, lunchtime customers spilling out of the doors. "How much do I owe you, Ian? Thank you for the best morning ever, lots of interesting information and such good company."

"How much do you owe me? Now child – don't you go offending an old friend of Miss Dorothy's! I would drive her to the ends of the earth, I surely would, and the same promise goes to you. You join your friends and I hope we'll have the opportunity to get to know each other better at some later point."

Rose saw Shane and Jamie waving at her from one of the tables outside the restaurant. She leant over to give Ian a kiss on the cheek, and he seemed very touched. "Thank you Ian, and I hope I see you again soon."

"Oh you will if the good Lord intends it," replied Ian, and the car moved away.

The next few hours were a blur of laughter, happiness and great companionship for Rose. She hadn't been as happy for many years. Tilly, Jane and Greta made her giggle, they teased Shane and Jamie mercilessly and promised to show her nightclubs with great offers for females to get in free. Jokingly – with mock disparaging looks at Shane and Jamie – they suggested that way they could meet some properly handsome guys.

The food at LBW's was first class. As predicted, Rose was not seriously hungry after her breakfast, but she enjoyed sharing bits from the boys' plates and agreed that the lobster pizza was indeed to die for. She wished they'd been meeting up for an evening meal to give her time to make room!

Greta stood up. "Sorry gang, but Jane and I start work in an hour and we have to get back and change – if we're late there'll be big trouble, but this has been fun. We must do it again!"

Jamie checked his watch. "I need to make a move too. Rose – I'll give you a lift back to the hotel?"

"That would be brilliant thanks; I'm meeting John and Kathleen in the lobby at six so I need to get a move on too. Where's your car?"

Shane whistled nonchalantly. Greta giggled as she and Jane left, waving and smiling. "What's the joke?" asked Rose.

"Oh shut up you lot, Rose will be fine."

"Fine?"

"You don't mind riding on a bike do you? I'll be back in a mo."

Rose had visions of a bicycle made for two and hoped it wasn't far back to the hotel; she wasn't fit enough to pedal for too many miles. Jamie came round the corner of the restaurant on a large but elderly looking motorbike. The noise was immense and everyone else sitting outside stopped talking.

"Is it safe?" asked Rose. "Perfectly, hop on." He handed Rose a crash helmet and she put it on, feeling very unsure, and climbed on board. She had never travelled on a motorbike before and felt a bit nervous.

"Come on hold tight, I'm a good driver!"

Rose wrapped her arms around him (which, despite herself, she rather enjoyed) and clung on for dear life. "I do have to breathe while I drive, tiny bit looser maybe?" They raced off down the road and Rose felt half exhilarated, half scared, but it certainly wasn't an experience she would forget.

Standing talking at the entrance to reception were John and his wife. Kathleen beamed broadly when she saw Rose dismount from the bike. "That looks fun, have you had a lovely day?"

"I have Kathleen – and thank you for the lift, Jamie."

"Can I ring you later? You gave me your mobile number?" His smile, just visible under his helmet, suggested he was pleased with that idea, but still Rose didn't know how she felt. She just shrugged, and waved as he left.

"There will be a taxi here in about ten minutes, Rose," said

John. "Do you have a slightly dressier outfit, perhaps?"

Rose felt embarrassed at her lack of forethought. "I only have my jeans or another pair of shorts, John. I'm sorry – I totally miscalculated what to bring on this trip."

"Jeans will be fine dear," Kathleen chipped in. "It's a very casual place tonight and John and I have discussed a shopping trip tomorrow for us girls, to get you kitted out as you'll need a more professional outfit for tomorrow afternoon."

"I, I mean…" Rose felt embarrassed and out of her depth and far from flush money-wise. "Not to worry for now, dear; get changed and we'll discuss all of this over dinner."

Dinner was another wonderful experience that Rose filed away to treasure on a cold miserable British evening in the future. The restaurant, surrounded by exotic flowers and palms, sat on the edge of a beach with lovely views. The food had been out of this world and Rose enjoyed every morsel.

As they sat over coffee and delicious chocolate-dipped fruits, John looked serious. "Rose, I need to talk to you about the meeting we have to attend tomorrow afternoon."

"Yes, Kathleen mentioned needing smarter clothes… what is the meeting?"

"Events seem to have gathered momentum over the past twenty-four hours, bad news travels fast. The bank manager for the hotel rang me and said he'd received a call from the hotel manager – nothing good I'm sure, that man is revolting. However, the difficulty is that we need to introduce you to the bank manager, the hotel accountants and tax specialists here on the island. The hotel manager should be introduced to you formally and Eric Somerville, a property developer, will be joining us. He has been discussing the hotel with both the bank manager and accountant without my knowledge."

"That sounds a seriously heavy group of people to see all at once." Rose tried to sound braver than she felt.

"Indeed, a heavyweight introduction for you, but I believe you'll cope. I'll be there and will watch your back. There are quite a few pieces of the puzzle of which they have no knowledge at all."

"Me too, I fear."

"You hold the main piece of the puzzle and they aren't aware of that. It's rushing you, I know, but events seem to be running away with us. Although we always had to have a decision tomorrow, now there will be an audience helping you make it."

"It's all so scary," replied Rose.

"Before tomorrow afternoon we need you to decide what your future will be. Do you want to stay and run The Summer House, or do you want to sell off the land? I can't influence you either way, as Dorothy wanted you to have a free choice."

Rose's heart sank. At twenty-six she may have been mature for her age and felt she had a real flair for business, but this was way out of her league.

"I can't make a decision," she faltered. "What are the books like – can we afford to run the hotel? It seems to have been run into the ground… I haven't had a chance to see anything, talk to anyone…" She stopped, and for the first time felt just a bit irritated with John and Dorothy's plan for her.

"The bank wants to foreclose on the hotel as the account is overdrawn, and they want to tell you tomorrow that they have no faith in your ability to manage the hotel. Aided and abetted, I'm sure, by poisonous reports from McGuyver." John paused. "But you would get several million with no effort from the property developer, I'm sure…"

"What a decision to have to make, virtually on the spur of the moment."

"John, explain about the trust fund, come along."

"Dorothy left a large chunk of money in a trust fund should you decide to run the hotel. If you choose to sell, then that trust fund will be split between her favourite charities. Dorothy wanted me to wait until you'd made your decision but she couldn't have guessed the hotel had been so badly damaged. The point being there would be plenty of funds to stop the hotel going bankrupt."

Rose closed her eyes – she felt like Alice in Wonderland. The land she had inherited would be worth millions apparently, or the hotel could be run with a trust fund should she want to take up the challenge. This was somebody else's life, not hers. How could she pass up such a wonderful opportunity – but at the same time was she capable of taking it on? It was all too much.

"I'm asking a lot, I know, but I need your answer by tomorrow lunchtime, before the meeting."

Chapter 5

Rose and Kathleen staggered into the lobby under the weight of their purchases, laughing and congratulating each other on a good morning's work. Much to Rose's joy, Kathleen had insisted that hundreds of dollars spent on clothes was just fine with John as part of the travelling and research fund Dorothy had left. So they had been shopping at the island's largest department store and Rose was now the proud owner of a couple of beautiful new outfits: a navy blue designer suit that made her look a million dollars, and a very lovely dress in a floral print that was gorgeously feminine. As soon as Kathleen had seen it she insisted Rose needed it, and made a sly comment about the young man they had met on the beach.

"We'll come and collect you from your suite to get some lunch shall we, say thirty minutes?" Kathleen waved as she walked towards the lift.

"Hey Rose!" There was a loud shout. "Rose – over here!"

Rose turned around and tried to see who was calling her, then realised it was the tipsy woman she had met on the flight from London; definitely not the type she wanted to hang around with.

"It's me, Cheryl! Remember we met on the plane, hell of a ride, eh?"

"Oh vaguely – yes, of course! We sat at the bar for a while. Are you staying here too?"

"Me, nah, wouldn't touch it with a barge pole, McGuyver is a dirty old man and nobody in their right mind stays here! Nah – my boss is here for a meeting, so I thought I would scrounge some free wifi while I wait for him. Never enough time for Facebook or emails at the grubby place Eric makes us stay."

"A meeting?" said Rose nervously, a strange feeling crawling up her back.

"Yeah, two actually. First the old chap needs to have a meet up with McGuyver, just sorting the pay-off really. I reckon he's done his job now, rumour was the bank is going to foreclose so that should be enough. Then bit later he's meeting the new owner, should be a piece of cake, no one in their right mind would want to keep this place if they could sell instantly. Eric's hoping for a massive bargain – even including McGuyver's cut – so I'm researching good places to go for a romantic celebration tonight. It'd better be champagne all night the amount Eric should make out of this."

To emphasise the point Cheryl kicked her tanned legs and one of her gold designer flip-flops tumbled to the floor. Leaning down to see where it had ended up she missed the look of rage darkening Rose's face.

"Well I wish you the best of luck," said Rose. Had Cheryl been even half aware of her surroundings she might have caught an unusual note in Rose's voice. "I have to dash, meeting Kathleen for lunch."

"Oh yeah I saw her, that your mum? Nice to give the oldies a break I guess – you must be a saint. Let me know if you ever want an escape, I can show you where the good times are on this island!"

"That's so kind of you," replied Rose, teeth clenched. She was sure Cheryl would spot her fake smile, but it seemed not. The latter was looking down at her iPad screen and didn't even notice Rose had marched away towards the lift.

Back in her room, Rose picked up the phone. "John?"

"Yes is that you Rose? I thought we were collecting you – is anything wrong?"

"Yup," replied Rose, so angry she felt tears welling up. "The meeting this afternoon… well… we are going to war! I hope I don't let you down but I will *never* let those men beat me, not ever!"

"Right," said John," let's meet up for lunch right now and you can tell me more and we can discuss tactics. You are all right, though? I am worried something has happened."

"It has John, but nothing I can't manage." As she listened to herself she wondered what the heck she was doing – but they would see.

She dialled the numbers she knew by heart. "Mum, is that you?"

"Yes darling, how lovely to hear your voice, everything OK?" Rose held the phone close, wishing she could hug her mother right now instead of making do with a quick phone call.

"It sort of is and it isn't Mum. I am safe and John and Kathleen are being very supportive as I said last night, but there's a big meeting this afternoon and I just wanted to hear your voice for a couple of minutes. I think I feel a bit frightened." Rose laughed at herself; she 'thought' she felt a bit frightened? Hmm… really, Rose?

"I wish I could be there to give you a hug," replied Pearl, "but I trust you and I know my little girl has got more talent in one little finger than everyone else in that room will have, apart from John of course – I assume he'll be with you to help you do the right thing?"

"Oh yes he definitely will; we're just going to have lunch and talk it all through. I'll ring you later and tell all, but I just needed you for a moment. Oh – I can hear John and Kathleen knocking on the door – I have to go. Thank you, Mum." Rose wondered why just a few moments of listening to Pearl's voice had comforted her, but knew she felt stronger and hoped she could pull off this meeting.

Kathleen was wearing the beautiful but enormous pink sunhat purchased in town earlier, and John looked every inch the colonial in his white linen suit. Rose hadn't changed yet, but they reassured her that it could wait.

"It will have to be a relatively quick lunch," said John. "We only have an hour before the meeting, so I have made an executive decision. Kathleen has been down to the kitchen and dear Yvonne has rustled up some lemonade and a pile of sandwiches. I thought we could eat out on the balcony?"

"Anywhere is fine," said Rose. "I suspect I'm too upset to eat much anyway."

They all moved out to the balcony and within what seemed like moments there was another knock at the bedroom door. Rose opened it and in came Yvonne bearing a tray with everything Kathleen had ordered. "Oh thank you so much… Yvonne, isn't it?" asked Rose, peering at a very tear-stained young waitress.

"My pleasure Miss Rose, I am so pleased you are here." Rose smiled: Yvonne was the first person in the hotel to have either welcomed her or acknowledged her existence! "Please excuse the way I look, I just had some bad news… but you enjoy your lunch." She turned to go, but Rose held her back.

"Was it anything I can help with?"

"No Miss Rose," replied Yvonne, almost curtseying. "The manager just informed me that this would be my last week as the hotel was closing and I love my job so much – well most of the time – and the difference the money has made to my kids is like a miracle."

John came up behind Rose just in time to hear what she was saying. "Yvonne, Yvonne – look at me." The maid, who had been staring dismally at the floor, looked up. "I can't tell you any details yet, but I can promise you a job with a good pay rise by the end of this week and we will have a talk about it tomorrow, OK?"

Yvonne looked into Rose's eyes, not quite believing what she had heard. "If you say so Miss Rose, but I can't believe you would help me?" Rose took her hand and squeezed it. "Believe me, Yvonne."

"Well," said John as he closed the door, "I guess that tells me everything I needed to know about your decision for the meeting!" He looked happy and as though a weight had lifted from his shoulders.

"Not everything," said Rose. "Come on, let's go and sit down – I might just fancy a sandwich now I've decided what to do. I feel quite excited!"

"So tell us all," said Kathleen, her new pink hat making her look very glamorous.

Rose explained her meeting with Cheryl in the lobby, and John's face was a picture as the story unfolded. "My God, that man should be shot! Poor Dorothy – she didn't deserve this."

Kathleen leant over and took his arm. "Blood pressure, remember." John shook his head. "Oh I could curse getting older some days, if I was twenty years younger I would have punched the man to the ground." He was quivering with rage.

"Fat lot of use that would have done," replied Rose, smiling at his loyalty to Dorothy, "then he'd have got money from us by suing."

"True," said John, "very true. So do we have a plan?"

"Well," said Rose, "just at the minute I am so angry with them all, especially this Eric bloke, that I really want to scream at them. Tell me – will I have a problem getting new accountants and a bank?"

"Oh truly not my dear. I've already had a word with another bank as we were unhappy about the deposit rates with the hotel's current bank. Replacing the accountants may be a bit tougher as they were the best, but plenty more in the sea."

Kathleen winked at her. "If you've had enough to eat my love, you should go and change. We want you to knock'em dead, and that new suit and accessories should do the trick."

Rose rushed into her bedroom and looked at the beautiful designer suit. She'd never owned anything this expensive in her life, and the silk blouse that went with it had been several more hundred dollars. Perhaps she could get used to having money! But right now she had to focus. She brushed her hair vigorously, then indulged herself in a nostalgic memory of Dorothy teaching her how to put her hair up just like the debutantes had done in her day. The new Chanel make-up she and Kathleen had chosen was so lovely to use and she had her pearl earrings too (they went everywhere with her), a twenty-first present from her parents.

Giggling as she slipped on the designer shoes, she hoped the high heels would impress and not lead to her falling into the meeting and making a fool of herself.

"Good heavens, I would barely know it was you!" said John as she walked into the seating area outside the meeting room. "You look beautiful. Well done girls! Great choices – and I see what you mean, Kathleen." He nodded at Kathleen, obviously referring to a previous conversation.

"Here my love," said Kathleen, "just a loan as they are too sentimentally precious, but you'll be able to buy your own before you know it." She proffered a pretty pearl necklace. "The neckline of that blouse just calls out for pearls and they might just bring you luck – I wore them on my wedding day." Rose felt quite a lump in her throat knowing how valuable they were to Kathleen, but it was a lovely gesture. She was so lucky to have their help and support.

John took her arm, "Miss Hill, may I escort you to your meeting?" The last thing Rose heard was a whisper from Kathleen in John's ear, "Go get 'em, tiger!" Rose hoped yet again that one day she would have a relationship that precious and enduring.

John opened the door to the meeting room and stood back to let Rose to walk past him. Rose thought she might have heard a sharp intake of breath, but she wasn't sure. John walked in behind her. "Good afternoon gentlemen, my apologies for keeping you waiting."

"Some of us do have busy schedules Mr McKay, tardiness is never an attractive attribute."

Oo-err, thought Rose! Why do I feel he would never have said that if he knew what was coming? John smiled somewhat tepidly, and turned to Rose. "Let me introduce these people to you, Miss Hill. Mr Wallgood, the manager from the local Bank of America branch; Mr Allthrupp, senior partner at the accountants Allthrupp & Weston." He hesitated; there was a much younger man to the right of the latter, and he looked questioningly at Allthrupp.

"Forgive me," said Allthrupp, "this is Mark Beard, a very junior partner. If it is acceptable I just brought him along to see how successful business is carried out and so that he is privy to any works that have to be carried out post meeting."

John nodded formally and continued, "Mr Somerfield I presume? We haven't met before."

"Absolutely old chap, good to meet you." Eric Somerville leapt up and pumped John's hand rather excessively. He didn't offer the same courtesy to Rose.

"Finally McGuyver, I believe we have all met several times previously." The lack of formality on John's part was meant as a huge slight, but Rose suspected McGuyver barely noticed.

Allthrupp stood up. "If you will forgive me Mr McKay, I thought it best if I take control of the meeting as the bank has some serious input. Once the first item on the agenda has been discussed we can progress from there."

John looked across at Rose and smiled secretively, and she nodded. "Absolutely fine, you take the lead Allthrupp." A fleeting unease crossed the latter's eyes, presumably at John's use of his surname only and the latter's casual attitude towards him.

"Gentlemen: if I could ask each of you to give the meeting a report so we can wrap up this matter as soon as convenient?" Everyone nodded, and Rose tried not to feel sick with excitement at the fun she and John would have with them all shortly.

"Mr McGuyver – if you would?"

The overweight and unkempt hotel manager had barely brushed up any better in his preparation for the meeting, but he did at least seem to be clean and not under the influence of alcohol.

"Not a lot to report that we haven't all been aware of for some time: bookings are still down and some weeks non-existent, and we tend to keep the dining room closed most days as so few takers are about. I have warned the staff there will be redundancies at the end of the week." He slumped down into his chair in a very disrespectful manner, perhaps that of a man who anticipated a big celebration over the coming evening.

Allthrupp stood up again. "As accountants to the business I fear I have to report a loss this year and can only foresee more losses in the future. Since the demise of the hotel's owner, funds have been severely restricted," here he glared at John, "and we as the official accountants would have to put on record that we have officially said this at this meeting." He gesticulated to the young man beside him who was scribbling furiously.

He then signalled to Wallgood, the bank manager. "A very short but not very sweet report from us," announced the Bank of America's representative. "The client's accounts are currently overdrawn and we will have no alternative but to foreclose in the very near future as loaning a failing business money is ludicrous." He sat down very self-importantly and looked to John, maybe expecting a shocked reaction. John just nodded as though he had expected it, causing a slightly bemused look to cross the banker's face.

Allthrupp stood again and thrust out his chest. "However, all is not lost and I believe we have the cavalry on hand to rescue us as I speak." Laughing at his own joke he gestured to Eric Somerville to stand.

"I perhaps alone have extremely good news for all concerned. I run a company called Ocean Front Marinas. Mr Wallgood: I believe you can vouch for the strength of my company and my bank account." He paused to accommodate any laughter but none appeared to be forthcoming; the speech had obviously worked better in other circumstances. A touch flustered he continued, "I would be very interested in buying the plot of land upon which The Summer House stands, and would be prepared to offer an extremely generous one point two million dollars." He sat down and looked around the members of the meeting.

Rose stood up slowly. "Can I just ask all those present for a personal opinion on that offer?" The men looked at each other in some confusion.

Allthrupp looked up at her and said, "Excuse me Miss... sorry I didn't catch your name.... fascinating though it is to know Mr McKay has an enthusiastic secretary... or are you a paralegal? Never can tell the difference these days!" Again he laughed at his own joke. The awkward silence in the room failed to prevent him from continuing. "I really feel Mr McKay should be handling any business at this moment." The younger man beside him leant over and whispered urgently in his ear and then pulled a 'so sorry' face at Rose, and she couldn't help but smile at him.

"Aha, my misunderstanding Miss Hill, of course, so many

clients don'tcha know, of course as the new owner you are bound to need guidance. Well – as your accountant – I would say this was an extremely fair offer and should be accepted with alacrity." Mark Beard gave Rose an agitated shake of his head, still trying to hide his opinion from his senior partner but clearly informing Rose what he thought. She smiled at him again.

She nodded at the banker. "And you Mr Wallgood, your opinion?"

He replied, perhaps a little hesitantly as he may have decided she was not the idiot he had assumed: "Well, Miss Hill," he nodded at John as if to apologise for not speaking directly to him, "as you will understand as bankers we cannot take unsupported risk and it is blatantly obvious that this establishment has nowhere to go from the depths the books have been showing recently. I have to, in all conscience, say this is an excellent offer that should be taken before it is removed from the table."

McGuyver sat up as if expecting to speak, Rose noticed this and, trying to control her rage, said in a clipped tone, "McGuyver: I won't be needing an opinion from a member of staff, but you may stay for the rest of the meeting if you desire?"

McGuyver looked as though he had been slapped round the face, which was indeed just what Rose would have loved to do had it been an option. She saw John biting his lip and assumed that, like her, he was enjoying their little war game.

Eric Somerville looked over to McGuyver with an irritated expression. The two men, worried that they may have taken a wrong turn, exchanged a glance. How true, thought Rose, and then she continued. "Gentlemen, you are the trusted advisors for this business, you used to be well thought of by Dorothy and her executors. However, knowing everything I have learned in the past two days, I am sad for Dorothy that she trusted such unprofessional crooks and disappointed for myself that I will have to make such radical changes to my team..." There was a lot of shuffling and quiet coughing and furtive glances exchanged.

"Let me tell you, I have done my own research, and this plot should be valued between four and five million dollars," she glanced down at the papers John had placed in front of her, "and that's just empty land value. I wonder if it might not be worth even more were it to be developed by a sympathetic and historically aware property company. The Summer House is renowned worldwide, with a fabulous array of celebrity visitors over the past hundred years." Rose looked around the table and smiled at the collection of surprised and now anxious faces.

"I will therefore not only be turning down your 'kind' offer, Mr Somerville, I will be speaking to the island police in an attempt to stop you playing this game with another less fortunate individual. Mr Wallgood, you will find sufficient funds to level our account in your bank shortly and we wish to close the account as of that moment. Mr Allthrupp, I am disappointed that as my accountant you were not able to advise me of the true value of the land." Rose paused; her courage was waning, but getting rid of McGuyver was something she wanted to do, for Jamie if nothing else.

"Mr McGuyver, I not only want to fire both you and your daughter, I will be arranging an injunction to make sure neither of you comes onto my property again. I have rarely come across a nastier person than your daughter and your actions and hopes of conning me mean I will also be talking to the island police about you. I would like both of you and your belongings off the property by close of play today."

McGuyver stood and threw the bundle of papers (possibly his speech she wondered, or some accounts?) across the table at her. "And you, idiot child, can just rot in hell! Never think you can slight

McGuyver and get away with it!" With that he stormed out.

John turned to the banker. "I have organised the transfer, and I suspect the balance is at zero right now, so closing the account should only take you a short while – if I could have the papers in the morning?" He looked across at Rose to see if she wished to add anything.

"Thank you, Mr Wallgood. Before you leave can I say again I am disappointed that a professional such as yourself should have seen fit to join in this charade and incorrect valuation of the property. I am sure Mr McKay plays golf with some of your superiors and might see fit to mention our disappointment and removal of an account that you have had for over thirty years." A very morose Wallgood swept up his papers and briefcase and departed.

Somerville and Allthrupp seemed frozen to the spot , which amused Rose enormously. She leant over to John and whispered; he shrugged and then nodded.

"Mr Allthrupp, I have a slightly different suggestion to put to you. As far as I am aware, Mr McKay has noticed no irregularities in your ability to administer the correct island tax information or indeed in keeping the books completely straight. I would therefore say that I might like to retain the services of Allthrupp & Weston, with one proviso." Allthrupp's glazed look seemed to snap back into narrow-eyed accountant's focus.

"My proviso, Mr Allthrupp, is that you personally have no connection with my books, accounts, no personal knowledge of this client at all, and that all matters are to be handled personally and solely by Mark Beard. Are you agreeable if we were to organise a contract? Should Mark decide to leave your firm then the account would go with him, naturally."

Rose thought she heard a splutter of laughter coming from Mark, but it was just a cough. Allthrupp was red-faced and very angry. "I have never been more insulted in my life, but if that clause retains the business for the company then I can only agree. Now if you will excuse me I have better matters to attend to! Come along, Mark."

With Allthrupp, Wallgood and McGuyver out of the room, it left Eric Somerville sitting to her right and Mark (who had ignored Allthrupp's command) to her left. Somerville seemed a little dazed at what he saw as a done deal melting away before him.

"Now Mr Somerville, I believe that is the conclusion of our business. I think it was a poor business decision on your part to ally yourself with men of that calibre, but that was your choice obviously."

Somerville rose and walked towards the door. "Oh Eric," added Rose, "You might want to have a little chat with Cheryl over the celebration dinner tonight that she is booking downstairs in the lobby... she might have been another of your poor decisions..."

As the door shut, John began to rock with laughter. "Oh Rose, Dorothy is up there clapping at your virtuoso performance and having the time of her life, so to speak! She would have been endlessly proud of you."

Mark Beard reached over to shake her hand. "I have a wife and two children, so I am completely safe, but you know I'd have given you a totally inappropriate hug if I could have. I loved the way you handled them all, and I am thrilled that I get to work with you on the project – what are we doing?"

John interjected. "Well Mark, I know your firm has been good for several of my friends and clients in the past, so I was happy that Rose chose to retain you, but you have yourself to thank. Whatever you did or said something changed her mind – before the meeting your company was gone!"

Rose smiled. "I could see you were honest Mark, and when

you shook your head at that valuation I also realised that you were being pretty brave with your boss sitting beside you!"

"Senior partner, please!" grinned Mark. "And yes – I will still get hell for it – but heck it was worth it."

"As to business," said John, "I think we need a little space. Rose has been plunged into this with very difficult timing and I want her to have a day or so to consider her options. As The Summer House's new accountant I can tell you that there is a considerable trust fund available to renovate and run it, but apart from that I am as much in the dark as you. Rose, I suspect, feels the same – eh Rose?"

"I just knew I was angry and that I had the resources to smash their smug little trick, once Cheryl had told me that McGuyver was involved in the con too. I suppose I just sort of snapped. It's all a bit real now… sorry… I feel a bit shaky…"

Rose really was shivering so John dispatched Mark with a plan to meet in a couple of days and shepherded her up to rejoin Kathleen. The tears began to flow as soon as Kathleen put her arms around her, and all Rose's fear and anxiety came out with huge sobs and shudders.

"Come on now my love, we can do this! Dorothy would be really proud and you'll have a lot of fun deciding exactly what you want to do. And you can still sell up if that's what you want – nothing is written in stone, except that she wanted you to be happy."

As the sobs subsided Rose heard her phone ping with a text message. "Any chance of a meal tonight, just us? Jamie x."

"Is that the nice young man who brought you back to the hotel on his bike?" said Kathleen, smiling at her with maternal eyes. "Yes," hiccupped Rose, "he wants to take me out for dinner."

"Well I would definitely say yes then, just the occasion to wear that pretty dress we bought this morning and plenty of time to redo that make-up that made you look so beautiful."

Despite her earlier misgivings Rose texted back. "Yes Jamie, need a friend tonight so perfect timing."

Chapter 6

Rose stood in front of the mirror and smoothed her hands over the skirt of her new dress. Kathleen had been right: it did look pretty. A cold flannel laid across her face and half an hour's rest had helped clear the blotchy skin and puffy eyes that always developed when she had been crying.

Stay or go – what should she do? The whole project seemed overwhelming, and it was ridiculous to contemplate handling it alone. John and Kathleen might be here this week but they would be gone soon and she knew she had neither the experience nor strength to cope. Tears started to well up again but she brushed them away firmly. Tonight she would have fun with Jamie; he had always made her smile, even if she felt unsure of his loyalty and was still, to be honest, cross with him.

Her phone bleeped and a text message appeared. 'Waiting in lobby J.' Taking a last look in the mirror, Rose grabbed her new bag and felt her mood lift.

Jamie whistled as she approached, "Hi gorgeous, goodness me! I'd forgotten."

"You cut that out, Mister! We're going to try and be friends, right?"

"Surely I can tell a friend she looks amazing?"

As they headed out of the door Rose found herself blushing, and grateful for the cover of night.

"Shane leant me his car – I guessed you might not be in the mood for my bike?"

"I'd love to lie and say it wouldn't have mattered but yes, I'm truly grateful, thank you Shane."

They drove out of the car park in silence. "Where are we eating?" asked Rose.

"It's a place I like, but better suited to couples and quiet conversation than when we all go out as a group. It's called Monkey Beach, a mix of American cuisine and local food, there's usually something for everyone."

"It's worked for you before with all the girls you have taken there then?" Jamie narrowed his eyes. "Mean point scoring, Hill."

Rose sighed. "It is nice to be with someone I know, it's been one hell of a day. Talk about being a gift that turns out to be a ticking bomb!"

"Hang on – let me get parked, then you can tell me all about it." A valet appeared from the entrance and Jamie shook his head. "Sorry mate, I'll put it in the car park myself." The valet shrugged and walked back inside.

"Sorry to be mean but the guy expects a huge tip and there are always loads of spaces." He stopped the car in an empty row and jumped out, planning to open Rose's door. "I'm quite capable of opening my own door, but thank you for the gallantry." Rose eased herself out of the car.

The restaurant was painted a strong but attractive pink, with windows and doors picked out in gleaming white. Feathery palm trees flanked the building and sparkling fairy lights decorated the trunks and foliage. Soft music filtered through the open windows and Rose realised how much she was looking forward to the evening and how much she was hoping for closure on the sad ending to their relationship.

They were seated in a quiet part of the restaurant, overlooking the sea, exotic flowers in a small vase on the table. Jamie spoke to the wine waiter and checked with Rose that a sparkling white would be OK with her. They sat back to relax and peruse the menu.

"Come on Rose – there has to be one big story to tell! Shall we talk about it?"

Rose shot Jamie a flustered glance. "The only problem is that I may end up in tears if I get into it too much."

"Deal. How about if we wait until coffee to talk unless it happens naturally earlier?"

"Thanks. I feel a bit stupid but it would be great to have a reprieve."

"Sounds heavy. Let me tell you about Tilly – you won't believe the job she's taken!"

Rose sat back in her seat. The food came and she thoroughly enjoyed the Caribbean prawns she had chosen. She teased Jamie for picking a burger, although he protested it was the best on the island.

At long last Jamie put his dessertspoon onto the empty plate and sighed appreciatively. "That chocolate mousse is the best, full stop, in the world."

"Mmm… I agree. I'm glad you persuaded me to choose that – it means I have to come here again to have that wonderful sounding flambé thing I decided against this time."

"It would be my pleasure."

"Slow down Jamie – we have a lot of fixing to do. I spent months feeling sure I'd done something wrong or that you hated me. It'll take time to heal everything, but yes, sure, we can come here again as friends. But we really need to get rid of the 'elephant in the room'. You just walked out and disappeared. No contact, none of us knew where you were. I was devastated."

"In all honesty the budget would struggle bringing you here again this week before you go home, it's probably for the best," Jamie hesitated for an uncomfortable moment. "I think there may be a better time and place to go over all the old stuff. Let's just let things flow on for a bit for now."

Rose felt frustrated; she and Jamie had been inseparable for nearly a year, and then he had disappeared overnight. All their friends had searched and phoned but no one could find him; even the university couldn't help, apart from telling her that he had officially left.

As the waiter brought their coffees, Jamie looked at her curiously. "Tell me about your day?"

"I'd like to explain to you, but where to start?" Rose took a deep breath, then filled him in as succinctly as she could about Dorothy, the will and today's meeting. "You're quiet? No comments?"

"To be honest I'm totally and utterly gobsmacked – I never saw this coming! I assumed you had personal problems and I was going to be the old agony aunt."

"I have… in a way."

"Hell of an exciting personal problem though, you have to admit."

"Yes, but I'm way out of my comfort zone and that has taken away any of the nice bits. I'm grateful to Dorothy for thinking I could ever cope with this, but she didn't expect the hotel and staff to have been damaged and ripped off. It's bigger than any dream I had and hard to take on board."

"It's a dream I'd kill for," said Jamie sadly, "but I understand if you feel selling out is the easiest option."

"I see what you are doing – don't think you're goading me into taking it on to prove you wrong!" They looked into each other's eyes for a long moment. "Are you thinking what I think you are thinking?" said Rose.

"That would depend on whether you are thinking what I'm thinking or what you think I might be thinking!"

"Right, you first."

Jamie took a breath. "I may be overstepping here, but if you would like some help, I'd love to be involved in the project with you. I'm no internationally proven managerial golden boy, but I have had experience and I would work endlessly. I realise we have some personal issues to get past but..."

"Yup, quite a few personal issues I would say!"

"Rose I'm so sorry, truly and I will explain it all to you one day, I promise. I carried on studying like you did but in a more hands on way. True I only finished the first year of our management degree and only have a limited number of diplomas, like zero, but I do have a lot of practise and was given loads of responsibility in some of the jobs I have been doing."

"I just don't know how John, my lawyer will feel about it, he's very involved with the project and – oh I guess we could ask his opinion."

"It doesn't sound easy but hey, we have enthusiasm, hopefully we could mend our friendship… and best of all we could employ Tilly and stop her becoming an exotic dancer."

Rose giggled. "Don't tell me, you have one proviso: not until you've been to the club and seen her act."

"Excuse me," said Jamie self-righteously, "that never crossed my… OK… maybe!"

"Seriously though Jamie, it's a big step to allow you back into my life after all this time. But let's try, would you be able to come over to the hotel tomorrow and have a meeting with John? He's such a wise man and I trust his opinion?"

"I have a delivery to do early morning, but eleven possible?"

"Sorted. I hope John thinks it's a possible solution."

* * * * *

"Morning Rose! Beautiful day, don't you think?" John looked dapper again in his colonial whites. Rose joined him in the hotel lounge, and sat down.

"You seem pleased with yourself?" Rose smiled at John, he was such a rock for her.

"I hope you'll be pleased with me too; either that or you'll be cross, not sure which." John seemed a little on edge, which was unusual.

"That's got me worried – what's happened, John? What have you done?"

"I had a long chat with your mother last night. She rang me when she couldn't get you on your mobile, and she was worried sick about what was happening."

"I forgot to charge my phone and it died on me late afternoon – and going out for the evening with Jamie I forgot to phone her. Oh – I do feel bad. What do they think about our meeting yesterday?"

"You'll be able to ask them yourself in about four hours. I offered them the chance to take a flight over here and stay to help you decide what you are going to do."

Rose jumped up, threw her arms around John and hugged him fiercely. "I don't care one bit that you are only meant to be my solicitor, I'm still hugging you – I'm so thrilled – thank you! They will love it."

"I hope so. I sent the same limo for them to make sure your mother didn't think you got preferential treatment."

"Poor Dad will feel duty bound to discuss the route with the driver all the way to the airport, and argue about parking." They both laughed and the atmosphere lightened.

"Let me fill you in on the discussions I had last night with Jamie in the restaurant." Rose explained that he had experience in hospitality and had done the first year of the same management degree course that she had studied, which was where they had met. "I invited him here this morning to have a chat with you and to see if you think it's a good idea that I let him help with the project."

John was serious, and concerned about their personal relationship. "The first and main worry I'd have is what would happen if you two fell out and stopped being boyfriend and girlfriend – could you continue past that? We would have to draw up legal documents to protect you and make things a bit bomb proof I think"

"We're definitely only going to be friends; there's no chance of romance on the cards. We have quite a bit of history and we both agree that friendship is all we want, despite having been close many years ago. It'll be fine and yes of course we would need to get everything sorted out on a legal footing."

John nodded, but said nothing. There was a knock at the door and, right on cue, Jamie appeared with a tray of coffee. "Sorry, I tried to find someone to ask at reception, but there was nobody around, then a sweet little lady passed carrying this. I guessed you might be her destination and so I offered to bring it in return for directions."

Rose stood up. "John – this is Jamie, Jamie French."

"Good morning Jamie! Rose had been telling me all about you. Please put the tray down here." Rose poured coffee for the three of them, and pushed the milk and sugar towards John.

"Jamie, John and I have been discussing everything, and I've explained the plans we made last night. How do you feel this morning – are you still keen to join me?"

87

"I'd be interested to learn more from John about the financial side, to make sure the hotel is safe and not on rocky ground before we start. I remember the layout as I worked here for a couple of weeks – and I do trust you, but it seems a huge undertaking. I'm definitely up for it, but I'm sure you both have more to say."

Rose was watching John, who was sorting some papers. He looked up and considered his two young companions. "I think the main thing to go over with you both is the fund that's available and the current hotel figures and facts. Sadly we're lacking a lot of input that should have been available from any decent managerial set-up, but we'll have to make do. There is what Dorothy and I felt was a generous fund to help you make changes and soften any financial gaps, but that was before we knew what we were faced with. It's enough, but you'll still have a steep learning curve I guess."

Their deliberations took the rest of the morning. A couple of hours later Kathleen appeared with a tray of sandwiches and bottles of water. "I wondered if you might all be hungry, it's after one now?"

"Is it? Thank you Kathleen. I don't suppose you fancy joining in the discussion? I'd value your input." Rose patted the seat beside her.

"Oh I'm not sure – I've never been one for facts and figures. I leave that to my John." Kathleen gave John a look that again made Rose's heart ache for a relationship with the same depth of love and trust. "I think we've got past the facts and figures stage, Kathleen. Your opinions would be of huge value at this point." John smiled back at her.

"Of course I'd love to help."

Rose pulled out her notepad again. "Have you got any comments on what you've seen around the hotel over the last couple of days that we may have missed or that you think is important?"

"What, apart from the fact there are no guests?" The others laughed. "I checked the registration book, nobody – we're on our own, and Yvonne confirmed it."

"Kath, I always knew you were my secret weapon! You're quite right, it wasn't discussed, we only got as far as checking future bookings."

"I suspect you'll find them far and few between," added Kathleen. "I heard the staff saying how they all knew the hotel was going to close and they were only working because they hadn't been paid yet this month."

"I think speed is of the essence," said Jamie. "Every hour that goes past McGuyver will be poisoning any remaining staff, even though he's left the property, or they will be talking themselves out of a job and leaving anyway. We need to see how many staff are fit to be kept on."

"How about calling a staff meeting?" said John. "Let's get everyone together and we can organise who is staying and who isn't. In the meantime…"

Rose interrupted, "In the meantime I suggest we check out how many guests are booked for future dates and ring and cancel them all so we have a clear month to get our house in order."

"I checked: one booking for two weeks' time and that's it."

"Thank you Kathleen. I don't suppose you fancy staying and being my right-hand man, I mean woman?" Kathleen smiled, and shook her head.

* * * * *

Rose stood in front of the motley crew comprising the staff of The Summer House.

"Thank you everyone for coming to have a discussion with me."

A low buzz of whispering emanated from the assembled company. "I'm sure you have all heard already that I'm the new owner of The Summer House. I inherited the hotel from my friend Dorothy West who some of you may have met. She hoped with my enthusiasm I might restore the hotel to its former self and bring back some of the glamour that she enjoyed creating here."

Another buzz of comment skittered around the room. "I suspect many of you may be thinking I'm too young for such an onerous job. I may only be twenty-six, but I have spent the last eight years working on a business degree, hospitality management course and practical experience in a large hotel in England. I'll be passionate and hardworking and that's been lacking in your leadership recently."

Rose gazed at the faces turned towards her and saw hope in some eyes, distain in others. "I'll be offering many of you a job with the new ownership, but some of you may feel it's too risky a project to be part of. We'll be having a management meeting later today. Those of you who want to stay and continue to be part of The Summer House team please go and see Mr McKay, who is sitting at the table at the back, and he'll take your details. I'll be calling a daily meeting to keep you up to date with what is happening. Thank you."

Jamie came over and whispered in her ear. "Good job Rose, rallied the troops – now let's see who wants to stay."

They tried to appear casual and as though they weren't counting the bodies who wanted to stay. Somewhat unnervingly at least fifty percent of the staff had walked straight out of the door without talking to John.

A young girl came up to Rose. "Excuse me, may I talk with you?"

"Of course, Yvonne." She spotted Kathleen gesticulating at her and, trying hard to read between the lines, Rose guessed that she was trying to give her the thumbs up. "What is it, Yvonne?"

"Sorry to bother you, Ma'am."

"Oh please call me Rose, I'm much more comfortable with that. Let's leave the 'Madam' bit for the guests."

Rose led Yvonne over to a couple of chairs set apart from the others and they sat down. "So Yvonne, what did you want to talk to me about?"

"There's a lady called Bessie that does washing up, she was too scared to come to the meeting as she's shy and she was worried she might lose her job if she didn't come. I promised to speak on her behalf."

"Yvonne, I promised you a good job and security and I'll follow through on that promise – and I am sure we can help Bessie too. You seem to have a good understanding of how everything runs in the hotel. I'd love to promote you to a much higher level – bear with me while we sort out who is staying and who is going."

"Of course! I'd love to help in any way – it's such a happy time for me."

Kathleen walked over to join them. "Rose, I hope you don't mind me joining in the conversation, but I had an idea that might be useful."

"Of course Kathleen."

"Yvonne, you have been kind and sweet to me, I trust your judgement. I wonder dear, if you would have a chat with Rose about who you think loves their job and who you would say isn't reliable or kind?"

Rose nodded. "Smart idea, Kathleen."

Kathleen took Yvonne's hand and squeezed it gently. "Come on my love – there's no need to cry! Be strong – you have three children, you said? And the girls are twins?"

Yvonne blew her nose and straightened up. "They are indeed, Miss Kathleen, and the apple of their Daddy's eye."

"Come on, you're earning this money to help them and we'll make sure you enjoy your job while you're at it."

"So Bessie is a nice lady, is she?" asked Rose, eager to get going.

"Oh yes Rose, she is indeed and she works more hours than she ever lets on. Think that's because she'd rather be here than at home. Her man isn't too kind to her and she gets free food here."

"That's good – we'll make sure she keeps her job too. Is there anyone else who is specially kind or good at their job?"

"My friend's a cleaner here, she does most bits of the hotel but she's especially good at the brass bits and mirrors. We all call her Sparkle, we aren't sure what her real name is, jus' bin Sparkle for always!"

"Good – and any others?"

"To be honest, not many. "

"OK. Let me put it another way Yvonne; I understand this may be difficult for you. Are there any members of staff we should be wary about as they're dishonest or mean to people?"

"What, apart from Summer and her Dad? There is another but I think maybe he'll leave anyway. That's Gill the bartender. He has been stealing bar stocks for years and boasts about it in the staff room – and then there's John the swimming pool man. He doesn't work here, he visits to clean the pool, but he's a nasty man and has hurt some of the young girls who worked as maids. I would feel much safer if he didn't come here again."

"Thank you – that will make such a difference to us. I'm sorry I don't have details of your job and wages yet but we'll tell you soon, I promise!" Yvonne's eyes filled with tears yet again, and she disappeared out of the room.

"That wasn't a huge list of people to keep on, was it?" Rose walked over to John's table and raised her eyebrows. "Any takers?"

"Worryingly not many," replied John, as he scanned the list. "Gill the barman was ingratiating and seems keen to stay. The chef was horribly pompous and was suggesting, I think, that we would be lucky if we retained his services, but the fact he came to see me implies he does want to stay. There were two maids who seemed pleasant enough, but we should check them out. Apart from that – nothing." He checked his watch. "Your parents will be arriving soon, Rose. Do you want to go to the airport to meet them or let Ian do it and bring them here?"

"I don't think they will ever have been met with a sign and a limo! Why don't we let Ian greet them at the airport? Perhaps Ian could text you or me to say when they're outside?"

"Good idea," replied Jamie. "Now since we may have a short lull, could we do a tour of the property to let me reacclimatise?"

"That's perfect, you two have a wander round and see what's what." Yet again Rose had a sneaking suspicion that John was hell-bent on matchmaking!

* * * * *

Rose gazed out of the window of the bedroom they were checking out. "All the rooms have the most fabulous sea views don't they? Jamie?"

"Sorry, measuring." Jamie had a gadget that seemed to be sending a red light across the space between him and the far wall of the room.

"What is that?"

"It's a laser measuring tool. I borrowed it from Shane this morning. He's more gadget-minded than I am."

"Oh right, if you say so." Rose didn't feel she understood a lot more than before she had asked the question, but it was probably best to keep quiet.

"What was the number of this room again?"

"Six it says on the door. I wish the rooms had names; I love staying in hotels where each room has a name or a theme."

Jamie looked up at her. "Err hello – who owns a hotel now? Why would you not name the rooms if you want to?"

"True," replied Rose. She still couldn't believe that this project was real; it had happened too fast and she was struggling to take it all in.

"Come on – there are two more rooms to do – let's try and squeeze them in before your Mum and Dad arrive." Jamie darted off enthusiastically and Rose felt happy she had him as both friend and business partner.

"Wifi is a bit rubbish down here," said Jamie as they reached the kitchen. "Why would we need that?" asked Rose.

"I'm plotting everything into an online project management programme. We have to do official planning and budgeting somehow."

"I was thinking of using rather more old-fashioned methods, but yes, good idea, as long as we discuss projects along the way that should work."

Rose looked around at the kitchen. The size was good but it seemed dated. "I don't think this would come up to health and safety standards in the UK, and the cleanliness level leaves a great deal to be desired. I'm surprised chef let it slip this far."

A large red-faced man appeared from behind the cupboard in the far corner of the room.

"You dare to speak of my kitchen in those tones, a young nothing tells me what is acceptable in my own kitchen – I think not! I told Mr McKay I would graciously stay on to help you out and see you into your new project, but with this type of interference, NO! Never!" With that he ripped off his chef's hat and jacket and threw them on the floor with an excessive gesture of disdain. He paused, but as neither Rose nor Jamie spoke, swept dramatically out of the kitchen.

"I think you were meant to throw yourself at his feet and beg him to stay."

"If he thought that was rude, he should hear what I'm thinking about the dirty insides of these cupboards and the floor over there! Good riddance I say. We have no guests, so no rush to find a new chef."

"Bit of a clean sweep on the staff front then! I guess it'll all sort itself. I have loads of contacts on the island."

Rose's phone rang. "Hello. Ian thanks for ringing – you're turning in now? I'll come straight up."

"Quick Jamie!" Rose flew out of the kitchen, her heart beating with excitement. How wonderful to have her parents there; how much she had to tell them about her plans, and how much they would enjoy this wonderful island.

Chapter 7

Rose rushed across reception to open the front door and saw her mother getting out of the car. Ian carefully escorted her into the hotel as though she was a treasured VIP. Pearl's face was wreathed with smiles, which grew ever wider when she spotted Rose. "Sweetheart, isn't this exciting! How are you?"

"Mum, I'm so, SO happy to see you." Rose hugged her mother as tightly as she could.

"Not fussed about seeing me, I suppose!" Rose spun round and repeated the hug with her father.

"Come on – I'm dying to show you round,"

Jamie approached and shook hands with both her parents. "Mum, Dad… this is Jamie French, do you remember… from uni…"

Pearl looked serious for a minute, then looked over at Ted and they both shrugged. "Of course we remember dear, how nice that you two have met up again." Rose looked awkwardly at her Mum. "It's OK, we're friends…" She hoped by saying the minimum her mother would understand all the things she didn't say!

"Come on – let's be seeing what you've gone and inherited, young lady." Ted took her arm.

"Jamie, perhaps I could have a few minutes of your time to discuss the financial side?" John looked at Rose as he spoke, silently OK-ing it with her. "Sure, come on –let's find a quiet spot. Kathleen, are you going to meet us for dinner?"

Kathleen, resourceful as ever, replied, "I thought I might go and have a chat with Yvonne and Bessie down in the kitchen, see if I can rustle up some food for us tonight."

"Excellent idea – we'll see you later."

"How about we all meet in a couple of hours – Mum, Dad – you're not too tired for that?"

"We're fine dear – dinner at seven sounds good to me. Come on, let's have a look around – ready, Ted?"

"Yes dear," he replied.

* * * * *

After a thorough tour of the building and some of the grounds, Pearl and Ted lowered themselves gratefully into the sofa in their room.

"Are you two all right? I'm aware you've been travelling for a day and a half… are you sure you want to join us for the evening – maybe you'd rather have an early night?" asked Rose.

"Excuse me, young lady! We're not that old and fragile and you bet your life we want to be in on all the discussions, most exciting thing that's happened to this family in years!" Ted took Pearl's hand and squeezed it.

"Tell you what," said Pearl, "could you leave us for say twenty minutes and we'll join you downstairs at seven o'clock?"

"Great, I'll see you later! Maybe you could have a power nap?"

* * * * *

Seven o'clock saw them all duly assembled in the reception area. John looked round and beamed at everyone. "So it seems

Kathleen, as usual, has the whole thing organised. We're to go into the dining room and Yvonne and Bessie have ordered flying fish rolls from the van down the road. Internationally renowned I would add, no crummy roadside fare here!"

"Thank you so much," said Pearl and Rose in unison.

"No problem, it was fun fixing a picnic! Sitting at a table will be much easier for talking and making lists. Come on through."

Several of the tables had been pulled together and there were fresh flowers in a small vase and a huge fruit bowl at one end. The dining room looked a lot cleaner than the last time Rose had seen it, and there were sparkling glass lampshades and candles lit around the room.

"You've worked miracles, Kathleen!"

"Not only me – in fact mainly Yvonne, and the fruit for dessert was organised by Bessie. One of her family has a fruit stall in the market."

They all sat down and were stunned into silence when Yvonne entered carrying a tray piled high with carefully wrapped parcels that closely resembled burgers, but promised so much more. "Wow," said Jamie, "be still my beating heart! Yvonne – I may have to kiss you." Yvonne looked very happy, and just a little embarrassed.

Rose dished out plates, and everyone took a parcel. Apart from appreciative murmurs, nobody spoke for a while. The parcels turned out to be flat bread buns, filled with fish, mayonnaise and hot sauce, pickle, cheese and salad. To say there were hard to eat in a dignified way would be an understatement, but everyone seemed to enjoy them. There were several left, and Jamie looked around surreptitiously.

"Jamie, grab another one – there are loads. Dad, would you like one? It seems a shame to waste them." Jamie gave a broad grin and eagerly grabbed another bun as did Ted and, after a pause, Pearl.

Rose looked at Kathleen and John but they both shook their heads and nodded towards the fruit bowl.

Once Rose and Yvonne had cleared the plates (Jamie still finishing off his third bun) and put the fruit bowl in the centre of the table, John stood and manoeuvred into place a whiteboard.

"Apologies for the workmanlike addition to the furniture. Jamie and I discovered this in the office and we thought it might help us plan. Jamie, do you want to take over?" John sat down and squeezed Kathleen's arm.

"Rose, do you want to start? Or are you happy to listen to my initial ideas?"

"Oh please carry on, there's plenty for us all to discuss."

"My starting place is staff. We've already discussed cancelling the one guest booked in; we haven't been able to contact them, yet but we will. Now, thinking of the staff, I felt we should look at departments first. I'd be happy to talk about my experiences over the past few years Pearl and Ted, if that would help. I've had a chat with John and explained the work and responsibilities I have been handling"

Ted shook his head, "No lad, we have to leave things like that to John and my Rose, if you're good enough for them, then you're good enough for us."

"Thank you Ted," said Jamie and then perhaps lost for words he turned to the whiteboard. He sketched a grid with the words Housekeeping, Kitchen, Maintenance, Office and Reception written along the top.

"We have close to no staff, sadly – but perhaps that's a good thing? At the moment we have Yvonne, Bessie, Sparkle and possibly another couple of chambermaids yet to be approached, and of course myself and Rose. The hotel might need a lot more staff than that, even if we run a pared-down version. However, although we have a good back-up fund, as John explained, it's neither huge nor a bottomless pit so we have to play it carefully."

There was a knock on the door and Yvonne peeped round. "I'm sorry to disturb you, but Bessie and I thought you might like to try some banana bread?" Rose looked across at Jamie as she recognised the delicious brightly coloured slices Yvonne was handing round. "Did you make this, Yvonne?"

"Oh no, I have a friend who works with her mother and she makes the best baked goods on the island. She has agreed to help with some baking too."

As one, Jamie and Rose said, "Angel?" Yvonne looked amazed. "Why yes! How on earth did you know?"

"Her Mum has been trying to marry me off – and my mate Shane, for that matter – to Angel for months! I go there frequently and you're right, she's an excellent baker."

Kathleen caught Yvonne's arm as she passed. "Yvonne – tell them a bit about your dreams and the hopes we were chatting about earlier."

"Oh I couldn't, Ma'am."

"On the contrary, please – we want any input you could offer. You never know how it might help."

A touch nervously, Yvonne started to speak. "You see one day I'd dearly love a breakfast café and tearooms of my own. I understand it'll never be, as it would need much money, but it's fun dreaming of menus and thinking about what food we could serve."

"Now that's interesting Yvonne," said Rose encouragingly. "Don't ever give up as you can never tell when or where a dream could come true. We're deep in discussions now, but I'll talk to you again later." Yvonne scuttled out of the room.

"So," said Jamie, "did that give anyone else an idea, or just me?"

"I think it might be interesting to use those skills and help

Yvonne follow her dream," replied Kathleen. "It's down to Rose to decide, but that could be an important piece of the jigsaw."

"Let's fill in more of the chart," said John. "There are some obvious names to add, I think?"

"I assume that Rose and I could take it in turns to be in reception and in the office? Any problems with that, Rose?"

"Absolutely not. I take comfort in the fact I would never be as bad a receptionist as Summer, and I've done several courses in hospitality – and you Jamie, would be a natural charmer behind the desk I'm sure."

"So with that column filled we now have… umm… nothing much else to add. Do we put Yvonne in charge of the kitchen? It feels too big a responsibility for her to do main meals. Do we ask her to organise housekeeping? It seems a shame not to use some of her skills… and oh dear…"

Pearl raised her hand slightly. "I…" she looked nervously across at Ted. "I wondered if you would consider older applicants?"

"Mum? Dad? What do you mean?" Rose's heart leapt with a mixture of excitement and anticipation.

Ted spoke up. "Rightly or wrongly, we haven't taken much to the new owners up at The Manor and I rather suspect they haven't taken kindly," there was a smothered cough from Pearl, "to the fact that Dorothy sold us The Lodge some years ago."

"Well the full details are clearly in the deeds." John looked aggrieved.

"Be that as it may," continued Ted, "Amelia and Neil were not thrilled that we have rights to wander in the garden or indeed to park and unload shopping on the drive outside our home, and that's just two of the upsets in the last week!"

"I'm sorry," John looked angry and embarrassed. "Dorothy's family are markedly different from her. She would have been mortified to hear that."

"I reckon it may have a happy ending," Pearl's grin stretched from ear to ear. "Amelia came down to The Lodge as we were waiting for the airport taxi and, cutting a long story short, she offered us half a million for it if she could have immediate possession. I don't know a lot about estate agency, but I guess our little house is worth a whole lot less than that."

"Good grief!" said Rose. "That's possibly double what it's worth! She must be desperate. What did you say?"

"I mentioned I was off to Barbados but would no doubt be seeing John McKay shortly and would tell him to arrange the whole thing as soon as he's available."

Rose rushed over to her mother and hugged her tightly, then moved on to Ted. "I'm so excited for you! This means you must follow your dream and buy somewhere gorgeous for your retirement. Goodness – I'm grateful that Amelia is such a brat that she'll pay anything to get what she wants."

Ted looked at Pearl, then at Rose and Jamie, "That's why we have a suggestion. Since we're almost homeless – and of course your mother is unemployed now – we wanted to volunteer our services and be here for a while, it might put a roof over our heads?"

Kathleen was the first to speak. "What a lovely idea."

Jamie was looking pleased too. "I'm thrilled that you would want to help. What would you like to choose as jobs? You'd automatically be… err… senior management!"

Ted grinned at Jamie. "Don't panic lad – we don't want to be any sort of management. Give us jobs we might be good at and we'll be as hard-working as you like."

Rose looked up at the chart. "Mum, you have a real skill for cleaning and housekeeping and many years' experience too – would you accept a role as Head of Housekeeping?"

"I certainly would my love, a job made in heaven for me. Could we have a room at the back of the hotel – would that work?"

"No, no," said Jamie, "I have a far better idea. Pearl, Ted, why don't you have the bungalow in the garden? We'd get it done up for you, obviously. I'm sure Rose would rather keep the suite she's in at the moment, and I have some digs with Shane already."

"Yes perfect. Better still – Dad, do you think you could brush up your DIY skills and you and Mum tackle the bungalow yourselves? You used to be brilliant on that front before the taxi business kept you busy?"

"I could indeed! What a great project – I'm feeling excited already. The other thing I could do is run a car to and from the airport, pick up guests if it wouldn't tread on Ian's toes? Might I be allowed to apply for Head of Maintenance? I enjoy a spot of DIY on a good day!"

"It's certainly all coming together. Rose, did you have any other ideas?" Jamie looked across at her.

Rose paused. "When I was lying awake last night I was thinking about what a great hotel needs. I wonder if we could find a good barman who could chat up the customers, mix fancy cocktails and be the real bedrock of the hotel? Jamie – would Shane agree to come over to us from the bar he's working in now? He knows all about cocktails and such, doesn't he?"

"He does indeed. Good call Rose – he'd be perfect. He's big-headed and would see the bar as his own little empire! Trust me – and don't get any ideas about Tilly, by the way. Lovely girl, but no need for exotic dancing here!"

"That's all looking much better," John indicated the chart on the board, which was filling up nicely, "but there's the problem of a chef…"

Rose spoke up. "Perhaps it isn't a problem. Could we not offer, at least for a start, fantastic breakfasts, light lunches and special afternoon teas to keep the traditional British bit going? Maybe home-made bar nibbles…. and all of that, I reckon, Yvonne might be able to handle, with a helper or two?"

"It is true the island has a mass of good restaurants. Maybe we could offer a free taxi service to their choice of restaurant and a pick-up later?"

"I could do that," Ted was nodding, "happy to help."

Pearl sighed: the long hours of travel were catching up. "On that note, would you all mind if Ted and I called it a night? It's been a long day."

"Mum, I'm sorry – I didn't think about the time difference, please do. We'll talk again in the morning." Rose hugged her mother tightly, "And I can't say thank you enough for coming over and helping me. I love you."

As she hugged her father she thought his eyes looked suspiciously wet eyes, but he brushed her off with, "That's what Dads do for their kids, surely? Now we must get to bed."

"Kathleen and I'll hit the hay too. I agree we should all chat on in the morning, but we've made a good start. I think you've got some exciting ideas, and promising potential staff too." John took Kathleen's arm and they left the room.

"Are you tired Jamie?"

"Actually I'm so wired I'm not sure I could sleep if I wanted to. Fancy killing two birds with one stone? We could go and find Shane and have a night cap at the same time?"

"Brilliant… but I'm guessing I have to go on that motorbike again?"

"'Fraid so, but I'll take it slowly, promise! I'm sure Shane is working tonight. We'll head to the Flamingo Bay and see if he's standing decoratively behind the bar."

Jamie kept his promise but Rose still felt nervous. She had never been a great one for the fast rides at theme parks and rollercoasters were her idea of hell, but holding tightly around Jamie's waist made it all seem a lot more bearable. She loved the way he smelt; he must be using the same aftershave as all those years ago... She stopped herself and remembered how important it was that she did not slip back into loving him again. Once bitten, twice shy; just friends this time. She loosened her grip around him and felt sad but determined.

They roared into the car park of a brightly lit (mainly by neon flamingos) bar. Music belted out of the doors and windows with a heavy rhythmic bass, and the sounds of laughter and clinking glasses brightened the night.

There were no spaces in the car park so Jamie steered the bike round to what she assumed to be the staff parking area. The standard of the vehicles went right down and there were plenty of gaps between the rusted older model cars. As she removed her helmet, she heard shouting and a fierce argument ensuing. They crept around the corner, moving cautiously. A couple were standing beside a BMW, yelling loudly at each other; suddenly the woman slapped the man hard on the face.

"I don't bloody know who the owner is! I've not talked to anyone – more likely to be your bragging at the golf club meant that solicitor found out!"

"You, my dear, are no more than a stupid liability. Good entertainment doesn't make up for lack of basic brains – you've ruined it all for now, but nothing's going to stop me."

"You can whistle if you think I'm staying in this Godforsaken hole while you work on your vendetta. The hotel stinks, the food stinks and frankly your attitude stinks. You're mean as hell, and as for that old joke about moths flying out of your wallet – who the heck would know – you never open it!"

"Go then. Can't say I'll miss you, except in bed. You're not stopping me getting this land, but it'd help if you could ever keep your mouth shut. I'll send your bags on. Call a cab and get straight to the airport."

With that he climbed into the car, slammed the door and sped off, tyres chewing up the gravel as he screeched out of the car park. The woman stamped her foot and headed back into the bar.

"I know who that was – let's hope I can avoid her." Jamie frowned at her, then shrugged as they made their way inside. Shane was leaning over the bar chatting up two beautiful young ladies. Slightly further down the bar was an impatient Cheryl, trying to get his attention.

Shane spotted Jamie and Rose immediately and was about to serve them when Cheryl pushed past, "Excuse me, I was ahead of them."

"She was indeed, mate." Without any show of irritation Shane gave her a wide smile and asked what she wanted. She ordered a large whisky on the rocks. Once settled with her drink she turned and saw Rose. "Hey we keep running into each other, funny how it always revolves around drinks, eh?"

Rose felt anxious and wondered if Cheryl might put two and two together, but it seemed not. "Yes indeed, it seemed a nice night for a drink."

"Pah! I thought the same, until the stupid old man threw a wobbly and now everything is messed up. Gotta go home for a bit, let him get over his strop. He'll soon be on the phone wanting me back." This positive statement was not reflected in her face; maybe she didn't believe her own words.

Rose breathed a quiet sigh of relief once she realised Cheryl hadn't joined the dots at all. Perhaps she could use this for her own ends. "You're welcome to join us for a drink if you're not in a rush. This is a friend of mine, Jamie; and Jamie, this is Cheryl – we met on the plane on the way over."

Cheryl held out her hand to Jamie. "Have to say love, you sure pick 'em. This one's a lot better looking than the old man."

Jamie ordered some drinks, including another whisky for Cheryl, and they sat round a table. Jamie kept flashing Rose 'what the hell are we doing and who is that?' looks. Out of sight Rose squeezed his knee as a signal to follow her lead. "What are your plans?" she asked Cheryl.

"Going to use the return half of my ticket and bugger off, I guess. No point in staying when he's in killer mode, he's no fun and there are no treats."

"In killer mode?" Jamie's eyebrows rose. "Yeah, deal's gone sour on him and he never takes that lying down. He's got a mean temper and what he wants, he gets, never mind the cost."

"Ah," replied Jamie. "He's going to up his price?" Cheryl took the last swig of her second whisky (both doubles) and pushed the glass towards Jamie. "Be a dear." Jamie went to the bar and Cheryl muttered, "Good move girl, he's gorgeous, wanna share?"

Rose blushed. "It is not like that, he's only a friend."

"Great: nothing in my way then," smirked Cheryl as Jamie returned with another double. "If your guy never loses, what will he do next?" Jamie handed her the drink.

"What, once he stops sulking that I've gone home? Not sure, but he has great contacts on the island, not nice people but they get results. He'll bully, bribe or kick people till they give him what he wants, not been a part of the relationship I've liked."

Shane came over to the table. "You rang for a taxi, Madam?"

"It's here already? Always the way when you're not in a hurry…" she stroked Jamie's hand, "unless of course you want some company for the night?"

"I'm sorry, I have to be up early; shift starts at five, I need to sleep soon. Nice offer though – maybe another time?" Rose kicked him hard under the table, and smiled to herself when he struggled not to wince.

"Bye Rose – maybe we'll meet again when I come back over."

"Sure, safe travelling Cheryl, take care."

Cheryl sashayed out of the bar, well aware that both Jamie and Shane were watching, and disappeared into the taxi.

"Excuse me! 'Maybe another time'?"

"Hey, I was undercover, important to lull her into a false sense of security! Who was she, anyway? But more importantly, I didn't like the sound of what that guy might do to get his own way."

"I'm sorry, but there was no way to tell you – that was Cheryl. Girlfriend or mistress, whatever, to Eric Somerville, the property developer I turned down."

"Jesus, I'm glad I didn't know! That guy sounds mean – should we be worried?"

"I don't see there's a lot he could do. I'm not going to change my mind, and if I did I'd sell to someone else, *anyone* else rather than him. I'm going to try and ignore the whole thing. Come on, let's see if Shane wants to talk."

Once the plan had been explained to Shane he was on board and hugely enthusiastic. "I'd definitely like the job; lucky us having a project like that to work on. Cool! Do you need any more staff?" Jamie looked at Rose, his head tilted slightly to one side. "Do we?"

"I think it's unlikely we'll need Tilly… I don't see exotic dancing featuring any time soon." Rose also felt uncomfortable about having Tilly around every day.

Jamie leapt to Tilly's defence. "She didn't always do that, that's just a gig she has taken to lately to improve her savings. Bar work is more her thing. She could be a good waitress?"

"I'm worried about all the staff being friends… what happens if we fall out?"

"True, but I do have one suggestion…" said Shane.

"Yes?" Jamie and Rose gazed intently at him.

"There's a waitress here who has the most divine voice. Once in a blue moon they get her up on the stage to do a session and the punters love it, huge talent I reckon."

"What's her name?" Rose liked the sound of someone who could sing *and* help with the waitressing.

"Nina."

"Nothing to do with the fact that Nina is your current lust, convenient to have her working within reach, mate?" Jamie laughed at him.

"No honestly, I mean it. I could get her to do a couple of numbers now, audition if you like?"

"That would be fun – would she mind?" Rose felt excited.

"Mind, nah! Any excuse! Nina! Nina – come here a minute."

A truly gorgeous young girl with beautiful skin and an enviable body came up to them. Her hair was exotic, with cornrows and masses of hair extensions, and her dress fabulous, in bold colours and with a plunging neckline. But most noticeable was her wonderful smile. "Hi?" she said with an enquiring look.

"Hi Nina," replied Rose. "Is there any chance you could do a couple of songs for us? Shane was singing your praises and we would love to hear you." Nina looked questioningly at Shane and he nodded. "Sure," she almost purred. Her voice was husky and definitely memorable.

She walked across the floor to a small raised area and fiddled with some sound technology for a moment, then tapped the microphone and coughed quietly. The buzz of talking stopped once she turned off the loud music and all eyes were turned expectantly towards the stage.

Nina launched into a soft, smoochy ballad which had the whole audience enthralled, then moved onto a song made famous by her namesake Nina Simone ('You've got life'). Rose wasn't sure whether to smile or cry. Nina's voice was a miracle; it sent shivers down her back and she recognised a God-given gift.

"Jamie – it would be wonderful to have her in the bar in the evenings. Could we offer her a part-waitress part-singer's job?"

"How could we not? Shane – that girl is golden! Don't mess up with that one… those looks, that voice… jackpot or what?"

"Tell me about it! I have no chance of moving on and leaving the island now, chained to my destiny!"

The two men laughed and Rose smiled indulgently; tough for a travelling soul to find he might need to settle down somewhere. She wandered over to have a word with Nina. She could see why the guys were star-struck; goodness, she was beautiful.

"Nina, could we talk for a moment?"

"Sure, let me get some water, singing always makes me thirsty."

"Could I have one too please?"

Nina carried the glasses over to a table. Rose explained their ideas, reassuring Nina they had plenty of capital behind them and that it would be a fun place to work. She asked if she would mind working with Shane. "Mind? I'm mad about the man at the minute! I'd do anything to be with him – but who knows how long these things will last."

"Sounds as though you two have something good going on, then."

"We just might have, and yes – I'd love to accept your offer."

"It is going to be a long haul rebuilding the business, but I think it may be fun."

"I'm so happy to be joining the team. I need to get back to work now though, can't let them down just because I've found a way to have more fun with my life." She smiled, flashing pearly white teeth, then wandered round the tables chatting and asking if anyone wanted drinks.

Rose walked back to the bar, where Jamie was talking to Shane earnestly. As she got closer Rose overheard "and not a word to Rose" and "don't worry, I've got your back", which puzzled her.

Jamie turned round. "I was talking to Shane about our plans, and I think it's going to work, but thank goodness we have a few people who know what they're talking about. Shane has all the contacts we need for the bar area, so that's one thing we can tick off our list."

As the evening progressed the bar clientele became more unruly and the music got louder. Twice Shane had to break up a fight. Rose was tired and wanted to go but she could see Jamie was having fun. Suddenly she noticed a couple of men moving down the bar towards her, and instinctively she flinched.

"So my little lovely," the reek of rum and body odour preceded the words, and Rose recoiled again. These kind of people really freaked her out. "Fancy a dance, pretty lady?" One of the guys had gold-capped teeth and a long scar across his cheek. She felt more than a bit nervous and on the edge of full-blown panic.

"Thank you but I'm with someone." She tried to be calm and polite, and edged nearer to Jamie.

"But I know how to show a girl a good time, plenty of money me – and plenty something else too." He leered at her, waving a huge wad of dollars. "My boss says you ken always gets what you want, one way or another, and money ain't a bad way. He sure paid me enough for what he wants, now I ken pay you."

Jamie stepped in. "Sorry mate, she's with me… another time, maybe?"

The second guy appeared on the other side of Jamie, leering, "Hey! His boss says whatever you want you can git, maybe we just will git now we have the cash."

Shane came round to the front of the bar and put his arm around one of the guy's shoulders in a nonchalant yet firm manner. "Sorry Lenny – but the only 'gitting' you 'gitting' tonight is to 'git' out. Never mind what anybody's boss says – Shane says leave this little lady alone, so goodnight boys."

The two guys narrowed their eyes at Shane, Jamie and Rose. "This ain't over, I didn't git this money for nothing." They left fairly peaceably, bar a random kick at the door on their way out.

Rose breathed a sigh of relief. "I was so frightened! Do you get loads of bully boys in the bar?"

"No, that sort often head for the cheaper bars, but they were flush tonight. Someone's paid them off for a job – could be drugs, protection racket – Lord knows what."

"We'll call it a night I think." Jamie had his arm protectively around Rose.

"You drive safely now," said Shane looking straight into his friend's eyes.

Chapter 8

Pearl and Ted were sitting in the sun on the balcony of Rose's room. Rose emerged from the bathroom, shook her hair, still wet from the shower and took a deep breath.

"Isn't it wonderful, waking up each morning to this sunshine and the smell of the sea?"

"It certainly is," replied Pearl. "I reckon this change will do you the power of good. But you realise we may all have to go home and tie up the loose ends there?"

"I could do that," said Ted.

"Thank you dear, but no – I'm going to have to help you or we'll never find what we put in storage again."

"What's the plan, Mum?"

"I think we could take a small storage unit. They had some of those down the road if you remember – I always wondered what people used them for, and now I know! We could put everything we think we don't need into storage and have the crucial stuff shipped. I'm sure we can cope while we settle in."

"I'd need my clothes, obviously," said Rose, "and maybe my old CDs and odds and ends from my bedroom?"

"Would it make sense to bring my tools and bits in the shed?" suggested Ted. "It would cost to freight them, but at least we'd know what I've got when it comes to maintenance?"

"I think your Dad and I could manage it on our own, and that way you can get on with reorganising things here. It's a month at least before you reopen?"

"Absolutely Mum, and yes Dad, I think it would be good to bring all your tools. We can organise a brand-new shed and you can get set up in that."

"I suppose I have to sell the car?"

"Sorry Dad, but it probably would be best unless you want to find a long-term parking arrangement somewhere?" Pearl jumped in. "Don't be daft Ted – of course we'll sell the car! You can always buy another with that huge fund you charmed out of poor Dorothy – £80,000 on a Jaguar, indeed!" Pearl smiled kindly, teasing him. Although the Jaguar had long been a dream of Ted's she knew he would always find an excuse to put family first.

There was a brisk knock on the door and Yvonne came in, bearing a large tray of breakfast goodies. "That looks wonderful Yvonne, thank you!" smiled Rose.

"They're bits I enjoy cooking up, I need to keep myself busy. There's my banana bread and some of my home-made granola and yogurt with fresh fruit, honey, jams and marmalades." She placed the tray on the table and put out the plates.

"Granola?" Ted perked up. "I love granola – is it a local recipe?" He moved straight for the cereal bowl and poured himself a large helping, adding milk.

"Oh no," said Yvonne, "a school friend of mine upped and marries this American. She had this breakfast called 'granola' and sent me a Christmas parcel with it in and I loved it. I asks for the recipe then changed it a bit."

"Yvonne, are you free to chat for a minute or two? I'd love to run an idea past you."

Yvonne frowned. "Is it bad, should I be worried?"

"We hope you'll think it's good, but let's see, shall we?"

Rose sat on one of the sofas and indicated to Yvonne to join her. "Jamie and I have been trying to work out how to relaunch the hotel with the minimum of fuss. We have to keep in mind we don't have any guests yet, and don't know how long it'll take to start filling up."

"You don't need me, I understand." Tears were shining in Yvonne's eyes as she spoke.

"Yvonne, you do make me cross sometimes!" said Rose, smiling at the tearful young woman. "Please believe that I'm going to help you and that you are truly valuable, it's all good." Rose paused to offer Yvonne a tissue. "We wondered if we might skip a full service evening restaurant and offer extra-super breakfasts, light lunches and traditional English teas… and we hoped you might be interested in running that for us, with a couple of staff to help you?"

"Me? Me run it? Me run it for you?" Now Yvonne was crying in earnest, tears rolling down her cheeks. Rose sighed and continued. "You have some great breakfast recipes and we have Bessie to help out in the kitchen. In the afternoons we have offered a waitressing job to a lady called Nina who is sort of a friend of a friend, and I know you'll love her. She's also a beautiful singer so she can work with you in the afternoons and sing in the bar during the evenings."

"Oh I can't believe it… it's my dream come true! I was only saying the other day… oh that's how you knew what I was dreaming! I can help with the bedrooms and perhaps reception?"

"Whoa… no way do you have to help on reception unless we're all struck down with the flu or whatever. Jamie and I'll work on reception and in the office. The bedrooms and cleaning are all going to be handled by my Mum, Pearl. Mum – come and meet Yvonne officially." Pearl came over and shook hands with Yvonne, then hugged her.

"Please call me Pearl – and can I start by asking your advice?"

Clever Mum, thought Rose.

"What do you think of the two remaining chambermaids – are they worth keeping? They didn't ask John if they could stay, but it would be nice to know your opinion?"

"I reckon they OK," replied Yvonne, "there's better, but these two knows the job already, and with you to look after them and chase 'em up... Of course there's always my friend Sparkle?" She looked across at Rose, keen to send the message that Sparkle wanted a job.

"Ah! I see what you are saying. I'll discuss it with Rose," smiled Pearl. "I'll see what we can do, but thank you for your offers of help. I reckon we're more likely to need to help you with the catering – I think your snacks and breakfasts will be an island-wide success."

"Oh hardly," said Yvonne, "but what excitement, I can feel my head fillin' with ideas already!"

"The granola gets a thumbs up from me," came a mumbled comment from Ted's corner, where a huge bowlful was disappearing fast.

"We're going to try making The Summer House somewhere different by having a special team behind the scenes, and you'll be an important part of that. I got John to check the wages and accounts and you don't get paid enough for the job you currently have. With all this new responsibility we'll need to more than double your wages to be fair."

Yvonne's tears started again and everyone laughed at her. "Oh dear – and I thought *I* was bad with my tearful reactions!" Pearl put her arm round Yvonne's shoulders. "We're going to have fun building this place up. I'm partly doing it because I loved Dorothy, but I guess you didn't know her?"

"Miss Dorothy was talked about a lot, but no, I never met her. Now would you 'scuse me, I got to tell Bessie the news."

An excited Yvonne sniffed her way out of the room and Rose felt comforted that at least the small staff she had would be unerringly loyal and make life happy along the way.

Shortly after Rose closed the door it was pushed open by a huffing and puffing Jamie, carrying a huge picnic basket marked with the initials 'F & M', travel rugs wrapped in leather straps and another basket with four compartments that Rose assumed was for carrying wine. "What have you got there?"

"Aha," said Jamie, "I was foraging in the rooms around the kitchen and I found a store room full of what I can only describe as picnic items. There are folding chairs, rugs, baskets and some shooting sticks. Maybe we could offer old-fashioned picnics too?"

"Good idea, lad," said Ted. "I could drive the guests to a nice setting, beach or whatever, and collect them later?"

"Great – I love this team brainstorming!" Jamie smiled and peered inside the picnic hamper. "Look at this, Fortnum & Mason with all the original cutlery, plates, cups and saucers… it must be worth a mint!"

"Great find, Jamie." Rose looked towards him and yet again felt her heart skip. No –she would not weaken and let herself get hurt again.

"Why don't you two go and test it out? I think we could all do with a day off and a bit of a holiday to let the new ideas sink in – we have so many life-changing events to get used to!"

Jamie nodded in agreement. "Perfect idea, Pearl. Rose, I can show you all the tourist attractions you haven't seen yet, there's so much I'm not sure where to start. Come on – let's go and raid the kitchen for food. I've borrowed Shane's car again, so we can play holidaymakers. Will you two be all right?"

"They'll be fine," came a voice from the doorway. John and Kathleen stood there, a light mac over Kathleen's arm and a capacious bag slung over John's. "We have supplies and a tour guide all sorted and waiting for you, Pearl and Ted; we could do the 'oldies tour of the island'. Ian has kindly agreed to escort us. He's arriving in ten minutes or so. How does that sound?"

"Fantastic," agreed Ted, and Pearl nodded.

Rose grabbed her bag and a bikini wrapped in a towel and she and Jamie disappeared, leaving the happy tour group behind.

* * * * *

"This is fun," Rose sighed, trailing her arm out of the car window and enjoying the rush of balmy air against her skin.

"You can look forward to a lot more sunny days – and frankly often when it rains it's warm rain, not the damp and chilly deal it can be at home."

"Did Shane mind lending you the car?"

"No, but he did get a couple of cracks in about how he didn't have a choice if the boss was asking to borrow his car. I know he was teasing, but it did make me think that maybe we should have at least one car between us."

"You're right; and probably we should both have a car as we don't want to spend every moment in each other's pockets." Rose tried to remember she must take care that they weren't repeatedly flung together.

"We'd better have a look at a budget. I assume I get an open-topped sporty number, making sure I charm the guests, and you perhaps could get a handy five-door small car or a small estate for shifting things?"

"It's a good job we're on the road or I'd smack you one. Yeah right, is my response to that. I suggest we go for a useful estate car for you and yes, I'm happy with a nippy hatchback-type thing.

Whatever we find on the market that's good value and will last for a bit."

"Maybe your Dad would enjoy coming along with us to help choose?"

"Brilliant idea – that would please him tremendously. In that case we'd better fix it sooner rather than later as they're going home shortly to clear the house."

"I'll have a word when we get back. I assume the finances will cover two cars?"

"Right now I suggest the finances will allow for almost anything we want. The trouble will start if we don't manage to make the hotel pay for itself quickly, but I'm confident we should be able to make it work."

They drew closer to the main town of Oistins and Rose spotted a billboard. "What was that Jamie, a submarine ride, 'Atlantis' or something?"

"Oh that, right, it's quite good fun if you don't scuba or snorkel I guess – good way for kids and oldies to see underwater life."

"Excuse me? Kids and oldies? Now I'm going to punch you, driving or not… would you like to rethink what you just said?"

Jamie flashed a confused look in her direction. "What do you mean? You *can* snorkel or scuba, can't you?"

"No, as it happens I can't. For starters I'm terrified of underwater life, beautiful to look at but no need to get too close – and also I've never had a chance to try it."

"Oh my God, we have to rectify that! There are loads of brilliant teachers on the island. You *have* to learn to snorkel – the turtles alone are worth it!"

"Hmm we'll see… maybe I'll be a bit busy… but I wouldn't mind trying the submarine ride 'for kids and oldies." Jamie flinched as she punched his arm. "Sure, why not? You don't usually have to book ahead... what is it now, eleven? Should be fine."

He took the next turning by a small poster and arrow indicating the 'Atlantis adventure', and stopped in the car park. "Over there under the tree would be better, then the car is in shade, thinking about our food and so on?" Rolling his eyes heavenwards Jamie repositioned the car. "You may have got a point... come on, let's get a move on."

There was quite a crowd waiting in reception and Rose's heart sunk. "Maybe we've missed the next one and it'll be hours to wait?"

"Nah, should be fine. It's quite big, hang on." Jamie went over to the till area, produced his credit card and chatted to the assistant for quite a while. Rose looked around for somewhere to sit. She resisted all the souvenirs; after all, they weren't on a real holiday. She took a deep breath as the reality of her recent acquisition hit her again. Oh Dorothy! You certainly knew how to pack a punch!

In front of her a blonde girl shifted her rucksack and indicated the spot next to her. "You're welcome to sit here if you like?"

"Oh thanks! I was wondering how long it might be before we get on a boat?"

"Shouldn't be long; they're running hourly in high season. I'm Kate, by the way."

"I'm Rose, and my friend who is hopefully organising our tickets over there is Jamie."

"You on holiday from England?"

"Long story: it was going to be a holiday but it sort of grew. How long are you here for?"

"Oh, I came for a week about two years ago." They both laughed. "Aha! Yours sort of grew too! Your story first – what's the draw?"

Kate shuffled the rucksack and propped it up between her legs. "It's hard to articulate quite how or why, but I had this strange feeling that my future was here. Whenever I contemplated returning home I felt down in the dumps. So as I'm a free spirit, here I stayed. I do all sorts of temporary work, occasionally a job sticks for six months, it's been a fun adventure."

"Good for you taking the plunge. What do you do – waitressing, bar work?"

"No, never, I hate doing that kind of stuff, more likely to tip a drink over someone than deliver it safely. I do travel articles, blogs, write-ups for mags, all that sort of thing. Today I'm doing a review of this attraction for an American mag. I've been on it before but it might have changed or I might have forgotten something, and I do try and stay current."

Jamie came over and confirmed that they had places on the next boat. Rose felt quite excited; it felt like a real adventure, and it was such a joy to get away from the hotel for a bit.

"Ladies and gentlemen – if you could have your tickets ready and follow me?"

Kate gathered up her rucksack and Jamie raised his eyebrows at Rose. "Sorry, I haven't introduced you – Kate, this is my friend Jamie, and Jamie this is Kate; she's doing a travel piece on the submarine."

"Cool, and good to meet you."

The crowd started moving onto the small boat that would take them to the submarine. The sun streamed onto the sea and magnified the sparkles and turquoise blue. Rose felt privileged to see such beauty. "Never stops stunning me – when I see that colour I almost purr with happiness," sighed Kate. "Oh me too, it's the most wonderful sight ever," agreed Rose.

Once they reached the submarine there was a slightly perilous crossing from boat to sub, then a tight squeeze down the vertical ladder into the vessel. Inside was surprisingly light and airy and there were seats on each side that faced a row of portholes. Jamie edged along the row first, followed by Rose and then Kate.

"All in and OK?" asked Jamie

"Yeah, fine."

Once they had got through all the instructions and questions, the engines started and Rose felt childishly excited once again. The submarine swooped through the water and dived deeper. Rose couldn't contain herself, 'oohing' and 'aahing' as brightly coloured fish darted past the windows. The pilot did a good job of pointing out any particularly exciting specimens, and Kate clapped wildly when they saw a large turtle swimming lazily not far away.

"Oh I do love turtles! I swear I must have been one in a previous life, the loveliest creatures." Rose agreed, although she felt Kate was rather more enthusiastic than she was.

Jamie leant over. "Kate, have you not done scuba diving or snorkelling off Brown's Beach? The turtles are everywhere, hawk-billed and green – you have to go."

"Sadly, although I feel a great kinship with turtles, I can't swim very well so there are limits to where I can see them."

A rather awkward silence followed, then Rose said, "See Jamie, we're both rubbish! Maybe you should teach us."

"That's a deal! I can't believe there can be *two* beautiful girls on this island who can't at least snorkel!"

"Jamie, bit over the top if you don't mind – great to be charming, but that one bombed!" Rose and Kate laughed together, and Jamie blushed furiously.

"Look at those brilliant blue fish – it's surprising that you can see this depth of colour so far underwater." Rose referred to the identification chart on the wall. "I think those might be blue parrot fish – and look at that big shoal over there! Groupers, I think?"

"Stingray," shouted a small boy behind them, and every head in the boat turned: there, about ten feet from the sub, a large stingray was lazily flapping along. "Isn't this exciting, Jason dear?" said the grey-haired lady sitting next to him. "Look at all the beautiful corals."

"I wanna see whales and sharks and PIRANHA fish!!!" shouted the child, and everyone sniggered. "Can't promise all of those," came the voice of the pilot, "but there are two beautiful turtles to starboard, right-hand side for any landlubbers on board."

Jason had to be physically restrained by his grandmother. Rose was starting to think she might have to do the same to Kate, who was now really excited.

Although the journey lasted forty minutes, it felt like ten to Rose; it was so thrilling, so different, and gave her mind a much-needed break from the huge changes life was thrusting at her. All too soon they were trooping off the boat and back into the reception area where fresh juices and intriguing snacks were on offer. Kate explained that some were like small samosas, and there were sticky spicy chicken wings too. Jamie, as always, ate enough for all of them, and Kate and Rose tried a samosa each.

While they ate Rose explained to Kate that she and Jamie were having a much-needed day off and, as a newcomer to Barbados, she was being shown the sights. "Oh Jamie – you have to take her to Parrot Beach! It's rare for anyone except locals to be there."

Jamie thought for a moment and frowned. "Parrot Beach – not sure I know that one?"

"Across on the Atlantic side, quiet, rugged and perfect."

"Do you fancy coming with us? We have room in the car and you could show us the way? Unless of course you need to work?" Rose wondered if she saw a flash of disappointment cross Jamie's eyes as she spoke, but he said nothing.

"If it's OK with both of you – I don't want to be a gooseberry."

"Oh no," said Jamie firmly, "we're old friends, aren't we Rose?"

Rose nodded, but inside the butterflies (more like large moths, it felt) did a lap of her stomach. It was probably a good thing they didn't have too many comfortable moments alone in romantic situations; it never pays to mix work and pleasure, she lectured herself.

Once back on the road, Kate sat in the front to give directions and managed to talk nonstop about tourist places they passed en route. "Barbados is actually well signposted and easy to get round; on some of the smaller islands you have to remember instructions like 'turn second left after the tethered goat' as there are no signs at all. Stop! Stop here!" she screamed. Rose jumped, and Jamie slammed on the brakes.

"Christ! What's happened?" he asked.

"Oh nothing – but if you turn down here there's a cottage that's literally covered in bougainvillea, a perfect photo opportunity, you mustn't miss it."

Rose felt Kate was great; a bit eccentric, maybe, but knowledgeable about the island, and a fun new person to have met.

A few minutes later they were back on the main road, and Kate pointed out the huge expanse of beach on the right. "There, there it is! You'll need to pull in over there, along the track." They followed her directions and parked in a grassy area alongside a couple of other cars. Once out of the car they paused for a moment, admiring the view.

"Come on Rose, let me show you, there were baby crabs on my last visit. Jamie, can I help carry?"

Jamie was struggling with the basket, rugs and general beach paraphernalia, but masculine pride stopped him from accepting any help. "No – you two go on ahead and look for a spot for us to have lunch."

Once they had all settled on the mats and rugs Jamie had

carried down, opened the bottles of water and fruit juice and selected sandwiches of their choice, a companionable silence reigned while they ate.

Kate leaned back. "This is why I never want to leave – it's a glorious day, the sea is blindingly beautiful and all is well with my world. I wish we didn't need to earn money for food and a roof over our heads. I haven't asked – what do you two do back in England?"

"Jamie lives over here at the moment, and I arrived almost a week ago."

Kate frowned at Jamie. "Sorry – I assumed you were a couple and had come over on holiday."

"Nope, we're definitely just friends, known each other for donkey's years – but workwise I guess you could say we're going to be working more closely together from now on." He looked over to Rose, unsure of how much more to say.

"It is a long story, and probably more fun over drinks and a meal than spoiling a sunbathe on the beach, but basically I have inherited a hotel over here and Jamie is going to help me run it."

Kate's eyes grew to the size of saucers. "Oh my, that is a really big deal." Rose smiled. "You have no idea of how much of a big deal it is! It's going to be a long rocky road to haul it out of the mess it's in at the moment."

"So where is it? Tell me more – this is a real-life adventure!"

"It's called The Summer House," chipped in Jamie.

Kate's eyes grew even larger. "What – THE Summer House? Oh my, oh my!" She let some sand trickle through her fingers. "I did an article on the history of Barbados ages ago which involved a lot of research. The Summer House was an important social centre for island society back in the middle of the twentieth century. There were loads of famous people and glitterati. It must be worth a great deal of money… I guess your family must be extremely wealthy."

"Not a bit," replied Rose, feeling uncomfortable, "my Dad drove a taxi and my Mum was a cleaner. The lady she worked for became a close family friend, but she died recently and left me this property. It was all a huge shock; I didn't know she owned property in Barbados, let alone a hotel."

"So how can you two run a hotel that big... don't you need training?"

"To be honest, right now it's not 'that big' at all. We have zero guests and a business that has been royally screwed by a corrupt manager, but we'll fight, we'll get there." Jamie touched Rose's arm gently as he spoke, no doubt as a friendly gesture, but Rose's heart did a double somersault and she pulled away abruptly.

"Would it be rude to ask if I could come and see round? I was refused a guided tour when I was doing research – I remember they were really snappy with me. But I have lovely pictures in my head and from newspaper cuttings I've managed to get hold of..."

"Are you thinking what I'm thinking?" asked Jamie.

"Depends what you're thinking," teased Rose, "but I was wondering, Kate, if you'd be interested in designing a small exhibition or display on the history of The Summer House? We could put it up in reception and people could read about what a fabulous place it has been over the years."

"Exactly-ish what I was thinking."

"Only 'ish'?" replied Rose

"I was thinking we could offer guided tours eventually, once we have everything done and sorted and yes, the same sort of thing."

"Yes to both ideas! I'd love to help, tours is what I'm good at... hey... if it's not being too forward, have you got anyone lined up to help guests plan what to do on the island, which tours are good or not and all that stuff?"

"Ace idea," Jamie paused, "but I'm not sure what we have in

the budget for more staff yet. Could we take your number and get back to you?"

"Actually it would mainly be self-financing. The attractions often give a commission to hotels booking their guests in. I'd need an area in the lobby and perhaps a small basic wage to make sure I could pay my rent each week, but apart from that…"

"It's a deal. Why not come over tomorrow morning and we can work out where you can have your area and get it set up, and you could advise us on the exhibition?"

"Done deal!"

"Hello pretty ladies!" They looked up and saw a stunningly good-looking, dark-skinned man standing over them. Slung over his shoulder he had a bag full of goods, and he held a few bracelets in his hand. "I saw you beautiful ladies and I 'mediately thought Westin, I thought, that being me name, Westin – there are beautiful women waiting to see if they can buy a pretty bracelet! These could have been designed for you."

He dangled the bead bracelets closer. Despite herself Rose had to look and was surprised to see that they were indeed gorgeous. "Are these glass beads?" she asked.

"A truly discerning customer for once! They are indeed, pretty lady, all made by my fair hand."

"You make the beads from scratch?" Kate stared at Westin with a knowing look. "Perhaps not the beads pretty lady. I helps me girlfriend, she makes those and gets me a-stringing and a-twisting."

"So your girlfriend makes the actual beads," asked Jamie, far less impressed than the two girls. "She does indeed, she bin to college an' all that too. I takes charge of the selling and the marketing of the tings."

"I think her work is so special," said Rose. "I don't suppose she has a card or somewhere I could look at these when I'm not trying to sunbathe and have fun with my friends on the beach?"

Westin, the full-of-talk salesman, was stilled for a moment. "You keen but not this moment now, you want me to bring them to your home?"

"No, some contact details please; if I want to see more of her work I could perhaps ring her or come and see them. I never feel comfortable with pressure salesmanship."

Jamie laughed. "I wouldn't push it mate! You may have met your match here."

Westin gave a huge gleaming smile. "I would be delighted to give you my Coralie's card – here you are".

He handed over a floral card with hand-painted bead images along one side. "That's a beautiful card, I'll keep it safely! Maybe we'll see you again."

"I do hope so. I don't suppose you, sir, would want to purchase an original book of love poetry, perfect to attract and keep a good woman and all written by yours truly?"

"No thank you, and now if it's OK with you we'd like to continue our lunch!"

Westin nodded as though he was considering an important issue. "Sir, never let it be said Westin didn't understand when he was being a gatecrasher."

As he walked away Kate burst into peals of laughter and rolled back onto the picnic rug. "Way to go you two! I have never seen Westin so expertly put down... boy, am I going to love spending time with you. That was pure unadulterated talent!" She wiped her eyes as she continued to rock with laughter.

"What's special about what we did – we only politely said 'not right now'?" Rose couldn't for the life of her see what was momentous about their exchange.

"Westin is a flat-out, honest-to-goodness sales god. I tell you

– not only could he sell ice to Eskimos, he could get them on a monthly pre-payment plan and fix a territorial deal with a fridge manufacturer. The guy is a legend round here, and he makes a good living out of hassling tourists. The only difference between him and all the other annoying bums that wander up and down the beaches is that he sells genuinely beautiful arts and crafts."

"The card he gave me is stunning."

"Yeah, Coralie is well known in town for her beading, beautiful work, can be pricy but it's worth it. His poems too, they're not all bad."

"Come on, let's make the most of the beach. Jamie – did you bring the swimming gear out of the car?"

"Sure, but Kate – have you got a costume?"

"I wear a bikini under my clothes – you never know when there might be a chance of some rays. I'll probably just paddle though."

The afternoon passed with much hilarity and laughter and time spent splashing about in the warm sea. The weight of Rose's new venture lifted from her shoulders, and the sunshine filled her heart.

At long last Jamie stood up and brushed the wet sand from his shorts. "Sorry to be a pain guys, but I just noticed the time. I need to be getting back – I have an appointment shortly."

"Right?" Rose didn't intend to be nosy, but realised it sounded that way. Jamie seemed slightly embarrassed, and shrugged it off with, "Only a work thing, I had to tidy up a few errands after I gave my notice in, can't leave them completely in the lurch."

For no good reason Rose felt anxious. But why should she? They were only friends, after all – but somehow it felt as though he wasn't being quite straight with her.

"That's fine. Kate – can we drop you anywhere en route?"

Chapter 9

"Mum, Dad, hi!"

Pearl and Ted staggered into reception, Ian following close behind. They were all burdened with large suitcases, holdalls and boxes. Rose rushed over to greet them and take some of the weight. "You must have the entire contents of the house here! Did you end up having to store anything at all?"

"I'll say so – took me forever loading up the car with her boxes and bags for the storage unit. I have no idea how your mother can accumulate this much stuff in a few years."

"Excuse me – some of the 'rubbish' was yours, and as for that shed… don't you start on me. *Your* bedroom was quite a project too, young lady; there are four packing cases in storage and several coming over with the shipment. To be fair I think we can all take some of the blame." Pearl dropped the cases and took a deep breath. "Fun to be back though, I found myself feeling quite excited on the way over."

"We've missed you," came a voice from the other side of reception. Jamie walked over to hug Pearl, then shook hands with Ted. "Let's get some of this stuff down to the bungalow and see what your verdict is on the revamp!"

"Oh I'd forgotten about that for a moment! Now – that *is* exciting – a new home. Planning to carry me over the threshold, Ted?"

"What, and ruin my back before I even start work? Not a chance! I'm sorry I didn't do more of the repair work myself before we left; I meant to do the whole thing."

After a concerted effort to transport everything over to the bungalow, Ian left with a cheery wave and Rose gave her mother the front door key. "Here, you do the honours. I do hope you'll be happy – obviously there's space for bits you've brought from home, but I got a package deal for most of it from a furniture shop in town."

"Ooh, I feel stupidly nervous." Pearl struggled to get the key into the lock. The door swung open to reveal a completely repainted interior, mostly white with a few pastel touches with pale blue sofas, country-style plaid curtains and a shiny white kitchen with all modern conveniences.

"I love it!" squealed Pearl, throwing her arms around her daughter. "You've got it just right – isn't it all gorgeous?"

"Nice dishwasher," added Ted, "not had a dishwasher before apart from our Pearl. Very fancy."

Rose took this to mean he was happy with the bungalow, and she hugged him too for good measure. "I'm glad it's all OK. I was worried about calling someone else to sort it out, but they really knew what they were doing *and* gave us good prices, a win-win situation really!"

Pearl opened one of the kitchen cupboards and cried out again. "Food, tea, coffee… you've thought of everything!"

"You can thank Yvonne for that; she did a supermarket run, and got you some fish and eggs from her relatives too. You'll find those in the fridge."

"This is the best moving in day we've ever had – how kind everyone has been."

Jamie chipped in. "Right, we must get on, there's a million and one jobs to organise. Ted, I think you have a DHL delivery due tomorrow with the contents of your tool shed, so we need to get that sorted. There are loads of handyman-type jobs to get done."

"Let them have the rest of the day, "said Rose, "try not to be too hard a taskmaster this early."

"Oops – sorry! I forgot how tired you must be after the flight."

"We'll let you unpack and relax. Shout if you need anything – there's a buzzer on the phone that gets through to reception. Shall we meet up for dinner later? Say seven o'clock in reception, and we'll organise what and when?"

"That sounds perfect, my love! We'll be up and running tomorrow, I promise – just a bit drowsy now. I think we both need a nap."

"If you get bored with napping, Ted, you might want to look at your new shed; you'll find it round the back." Jamie smiled at the older man, understanding what his priorities might be.

They walked back towards the hotel and passed Edmund, kneeling down and weeding one of the flowerbeds. "Hi Edmund! I've been trying to catch you all this week – where have you been hiding?"

"I just had a spell at home." Edmund kept looking down at the flowerbed as he talked, and Rose could tell something was wrong. "Edmund… what is it… have I done something to upset you?"

That comment made Edmund look up, and Rose tried to cover her shock. "What happened to your face, did you have an accident? Do you need more medical help? Can I do anything?" Jamie put his hand on her shoulder to signal that she was talking too much. "Edmund, what happened?"

Edmund looked down again and seemed unsure what to say. "I guess some folks took a disliking to me and I was lucky I didn't get hurt real bad."

"It looks bad to me." Rose felt saddened at the realisation that someone could have done this to him deliberately. Although she still hadn't found out the full story, she knew that Dorothy and Edmund had been great friends. Jamie's voice took on a steelier note. "Can you tell me why all of a sudden someone took a disliking to a gentle soul like you?"

"Some men came to my house to give me money to poison the garden with weedkiller. I couldn't do that. I couldn't poison my life and all those memories."

"But why on earth…?" Rose felt the tears welling up. "Was it because of us?"

"Somet'ing like dat." Edmund wasn't looking at either of them.

"Is there anything we can do to help you… pay medical bills? Did they hurt anyone else, or damage your house?" Jamie seemed upset by the news, more so than Rose would have expected.

"No, I don't have nothing valuable and I already mended the doors they smashed, so we're OK. My neighbours saw them off eventually. But you take care: there are some very bad people out there and they're not best pleased about what you are doing."

"I'm very, very sorry that our actions have brought you pain." Rose felt terribly guilty. "No, Miss Rose, your actions are lightening my heart. You are bringing Miss Dorothy back to me every day and that makes me happy."

"Thank you, Edmund," said Rose. Slowly and in silence Rose and Jamie continued walking back to the hotel. "I don't know if I'm sad, scared or angry."

"I'd go for all three. Shane told me he heard thugs bragging in the bar that they'd been paid to make sure we were sorry we messed with McGuyver. One of the lads working on your parents' bungalow mysteriously didn't turn up for work one day, and they had to get a replacement."

"Why didn't you tell me? What do we do?"

"Nothing is my best guess… what can we do? Employ an army of guards to keep this place and our staff safe?"

"I think we ought to have a staff meeting tomorrow and talk it through as a team. Everyone should be made aware that they need to take extra care."

"Agreed."

* * * * *

The next few days flew past without further mishap. Ted spent many hours preparing his precious shed. Pearl helped Rose and Yvonne to deep-clean the bedrooms and make lists of small jobs for Ted. The promised staff meeting never took place; on balance Rose and Jamie decided to let sleeping dogs lie and not upset everyone.

"We need to get on with naming the bedrooms," Rose said to her mother. "You're good with flower names – should we call them all after flowers?"

"Maybe," said Pearl, "but let me have a think. Kathleen and I were trying to come up with ideas on the plane on the way home, I have a few up my sleeve already! I'll miss those two – John may be our solicitor, but a better pair of friends you couldn't ask for. They've promised they'll be back in a couple of months, but to ring any time."

"I agree. John was so supportive and Kathleen is sweet, but she can be a really strong woman at just the right time!" Rose continued. "I want to get the bedrooms ready by tomorrow if we can – we've booked a photographer to take shots for the website." It felt comforting to have her Mum there as part of their team.

"Right, skates on," said Pearl, "I'll ask Yvonne if she can help out a bit longer. The other two chambermaids were meant to come in yesterday, but they didn't turn up – and when I rang the contact number I had for one of them and asked when she was starting there was a nasty cackle and the phone was put down. To be honest I reckon Sparkle is worth more than the other two put together, she's a really hard worker – and it's not as though we have any guests yet!" Pearl scribbled another idea in her notebook.

"That's why I want to crack on with the website. I need to start the whole PR thing going and talk about the hotel on Facebook and all that stuff."

"That's definitely down to you and Jamie – I never have understood that nonsense. Right, I'm off to finish the big bedroom on the second floor…. Yes, we must get the room names sorted."

Rose went downstairs, and peeped round the office door. "Got a few minutes for a coffee, Jamie? We need to discuss websites and social networking."

"Sure, can you give me five minutes? I have to make a quick phone call."

"I'll make some coffee and we can sit outside on the patio?"

"See you in a bit."

Rose laid out the coffee mugs and yet more of Yvonne's scones. They were both going to be the size of a house soon, she smiled to herself, if they didn't get guests in to help eat the constant stream of food resulting from Yvonne's experiments.

"Sorry to keep you waiting – trying to track down the DHL delivery for your Dad."

"Here, try these scones – Yvonne is a brilliant cook – our teas are going to be legendary."

"About as legendary as the size of my stomach! Twenty more laps of the grounds on my run tomorrow." Jamie took a large bite and closed his eyes in ecstasy. "Whoa – Yvonne is something else."

"How far have we got with the website? I don't feel I can do stuff on Facebook and Twitter until the website is perfect."

"Acshutsy…" Jamie failed to speak, hampered by a huge mouthful of scone and cream, the latter oozing out of the corner of his mouth. Rose handed him a paper napkin and Jamie gave a crooked smile as he wiped his face. "Sorry – food brings out the worst in me."

"Right if you're done…. Website?"

"It all seems to be going swimmingly. Darren is a mate I met a few months back, completely brilliant on anything IT related. We've found a local company willing to host it at a reasonable monthly fee and Darren's sending the files over to them later today. Once it's up and running we can all access it and send him corrections and ideas. I have organised admin rights for both of us, so we can keep it bang up to date too."

"The photographer is due shortly, so we'll take some pictures of the bedrooms and get some outdoor shots done as well. Maybe a few beach pics too. I think it's such a beautiful vista."

"Definitely. there's no real limit on how many pictures – there's plenty of space on the site."

"Right! Once we have that looking good I'll start a Facebook campaign. I wish I had more press contacts but I'll surf round relevant sites and collect as many addresses as I can so I can get a press release out."

They both jumped at a loud 'honk' from a van horn. Rose peered out of the window. "Jamie – your DHL… or rather Dad's DHL…. delivery is here."

"On my way – he'll need a lot of help with getting the crates into the shed." Ted had insisted that the layout and sorting of the shed and its contents was his job and no one was to cross him. Actually everyone felt he was welcome to what they all thought was a particularly dull task, but it was best that Ted felt real autonomy in his shed kingdom.

Rose had planned a barbecue on the patio that evening, but the weather was looking grim and the forecast predicted wild winds and heavy rain. Instead they ate in Pearl and Ted's bungalow. Pearl enjoyed entertaining and also sharing her new home for the first time.

"I don't suppose we have such a thing as an umbrella, do we?" Rose stared glumly out of the window. "It's raining cats and dogs – I'm going to get soaked running back to the hotel."

"Goodness me!" said Ted. "Who would have thought any daughter of mine was scared of a drop of rain!"

"Drop of rain, pah! That's no drop – it's a complete torrent." Rose pretended to glare at him.

"Here borrow my jacket, but make sure you give it back before I set off home," said Jamie.

Pearl looked up, "You're never going to ride home on that stupid motorbike in this weather? You'll get washed away!"

"The car isn't ready till the end of the week. I told them no rush as I wanted Rose's to be here first."

"Very noble lad, but you shouldn't be on the road in this weather; stay here with us. Pearl's got the guest room all set up ready for friends from home."

Pearl nodded in agreement. "He's right, Jamie; you shouldn't travel on your bike in this storm."

"Don't worry about me messing up your spare room, Pearl; you've only just got it looking spick and span. I'll sleep in the room at the end on the top floor. We haven't finished in there yet so it won't cause any extra work."

The lightning crashed again and Rose shivered. "If you don't mind Mum, I think we'll make a move – I hate storms."

"Of course my love, off you both go." Pearl gave Ted one of her 'don't argue' looks.

"Yeah, sleep well both of you," Ted mumbled.

Jamie handed Rose his jacket and they fled up the garden towards the hotel, the rain pouring down on them. Once safely under the porch the deluge seemed almost romantic, thundering down all around them. Despite the jacket Rose was soaking wet.

"You're drenched," Jamie said, looking down at her. Rose felt nervous. She could see where this was heading; she couldn't decide if it was what she wanted most in the world or was something she should avoid. "Come on, let's find that room for you," she replied, sounding much more formal than she felt.

"Yes of course," said Jamie, looking disappointed.

Peering round the door of the room on the top corridor, they could see that although as yet largely unfurnished it housed a perfectly good bed that had already been made up. On further inspection the en suite bathroom was fine too. "Looks OK, no problems there then."

"No, I'll… I'll see you in the morning." Rose turned tail and ran to her own suite, wondering if she was running from her destiny or saving her heart. She undressed, shivering as she pulled on a big T-shirt, and gazed out of the window. Storms like this were both terrifying and beautiful. She watched as the lightning illuminated the whole sky and the sea. Somehow storms over the sea were even more stunning than over the land.

There was a hesitant knock on the door, and without waiting for a response Jamie walked in, still dressed. "Umm, I don't want to cross any boundaries… but… err… I don't have a towel, could I borrow yours? Sorry – couldn't face getting into bed when I was as wet as this."

Rose went into her bathroom and came out with a bath towel and a couple of hand towels, which she put on the bed. "Here you are, I've got plenty. You poor thing – shall I find one of my huge T-shirts for you to sleep in? I'd choose one with a butch slogan on it, honest!" Rose giggled, and Jamie laughed too. As he stepped towards the bed he slipped his arms around her and she flinched as his wet clothes chilled her body and soaked her T-shirt.

"Aghh! You're soaking wet and cold! Gerroff!" Rose tried to be flippant. She was struggling to quash the feelings flooding through her, reminding her of how much love she had once felt for him and how he had hurt her. She pulled away. "I'm sorry Jamie, I can't do this."

Jamie's cheeks coloured and he bit his bottom lip gently. "No it's OK, I understand – maybe I was wrong, I'm sorry." With that he grabbed the towels and left the room.

Rose sat down on the bed. Should she forgive him for abandoning her all those years ago? It had been wrong, yes, but perhaps it was unfair to hold grudges too? She pondered for a while, wondering what she should do – and then decided. Gathering her courage, she went into the bathroom, grabbed a couple more towels and walked resolutely towards Jamie's door. She knocked gently.

"Yes?" came a gruff voice from inside.

"You forgot something!"

Jamie opened the door with a quizzical look on his face, but little else; he had a small towel wrapped around his waist and Rose's heart skipped a beat at the sight of his naked torso. "Umm... I didn't give you enough towels."

He raised one eyebrow. "And I need these because...?"

"Err... because if we're going to share a room, we ought to at least have plenty of towels?" Rose felt red hot; the embarrassment was killing her, and she almost turned and ran.

Jamie swept her up in his arms and carried her over to the bed. "You're an odd one and no mistake! I understood that I'd taken things too fast!"

"No, no… you hadn't – I needed to be a bit braver. I need to trust you, but it's just hard to get past all that stuff." With that she lay down on the bed, looked at Jamie and smiled tentatively.

Jamie laughed. "Come on – don't look as though you are going to your death! I knew you would come round in time, at least look as though something pleasurable is about to happen!"

Suddenly Rose's resolve failed. She felt her insides tighten, and knew she was stupid to weaken. Jamie had let her down; she still didn't know why, and she still sometimes felt that he wasn't always straight with her. She would be stupid to go through with this. She'd get hurt again.

"Sorry, I can't do this!" She leapt off the bed and went towards the door. Just at that moment a massive crash of thunder made her jump and cry out.

Jamie came over and took her hand. "Storms are never fun on your own. Let's just stay in the same room tonight and no, nothing has to happen." He led her slowly towards the bed and pulled over a threadbare chair lingering in the corner of the room.

"Now I feel mean, and there aren't enough bedclothes. Can I trust you to sleep on the bed but not to touch me?" She felt ridiculous suggesting this, and wished she had never come to his room in the first place.

"If that's OK with you… I'd like something to cover me?" Jamie settled down on the far side of the mattress. Fortunately it was a king-sized bed so there was plenty of room. Rose just hoped she would get past the embarrassment in the morning, and wondered if she would get any sleep at all.

* * * * *

Rose was woken by a huge commotion. She could hear her mother screaming alongside the sound of banging and a police siren.

"Jamie, Jamie, wake up!"

Jamie stirred sleepily then sat bolt upright as soon as the noise registered. "Christ, what's happened? Oh Lord – I hope they're OK." He pulled on his jeans and T-shirt, still damp from the previous evening's rain.

Rose realised awkwardly that all her clothes were back in her own room. Jamie raced off and she followed at a slightly slower pace, grateful that the T-shirt was a big one. She needed to check what had happened first before getting dressed.

About halfway down the corridor they spotted debris in the doorway of Rose's suite and water seeping into the carpet outside. Pearl came out and screamed again. "Rose, oh my God, Rose!" She ran to her daughter and hugged her as if her life depended on it. "Ted, Ted – quick – come here, she's safe!"

Ted emerged from the room, hair thick with plaster and hands bleeding. "Oh Rose, my baby Rose – I thought we'd lost you." Slowly he sank to his knees and Rose realised he was sobbing.

"What's happened?" Rose was scared by the trauma both her parents had obviously experienced, but couldn't work out what had been going on. But as they looked into her room they saw that the ceiling had collapsed; plaster and debris completely covered Rose's bed and the floor around it.

"Jesus," exclaimed Jamie. "If you'd been under that…" he trailed off as he realised Rose had been lucky to escape.

Pearl straightened up, obviously trying to regain her equilibrium. "I'm not sure I want to ask why you weren't sleeping in your own bed, Madam," she saw how scared and shocked Jamie seemed, "but in this instance I think we should all agree it was a good idea." Ted grumbled, sniffed again and fished out a handkerchief to blow his nose.

"So what exactly happened, I wonder?" said Jamie. "Must have been the storm, I suppose."

"Weird that only part of the roof collapsed. I hope it doesn't take too long to fix. Let me grab some clothes and I'll make strong coffees all round." Rose wondered whether to offer anything stronger than coffee.

Pearl was washing Ted's hands in the sink, and it made Rose's heart ache to think he had been scrabbling at the debris, believing she was under it. "We'll be down in a minute; let me just make sure your Dad's head is OK. Make us some coffee too please, Rose, and I think a couple of aspirin if you have some."

Luckily Rose could still get to her wardrobe and bathroom. She tied her hair back, pulled on some jeans then she and Jamie ran down to the kitchen to brew some coffee. Yvonne was just arriving; she looked scared and her eyes were like saucers. "Rose, Jamie, you OK, what happened? You can see a great hole in the roof, was it the storm?

"I guess so," replied Rose, "my parents are a bit shaken up. They saw the roof and ran in to check I was all right and found the debris all over my bed. Dad has hurt himself a bit I think, panicking and trying to rescue me. Luckily I didn't sleep in… err… that room last night."

"Ah! Good news mixed up in the bad news – that's the way of life." Yvonne smiled at Jamie.

"I must get some strong coffee on for them. Have we got anything sugary I can give them – Dad especially – for shock?"

"You asking me for sugary, girl? You out of your mind?" Yvonne laughed loudly and produced three large tins full to the brim with doughnuts, cake and biscuits. "Sure we got sugar!"

They all sat at the kitchen table and Rose sniffed her coffee. "Nothing beats coffee, the smell is everything first thing in the morning." Yvonne pushed a tin towards her, but Rose shook her head. Jamie however, took not one but two doughnuts.

Soon Pearl and Ted joined them and Rose felt sad when she saw how pale and shaken they both were, particularly her father. "Here Dad, coffee, an aspirin and one of Yvonne's doughnuts – just what the doctor ordered!"

Ted gave a weak smile. "Thanks my love, I bet I'll feel good after this lot."

Pearl was silent and drinking her coffee remarkably quickly, bearing in mind how hot it was. Still saying nothing she took one of the doughnuts. Everyone seemed lost in their own thoughts until Yvonne said, "So this old roof needs patching then? You need me to call Soli?"

Rose sat up. "Soli! Why does that name ring a bell? Mum – wasn't that the name mentioned in Dorothy's will?"

"I think you're right," Pearl replied. "Yvonne, you know this Soli?"

"Course we all do." Yvonne looked at Pearl as though she was crazy.

"Am I not understanding here?" asked Jamie, "I feel I've missed an episode in a soap…. Who is this Soli and why was he mentioned?"

"All John read out was that if we wanted any carpentry or building work done we had to go first to Soli. I suppose Dorothy was recommending him."

Yvonne laughed – not in her usual happy, twinkly way, but in a rather forced manner. "Recommending him – that's funny. I think John has missed a few facts in his tale of Dorothy and Barbados."

Pearl, Ted, Rose and Jamie all stared at her. "Yvonne?"

Yvonne looked back at them. "Soli and Dorothy lived as husband and wife for ten years. They never actually got married, but she lived with him and his family. Edmund is his brother. She lived with them and then came in to work here. It was almost a double life; she had one set of clothes at home with him, and her business clothes and English life, I guess, right here in that suite you're in now."

Nobody spoke. Rose gasped and lifted a hand to her mouth in surprise.

Yvonne shrugged. "Do y'want me to ring him and ask him to help with the roof? He'd be here in minutes."

Chapter 10

Rose looked Soli up and down. He was handsome for a man of his age, somewhere over seventy she guessed, tall and with well-defined cheekbones. His eyes twinkled and crinkled at the edges when he smiled, at the same time revealing a perfect set of white teeth.

"Soli, I'm happy to meet you." Rose held out her hand.

"And I you Rose," replied Soli. "Anyone Dorothy held dear is someone I admire." He gave a small and rather formal bow.

"Would you come for a meal sometime? There's so much I want to learn about Dorothy – if you feel you could talk to us?" asked Rose. "We have an emergency with the roof right now, but I loved Dorothy and I want to know more about her life."

"I loved Dorothy too," replied Soli, "so I'm sure we'll get along fine – and yes, I accept your invitation. Shall we look at the roof first while the weather is good? I understand it may rain again after lunch."

"Would you like a tea or coffee?" Rose wasn't sure how to treat Soli; he might have been the person closest to Dorothy in all the world, yet she was treating him as a workman – or at best a guest – when really he was almost family."

"Black tea would be most acceptable, thank you Rose. Now if you would show me the roof?"

They walked upstairs to Rose's suite and she thought she spotted a shadow of sadness cross Soli's face as they entered the room. "We felt it was strange that only the bit in the middle collapsed. I'd have expected it nearer the edge."

Soli peered skywards and walked round the pile of debris. "Have you had anyone up there recently to check if the roof needs work?"

"No, it didn't cross our minds; it all looked fine."

Soli was studying the hole in the roof intently. "I need my ladders and tools – I'll go fetch them from my van. Perhaps that tea?"

"Oh yes, right, I'll organise that right away." Rose felt as though he was dismissing her, but realised it was good that he wanted to get on with the job. Down in the kitchen she boiled the kettle. "Yvonne – have you got some spare biscuits or something for Soli? He's checking out the roof."

"I surely have, fresh out of the oven, brown sugar biscuits." Quick as a flash Jamie popped his head around the door. "I heard that Yvonne! Enough for a small taste for me?"

"Always, Jamie." She smiled at him with undisguised admiration. Perhaps I've got some competition? thought Rose.

"Did I hear right Rose – Soli is here already?" Jamie was tucking into a warm cookie. "Yup, I got the feeling I was being shooed out of the way so he could get on. I'm about to take this tea up to him. You want to come and meet him?"

"Why not? Here – I'll carry the biscuits."

"You keep those hands off till they get to where they's going!" Yvonne glared at him. Jamie felt suitably warned. He had always had a sweet tooth, but Yvonne's baking was making it all much worse.

When they reached the bedroom, Soli was up a ladder inspecting the damage. "You OK up there Soli? Tea's here."

"Thank you," Soli nodded gravely. "I need to get outside and inspect the roof too. I need to be sure of the best way to mend this."

"Thank you Soli. I'm grateful Dorothy insisted we call you first if we needed any practical help. You're are a complete godsend; we didn't know what else to do."

"The important thing, child, is that you are safe. It could quite easily have ended in another way."

Jamie interrupted. "Hello! I'm Jamie French, Rose's friend and colleague – are you suggesting this was sabotage?"

"No I'm not; that was a bad storm by any standard last night and roof problems happen. At the moment I have no proof that it was anything but a nasty accident."

Rose thought he seemed almost relieved, as though he may have initially suspected something more disturbing. Anyway, getting it mended ASAP was all that mattered. "Would it be too pushy to ask how long it will take to fix?"

"Too pushy as you say, indeed! I need to look on the roof before I say for sure. Did you make these biscuits? They're fine."

"No Yvonne is the cook when it comes to all things sugary! And I'm sorry if I seem to be nagging you; I'm just anxious as we hope to reopen before long."

Soli looked at her seriously. "You have my word, Rose, that the roof will be mended in plenty of time and won't spoil any of your plans. I have friends who'll want to help and we'll achieve your target, never fear."

Rose felt uncomfortable at the intensity of his words. It almost felt as if he had a hidden agenda. "Never let it be said that Soli hurt anyone's plans or destroyed their dreams." With that he downed the last of his tea and picked up his ladder and tool bag. "I'll be up on the roof for a while and will come and report to you when I've worked out what I need to do."

After Soli had left the room Rose looked at Jamie. "There has to be a hell of a story there somewhere. I hope he won't mind sharing it with us sometime."

"Oh there you are!" Kate's bright voice brought them back to the present. "Flippin' heck – what a mess!"

"Not good, is it?" said Jamie glumly.

"I assume the guy I passed on the landing is helping fix it?"

"Yeah," replied Rose, not feeling up to discussing Soli and his possible place in Dorothy's story.

"That's good. By the way," Kate continued, "I have lots of stuff for you. Presumably you want to send email shots out to the press? I have the full PR list I use when I'm trying to sell a travel article – might that be helpful?"

Jamie hugged her. "Kate – you are my favourite person on the planet right now! Brilliant – thank you – that's *exactly* what we need."

Kate looked a bit taken aback at his enthusiasm. "Sorry Kate, I think he's happy that something positive is happening at last; we've had a difficult day. Come on, let's get down to the office and see what we can concoct."

On the way down the stairs, they met Pearl. "Not using the lift, Mum?"

"Daren't – the stairs are the only secret weapon I have against Yvonne and her pies and biscuits! I was coming up to see you – you coming down to the office?"

"Yup, why?"

"I've come up with a list of room names which I wanted to run past you. I was also wondering it I could get the go ahead to order a few mail order bits and pieces to titivate the rooms a little?"

"That sounds intriguing," said Kate. "Am I allowed to listen in?"

Rose turned to her. "Kate, of course you can! You're an important part of the team. Mum, Kate has offered her PR list and as soon as I have all the photos grouped together we'll start a selling campaign!"

"That'll be exciting! It's all unbelievably fast nowadays, compared to the old way of posting mail and waiting for letters." Pearl shook her head. "I can't believe how easily this is all coming together! Anyway, can we talk room names now?"

In the office Jamie pulled out spare chairs and, as they were one short, he perched on the edge of the desk.

"Fire away, Mum."

"I hoped flowers were an easy choice and couldn't offend anyone. But I need to follow through the name with hangings or decorations within each room."

"Would you have plaques on the doors?" said Kate.

"Good idea I reckon." Jamie looked at Rose for agreement.

"Absolutely – not sure where to get them, though?"

"Hah! Easy peasy," said Kate triumphantly. "Coralie! She'll do them all for you, beautifully."

"Coralie?" said Jamie and Rose in unison.

"Yes, she's lovely. I met her a year or two ago when I was doing a feature on island crafts. Here, I think I have her card, it's gorgeous – I have it in my purse." Kate rummaged in her handbag and produced a card featuring images of hand-painted beads.

"Bracelets!" said Rose.

Pearl looked at her as if she was mad. "I hadn't thought of having bracelets in the rooms?"

"No – I'm right aren't I, Kate? This lady makes fabulous beads and bracelets. I was given her card the other day when I vanquished the world's pushiest salesman."

"Yes you're right – we met Westin on the beach. Pushy yes, but everything he sells is high quality as opposed to some of the unbearable tat that the tourists get offered. He's Coralie's other half."

"Right – so Coralie does room plaques as well as bracelets?" asked Rose.

"She paints beautiful flowers onto whatever she thinks might sell. Not long ago I saw a display of room plaques decorated with pretty flowers – nearly made me want to have one on my bedroom!"

"Great! Come on Mum, let's hear the names and ideas."

"I wondered if the big room on the second floor should be called the Bougainvillea suite as it's particularly beautiful. We could do Blue Lotus, Begonia, Red Water Lily, Poinsettia and Ginger Lily. They're all flowers here on the island. A nice painting of the flower or maybe a framed photo would be apt in each room."

"What about the beautiful suite on the first floor? I'd happily snaffle that for myself if I didn't think it was important to be able to offer it to guests." Rose was beginning to believe her dreams *could* all come true, and that at least this one was going to work.

"I'm not sure about this one: I love the idea, but you two may not. I wanted to call it the Sailor's Valentine suite." There was silence and puzzled expressions all round.

"What's that?" asked Jamie. "Not something I've heard of."

"A Sailor's Valentine is a box, often octagonal, divided into sections and filled with pretty things. Shells, beads, coral, anything the sailor could find to take home for his sweetheart. Sailors made them on their travels."

"Wasn't that theme used for the Barbados display at the Chelsea Flower Show one year?" Kate frowned, trying to remember. "It was all over the papers here. You could use pictures of the display in the room, maybe?"

"No, "replied Pearl. "I've found a shop in town that sells replicas of nineteenth-century originals. I fancied one for our bungalow and got chatting to the owners, and they're holding a couple for me that I think might look fabulous."

Rose laughed. "Sounds to me as though you have it all sewn up! Anything else you want to buy?"

"While I was wandering round the town I found some cushions and scarves, wall hangings and pictures which I might fit in the rooms. Can I have a budget and choose?"

"Of course," Jamie was scribbling down the suggested room names.

"On my way!" Pearl sailed out, clearly pleased with herself.

"Now printers… where do we stand with brochures to leave in reception?"

"They're doing a rush job for me," said Jamie, "might even be here this afternoon. Lucky we got the photos done before the storm! It'll take Edmund ages to clean up the grounds."

"Right. Kate, if you are happy to let us have the list, let's start writing our first mailshot! How exciting is this – makes it all seem real!" Rose picked up her pad and pen.

Suddenly a shout came from reception, and Rose recognised her Dad's voice. "Rose, Jamie, everyone, come quickly, come and see!" The events earlier in the day had left Rose a little nervy; hearing her Dad shouting scared her, and she dreaded what she might see.

They all hurried out of the office. "The cars, look! The cars have arrived!" Ted sounded as excited as a father delivering news of his firstborn.

Rose took a deep breath and tried to calm herself. She had to get a grip; a couple of nasty incidents didn't mean anyone would be able to spoil their dreams. And anyway, they didn't know that the roof fall was caused by anything other than the terrible storm of the previous night.

"Oh Dad, you got me worried – I thought it was something bad."

"Something bad! Heavens no, how brilliant is this, look at my new taxi! Dead posh we'll be now. Your car too, just the ticket I reckon; neat little jeep-style thing with only 20,000 on the clock – what more could a girl want."

"Technically Dad your 'taxi' is an eight-seater minibus or people carrier or some such thing?"

"Look, it's been Ted's Taxis for as long as I can remember, no need to get picky now and make me call a vehicle anything else. Taxi it is, and taxi it can stay."

Rose looked at the two vehicles parked outside the front door. She was happy that they were ticking items off the list and it would be wonderful to jump into her own car to go into town. But she knew she was going to have to try hard to look enthusiastic as cars had never been her thing, whereas her Dad…

"Ooh I love the colour of mine," Rose smiled at her pale-blue car. "Oh women lad, what do we do with 'em, eh?" Ted slapped Jamie on the back. "Always the darn colour, never a thought for what's under the bonnet!"

"Nice ride for airport collecting Ted, you'll look super-cool in that. How did you get the hotel's name done so fast?" They all walked over to the ivory-coloured Suzuki people carrier and saw 'The Summer House' and logo emblazoned on each side in gold.

"Guys at the garage were chuffed to get three car sales in one day. I leant on them to get the sign writing done and thrown in for free. Sorry your car isn't here today, but they want to give it a final service. It'll be good for a young lad, fun yet practical. Always fancied one of those SUV vehicles myself – wouldn't mind borrowing it for a spin once it gets here."

Rose couldn't help letting a giggle escape, and tried to turn it into a cough. She hoped her father was so wrapped up in the new cars that he wouldn't notice. It was great seeing him having the time of his life. The 'taxi' may not be his dream Jaguar, but he was enjoying his new acquisition.

Pearl came out of the front door. "Oh my goodness Ted! What have you gone and bought – can we afford it? You'll be a real chauffeur in that, what a treat." She leant towards Rose and whispered, "Boys and their toys." Pearl, Kate and Rose all laughed quietly.

"I think they're both fabulous, Dad. I'll take mine out for a drive later – would you mind if I left Jamie with you and finish a job I'm in the middle of?"

"That's good of you Rose. I wouldn't want you to miss out on the inaugural drive of the vehicle, but needs must I guess." Ted was on cloud nine and oblivious to the women's amused smiles.

Rose and Kate returned to the office, and Pearl soon put her head round the door. "We must let your Dad take us out for a drive later on; it would hurt his feelings if we didn't. I know you're busy now, but I think a bit of support for your Dad would be good?"

"Yes I'm sorry Mum, I was right in the middle of the emails and worrying whether I'm going to use the right wording. I'm grateful you're here, Kate; a second opinion is always good."

"Don't you worry, dear. I'm sure Kate will be a great help but you've always been brilliant with words. It's just that it matters more now."

"Thanks Mum! I promise we'll all go out in Dad's new taxi tonight – we need to celebrate! You want to join us, Kate? It seats eight apparently, so there's tons of room."

"Love to – and if we send this out soon we might even have something more to celebrate."

"True! Mum, would you mind ringing to organise a table at Monkey Beach?"

"Will do, now you two get on with the real work."

Rose read through her potential email. She checked for spelling mistakes, read and re-read it. "So Kate – do you think I've put enough – should I attach more photos?"

"I think what you've done is good enough, but let's check the website as that's where we're asking them to click through. We need to make sure it's all perfect."

They waited while the computer slowly opened 'www. thesummerhouse.bb'. Darren had done a great design job (and had charged them mates' rates too, which was a bonus). The home page showed the hotel in all its glory; different pages displayed the bedrooms and the bar, the view from the grounds and some brilliant shots taken in the garden, with Edmund looking as pleased as Punch.

Rose checked that she had the admin rights to make changes to the website, then turned to Kate. "Of course, the new taxi – we should add that in the airport collection. We could do with a picture, I suppose?"

"I've got a good camera on my phone – shall I go and take one?"

"Brilliant – if Dad wants to be at the wheel fine, but the side view of the vehicle would be enough."

Kate was back in a trice. "Mission accomplished. I've emailed the picture, and you should be able to access it now." Rose inserted it on the website and wrote a short piece announcing the free airport collection and delivery in the eight-seater people carrier. For larger parties they could offer further vehicles."

"Further vehicles?" queried Kate.

"Ian has already agreed to be our second taxi if we need help, and of course Jamie could whizz off and collect people in his SUV. We should be covered. Right now I'd be happy to have just one room occupied!"

Kate turned to her friend. "Right: questions for your tick-off list. Are you happy with the website?"

"Check," Rose smiled.

"Are you happy the email has been written correctly, and have you attached the logo and two photos?"

"Check."

"Have you got my press address list loaded so you can send the email automatically to them all at once?"

"Check."

"In that case I think you ought to consider pressing 'Send'… do you want to include Jamie in this?"

"No, I think we could do this on our own – it's my hotel, after all." Rose felt quite light-headed with excitement. She pressed the Send/Receive button. They waited for a moment, then collapsed with laughter.

"I'm not sure what I was expecting! A bang, and a flood of bookings, something that would happen instantly."

At that moment the machine bleeped as an email was received, and excitedly Rose clicked it open. "Delivery Status Notification (failure) attachments too large."

"What?" said Kate.

"Kate – I think I must have messed up."

"What did you mess up, Rose? Can I help?" Jamie had come back into the office.

"I… err… I sent out the email and now messages are coming back saying failed. What's happened? Is our broadband broken, or are they out-of-date addresses?"

"Hey – stop blaming the rest of the world! Let me sit down."

Jamie sat in front of the screen and flicked into the Sent box. "It doesn't take an Einstein to see what you've done. Most of these addresses, as they're corporate, will reject your message, and those that don't will curse you for sending pictures this size. Why didn't you wait and ask me for help?"

Rose's bit her lip and tried not to swear out loud. "I do feel stupid. I was sure I could do it and I wanted to surprise everyone at dinner tonight with news of a booking."

Kate tried to make a helpful suggestion. "Now Jamie is here perhaps we could resend?"

"But that'll look horrendous. Maybe we should wait. I've ruined everything!"

"Come on, cheer up! Jamie can sort it – it'll be fine. If you do a resend nobody will think anything of it – how often do repeated emails come in, after all?"

Jamie clicked on the two photographs Rose had wanted to send. He tweaked the files and Rose watched, feeling dumb. She was perfectly IT savvy but in her excitement at sending the press release had completely forgotten to reduce the image files.

"Right folks, we ready to send?" Jamie turned to them both. Kate and Rose nodded mutely. Jamie pressed 'Send' and the emails went safely on their way.

"Right – if you'll excuse me, Shane is coming over to discuss stocking the bar and then we're going to head off to the wholesalers." He smiled at Rose, nodded to Kate and left.

"I think he might have been disappointed that we excluded him," said Kate.

"I expect you're right – serves me right for being too big-headed and deciding to manage everything on my own. A lesson learned, I guess."

"Time I made a move," said Kate. "I'll go and find Coralie and see if she would do the room signs for you. Shall I get her to ring you?"

"Perfect, yes if you would."

Rose pondered what to get on with next. The website seemed done for now, although she would have to update it regularly. Facebook seemed a good next move. She could build the page, and hopefully start gathering 'Likes'. All her friends from the management course might be a place to start; they could share it around.

Suddenly hungry, she popped down to the kitchen, knowing that Yvonne would have something she could nibble: I'm definitely in need of comfort food, she thought. Banana cake in hand and a large mug of coffee on the desk, Rose settled down again and started work on a Facebook page. She chose the main shot of the hotel as the cover photo and wrote a few posts, adding photos and some bits of blurb from the brochure. Finally she sorted out the privacy settings.

She posted a message on her private Facebook account telling all her friends about The Summer House and adding a link in the hope they would 'Like' it and that the numbers of people following the site would swell. Within five minutes she had eleven 'Likes': not bad as a starter.

Taking another bite of cake she realised she should have mentioned the Facebook site in the press email, and felt inadequate again. Not her best day. She logged into the website to make sure there was a prominent symbol there to remind people to click through. She guessed she should set up Twitter too... she'd never been as keen on Twitter, possibly because she hated having to keep her words to a minimum. She laughed to herself: talking at length had always been her thing.

The computer pinged: her first email! She had a nasty feeling there was no point in getting excited; it would be some kind of spam telling her she had won yet another lottery or offering her something that somebody of her gender would rather not have.

Five emails, five emails and NONE of them seemed to be spam. Her heartbeat quickened and she desperately wanted to share the news, but no one was around. This was big – finally something might be happening!

She clicked on the first one: it was from *Barbados Today*, thanking her for her email and saying that they would be delighted to send round a reporter to take pictures and write a feature, and would tomorrow be convenient?

The second one seemed to be from a website, Island Travel. She clicked on the site and it showcased beautiful holidays for beautiful people exclusively on islands. The photographs were brilliant. They were asking for a free two-night stay next month for their reporters who were covering other stories in Barbados at the same time.

Two out of two! Neither seemed likely to bring in a mass of business but hey, it was all positive. She clicked on the third, this one from an American travel magazine. They seemed keen and again wanted free accommodation in the upcoming weeks and would write a feature based on their stay. Hmm… that sounded a bit mean, but they'd love it so all would be well anyway. Rose realised that this was how the world of travel writing worked: lots of requests for freebies!

The fourth one sent thrills through her: a holiday feature for *The Sunday Times*! The editor to whom she had sent the email had visited Barbados before and knew of The Summer House and was interested in the celebrity aspect, and Princess Margaret especially. Free accommodation again, but that could be huge! He promised to organise a reporter who would soon be in touch.

Feeling beautifully warm inside at this early positive response she clicked on the last email. What could top *The Sunday Times*?

"You may feel good that you have survived all attempts so far, but you have been warned, Rose Hill. This enterprise will not end well; go home before somebody dies."

There was no signature and no sign of where it came from, and no title…. Despite the bright sunshine outside, Rose felt horribly cold, and suddenly very alone. Who could it be from?

Chapter 11

Rose slumped forward onto the desk in tears, no longer able to control her emotions. She gulped and choked uncontrollably for several minutes, her body racked with sobs. Just as she was beginning to calm down a little, Jamie walked into the office. "Christ! What's wrong, Rose? Has someone hurt you? What's happened?"

"No," she sniffed, "no, sorry – I got a bit scared and once I started crying I couldn't stop."

"Got scared? About what, who?"

"There have been loads of problems, and now this…" She indicated the last email. Jamie leaned forward to read it and took a sharp intake of breath. "This isn't a joke any more Rose – we should contact the police."

"I agree, but what could they do? There's no way they can keep an eye on everything – and who on earth would wish us that much harm?"

"I think that might be an easy guess: McGuyver."

"But what does he stand to gain? He can't possibly think we would give him the job back, and all he's doing is risking the police going after him."

"Let me ring Darren. He's a whizz with emails and that stuff, far better than me. He may be able to help."

Rose wiped her eyes with a tissue, snuffling and hiccupping as

Jamie dialled. "Hi Darren? Yeah mate, I wonder if you could help – we've had a nasty threatening email… we hoped a heads up of where it came from was halfway to finding out who sent it? Right, yeah, right, yeah… I see that, hang on… typing one-handed… on that page… yeah I see, even illustrated, sure I can follow that. No other information available? Thanks for your help, anyway."

Jamie went quiet as he typed the information in and clicked back and forth from the email. He kept shaking his head, trying alternative ways of adding the information into the forms on the page Darren had recommended.

"Nope it's no good, all I can find is that yes, it did indeed come from a local IP address. It can't be a joke email from, say, the UK or America or anywhere else in the world and yes, it's someone here in Barbados. Bugger – I hoped I could follow it back more accurately. I'll forward it over to Jason in case there's more he can do. Anyway, what are all these other mails?"

Rose tried to be positive. "There's certainly some good news. *The Sunday Times*, no less, and a local paper, travel mags – so loads of interest already, which is great. I just couldn't cope when that last one came in."

Jamie stroked her hair gently. "Come on, perk up – someone may be mad at us, but we've done nothing wrong. It'll all work out in the end and we've got lots to work towards now. Let's go and tell Shane the good news – and maybe the bad news, too. He's a good mate when you're in trouble."

Shane already had the area behind the bar looking organised. As he saw them come in he descended from the top of the small stepladder where he was perched, placing the rarely used and expensive whisky onto the top shelf. "Jamie, whassup? Rose, you OK?" He registered Rose's tear-stained face. "Everyone OK?"

"We had a few emails, most of which were extremely good

news, but the last one, not good." Rose felt the tears welling up again. "I suppose you could say it resembled a death threat."

"Jesus Christ!" exclaimed Shane. "You are kidding me?"

"Sadly not. Anonymous, obviously, and basically saying we have been lucky so far but we should stop trading before somebody dies."

Shane leant back against the bar, open-mouthed. "I mean you hear about these things on TV shows and in films, but truly, a death threat… Have you rung the police?"

"Not yet no. I thought I'd leave Rose in your capable hands – could you find her a shot of brandy? – while I both ring the police and organise some coffee."

"Absolutely mate. Rose – I'm *so* sorry – what a grim thing to have to face. I expect it's just a jealous nutter, but not nice."

"If you could take care of Rose while I get this sorted?" Jamie moved quickly out of the room, obviously keen to contact the police. Rose realised that both guys were trying to make light of it, but that they too were scared.

"What would you like? We'll have to wait for coffee, but you could have a brandy or a whisky for now?"

"I don't know," replied Rose. "I'm scared – perhaps I've made the wrong decision about trying to run the hotel? I could be at home in luxury with a couple of million in the bank and instead no, I'm here in a strange place with someone wanting to kill me…" Her voice broke and she started to sob again.

Shane moved over and put his arms round her. She leant into his shoulder and tried to calm herself. Trying to distract her, he said quickly. "So what do you think… first-rate cappuccino machine in here? I rather fancy the waistcoated-barista look, and there could be a good trade for coffees when people come back here after dinner… and not everyone wants to get plastered every night of their holiday." He paused. "Might be popular at other times of day too?"

He gently stroked her back, comforting her, and gradually Rose found herself feeling calmer.

"I bloody knew it! You cheating double-crossing bastard – I'll show you for playing dirty!"

Shane flinched and Rose looked up to see who was screaming at them. In doing so she caught a blow that was probably intended for Shane. But bearing in mind the kick that followed, knocking her to the ground, possibly not.

Rose wished she could black out and escape this dreadful day. Who *was* that woman? Then she remembered: it was Shane's girlfriend Nina, the one with the wonderful singing voice. Stupid woman must have misunderstood Shane comforting her. Somehow her innocence made her feel even more affronted, and she felt her anger rising. She didn't often lose her temper, but when she did... she rose to her feet.

"Look you stupid cow, I don't want your bloody boyfriend. However, I also don't want an employee that has the brain of a gnat. Perhaps you should have checked what was going on before you launched into me."

"Sure, oldest trick in the book; offer Shane a job, he owes you one and then turn on the waterworks, everyone a winner. Females like you collect good men that can't see through your tricks." She raised her arm to hit Rose again and Rose, wound up by the day's traumas, did the unthinkable and punched Nina directly in the face. Blood spurted everywhere and Nina sank to the floor.

"I'll get you, I'll get you for this." Nina rolled over towards the fireplace and grabbed an old-fashioned poker. "Now see if you're so bloody clever, man stealer."

Suddenly a strong hand snatched the poker from her grasp.

Jamie grabbed Nina and pushed her roughly over to Shane. "For Christ's sake deal with her! Is she high?"

"Possibly," replied Shane "but I suspect she just lost it. I was trying to comfort Rose and Nina came flying in like a flippin' Ninja turtle!"

"Trying to comfort her, my arse! Caught you both red-handed."

"Caught nothing you idiot," hissed Shane, obviously worried for his job and Jamie's friendship. "Rose and Jamie have received a death threat by email, and I was just trying to stop Rose crying. I suspect Jamie would have done the same for you had the roles been reversed."

Jamie interrupted. "I've been on the phone to the police. They're sending a constable down to interview us, but I suspect they feel there's nothing to be done."

Nina opened her mouth to speak, but presumably thought better of it. Shane handed her a handkerchief and helped her wipe a not inconsiderable amount of blood off her face. It seemed to be coming from her nose.

"I'm a bit shaken and I think this is going to be a real shiner tomorrow, but apart from the shock, yeah I'm OK."

Jamie whispered, "Sorry love but you win hands down, far better punch. You might have broken her nose."

Rose felt terrible. "But that's awful!" She turned towards Nina. "You may have been wrong, Nina, but I shouldn't have hit you back – I'm sorry. Maybe you should get your nose checked at the hospital."

"Nah," Nina shook her head dismissively. "I know what a broken nose feels like and this isn't it. I apologise, seems for once Shane is keeping it in his pants, my mistake."

Rose felt it was a rather grudging apology and raised her eyebrows at Shane, but he shrugged and turned away. She wondered if Nina had previous experience of Shane misbehaving; this was a very different woman from the politely spoken singer she had met before.

"Come on Rose, I think you need to change before the police get here… perhaps a cold compress and a lie down might be a good idea."

Rose staggered slightly, and Jamie swept her up and carried her as though she was as light as a feather. As they neared the suite that Rose was using while hers was being repaired, Pearl appeared in the corridor brandishing a feather duster.

"Rose, Rose – what's happened? Rose, are you OK?" She turned to Jamie for information. "I wonder if the best thing to say might be that she got into a fight?"

Pearl's mouth dropped open in surprise. "Rose has never had a fight in her life!"

"To be fair she was acting in self-defence. Nina hit her in the face and followed through with a kick. Rose punched the bejesus out of Nina, as they say 'you should see the other guy'. Shane is taking Nina to get checked over now I think, to see if her nose is broken."

Pearl's mouth gaped and she turned to her daughter. "Is this all true?"

"She hit me first," replied Rose, "she decided I was stealing her boyfriend."

Pearl shook her head. "But Rose, I've never known you be violent, never."

"These are different times, Mum. I've had a truly shitty day and yes, maybe I was wrong to protect myself, but I did – and at least no one is dead." At that point the whole email threat came back to her and the tears started again. Pearl looked a little shocked, but went on to comfort her daughter. "I can't blame you Rose – I might have done the same myself! Bring her into the bedroom, Jamie."

"Is Ted around? I should tell him at the same time?"

"Tell him… tell him what?"

"Could you fetch Ted? I need to get Rose into the room."

Pearl opened one of the bedroom windows. "Ted, Ted!" she yelled through cupped hands. "Yes – get up here quick!"

A few minutes later Ted hurried into the room. Catching sight of Rose he rushed to her side. "Who was it – what happened? I'll do for him."

"It was a her not a him, Ted. There was a misunderstanding when Nina, Shane's girlfriend, saw him comforting Rose. We've had a death threat by email and understandably Rose is really upset about it. Anyway it all got a bit out of hand. Nina had a go at Rose so Rose got mad and punched her."

"Back up lad, never mind the fisticuffs… what was that about a death threat?"

"It seems someone saw fit to send a warning email, specifically mentioning Rose, saying we were lucky to have escaped so far but we should go home before somebody dies."

Ted slumped down onto a chair and exhaled loudly. "What have we got ourselves into? Dorothy would have had a fit."

"You stay here with Rose while I go and get first aid stuff and make some tea. Ted, you come with me." Pearl took his arm and they headed out of the door.

Rose lay back on the bed and sighed. "You can't say it gets boring round here!"

"True – but I suspect life with you would never be boring anyway. Do you think it would be better if I moved into a room at the hotel, rather than you being alone, especially at night?"

"That seems a bit much to ask, Jamie, but yes I would be so grateful. Presumably we'll need night cover once guests arrive, so maybe we should get a night porter I'm just not feeling too brave right now."

Jamie leant forward and kissed her on the forehead.

"Right, Prince Charming," Pearl's voice came from behind him, "I have salve and some plasters. Jamie, you could do with a sweet tea, must have been shocking for you too." Pearl fussed around Rose, cleaning the graze on her face and applying ointment. Rose sipped her sugary tea and began to feel better. "There's one stupid girl who's lost herself some good work," said Pearl.

"I'm not sure, Mum – I behaved badly too. It was all just a huge mountain being made out of a molehill. I bet Shane is giving her a prize telling off – he sounded so angry with her."

"Quite right too, dumb woman."

"I really don't want her anywhere near me, but on the other hand her singing could be a real draw for the hotel."

"It's your hotel, not mine, so you have to decide but keep her or no – but you can't expect me to like her."

A sudden commotion in the corridor made them all jump. "Eek, help!" Yvonne came running into the room, looking excited and pleased she had found them all. "Real guests, I don't know if I messed up, REAL guests!"

Everyone looked nonplussed, as if she were speaking a foreign language. Jamie was the first to speak. "Guests where Yvonne, downstairs? But we don't open until next week."

"No, on the phone – the phone rang and rang down in reception and no one was answering it, I thought I better, might have been important, and it was…"

"Yes?" chorused Ted and Rose.

"It was a lady, she wanted to book, but there's no book and I don't know the prices and I'm not sure which day we're opening and I didn't know what to say…"

"Calm down Yvonne, I'm sure you did fine. What did you say to them in the end?" Pearl patted her on the shoulder as a sign of solidarity. "I said that the receptionist was out of the office for a moment and that she would ring her back directly and apologised for the inconvenience."

"Yay!" Rose grinned at Yvonne. "That's a complete superstar performance – no one could have done better!" Yvonne stared down at the carpet. "I'm glad I did right."

"You did indeed. Jamie, could you possibly ring her back? I need to pull myself together a bit more." Rose turned, and Yvonne noticed her bruises. "Lord alive, who did that to you, you OK?"

"Right," said Jamie, "I'll leave you to tell Yvonne about the afternoon's dramas and I'll get back to what could be our first clients, something we could really celebrate tonight. Did you take their details, Yvonne?"

There was a long pause. Rose was sure everyone in the room thought the same: that, despite having done the right thing, Yvonne had forgotten to write down their details. "Ha – got you all!" laughed Yvonne. "It's all carefully written out and left on the front desk."

Jamie smiled at Yvonne and went down to book in their first precious guests. Having made sure that their daughter was all right, Ted and Pearl went back to their various tasks.

Rose washed her face again and sat calmly for a while. She no longer felt like crying, and her breathing had returned to normal. At last she decided she couldn't wait any longer to find out whether the guests had booked. She found Jamie in the office, checking the email and filling in the Bookings spreadsheet on the computer. "So what happened – tell me all?"

"Good actually. Seems your email and Facebook have started the ball rolling. The phone call was from an American couple.

They didn't recall where they saw that we were opening again, which seemed odd bearing in mind it was only a couple of hours previously they'd spotted it. Anyway, they weren't the most pleasant people in the world and bartered, saying we should be grateful to have guests to fill the empty spaces in the first week. I agreed to give them a discount of fifteen percent, more than I wanted but less than the twenty percent they asked for."

"How many nights?"

"Three nights in that first week we're open. And another couple has emailed, American too I think, and they want three nights too, starting a night earlier. Finally a third booking from Alice and Angus – do you remember them from college? I sort of do, but they seemed to know you well?"

"Alice and Angus – gosh yes! They were destined to be together forever from about week one of the first term."

"It seems they're getting married and when they saw your Facebook post they knew it was a sign that they should honeymoon here. They also asked if we did weddings."

"We could, but that's such a big thing – I'd need time to plan and get it right. "

"Oh don't worry – theirs is fixed at a local church with hordes of relations coming – but it's a good idea, for the future, isn't it?"

Rose's heart skipped a beat at the idea of having a good reason to plan a wedding, but she quickly ticked herself off for being so stupid. "Excellent idea – we should add it to the sooner-rather-than-later list, don't you think?"

There was a knock at the door of the office and in came Soli, with Edmund close behind. For some reason seeing them both there together worried Rose, but they seemed calm and she waited to hear what they had to say.

"Rose, Jamie," Soli gave his usual little bow. "I need to have a word please."

"Why of course Soli, what's the problem?"

"I feel that the main repairs to the roof are all progressing nicely. Given the help I have, we should be finished possibly tomorrow or the day after, which is all satisfactory."

"That's good news Soli – thank you for sharing that with us. We could do with some good news today." She noticed Soli was being tactful and not mentioning her fast-blackening eye." He continued. "I'm afraid what I need to bring to your attention is possibly not such good news, but it's important to tell you – that's what I said to Edmund when he showed them to me."

"Showed what to you, Soli?" asked Jamie.

Edmund produced a large pile of slates, weather-worn but not broken in any way. "These – and I'm sorry we have to tell you about it, but it matters."

Rose was now completely confused. "I'm sorry, I'm not quite getting what you need to tell us – please forgive me for being slow."

"These tiles were found by Edmund, in the shrubs underneath the window of your room. All piled neatly, no damage, just a pile." Soli looked grim-faced.

"What does that mean?"

"We assume the problem with your roof was definitely not the weather, although the forecast storm was indeed part of their plan. The reason your roof fell in was that someone had removed a considerable number of tiles immediately over your bed, and the pounding rain got through and caused the ceiling to collapse." Edmund had been looking down as he relayed the information, unhappy at his message.

Soli continued, "We also suspect that some sabotage was done to the rafters to make sure the ceiling caved in, but I wasn't able to spot that from the damaged pieces. It was only when Edmund found these tiles that we guessed the real truth."

Jamie and Rose stared at Soli and Edmund. "We're lucky that their plan backfired I guess," said Jamie slowly. "Thank you, both of you, for being loyal and helping us – we're up against such difficulties."

* * * * *

Rose peered into the mirror. She was trying to cover the ever-deepening bruise on her face with the thickest layer of make-up possible, to make it go away. Finally she admitted defeat; it was camouflaged, may be, but far from invisible.

Jamie knocked on her door. "You ready?"

"I'm as covered up as I can be."

"Oh I don't know!" Jamie smiled at her, noting her fairly low-cut dress. She and Kathleen had bought it on her first day in Barbados and it was useful for evenings out. She had worn it when she and Jamie last went to Monkey Beach.

"Right let's pick up your Mum and Dad – and Kate's in reception too. I'll fill her in so you don't have to talk about it if you don't feel like it."

Once everyone was assembled in Ted's taxi, the shiny new Barbadian version, he tried to lighten the atmosphere and suggested a sing-song, but no one was really in the mood. Nonetheless it was a pleasant drive over to the restaurant.

"I'm looking forward to my dinner," said Ted," you told me it was a good place and I'm starving."

Jamie whispered to Ted, "Let the valet park the taxi tonight, it looks busy here and the girls can all get out at the front door." Ted seemed about to say no, but then shrugged and handed the keys to the valet. The latter looked less enthusiastic about parking a people carrier than a cool sports car, but he smiled politely nevertheless.

Sitting at their table, Rose looked around and realised that these people were helping her to fulfil her dreams. Working with family, pulling together as a team, having friends to help and a goal to aim for: all this mattered to her more than everything else. She suddenly felt more confident, and tried to put the day's difficult events behind her – for this evening, at least.

Ted and Jamie certainly did the family proud, eating massive amounts of food, and Jamie finished off several leftover puddings. Kate, it seemed, was on one of her intermittent diets. Pearl and Rose were struggling after the day's happenings and neither of them managed to eat much, but the atmosphere was fun and the glasses of rum and wine cheered everyone up. Ted complained a few times because he couldn't drink, being the designated driver, but largely in jest.

"Let me propose a toast," said Ted. "Here's to our first guests – to The Summer House and all who sail in her!"

"To The Summer House," they chorused, clinking glasses.

"I'd give a short speech, but I think my daughter and my wife would stop me so I'm not going to try. But I will say I'm chuffed how the place is shaping up and look forward to the excitement of our first guests arriving!"

"Now sit down, Dad."

"Speeches and toasts or no, I think we should get the bill and make a move. It's been a hard day today and tomorrow's going to be another long one. Who knows – we might get more guests!" said Pearl.

"True," replied Jamie, motioning to a member of staff.

Bill paid and jackets and coats retrieved they all headed out through the door. Rose was glad they had gone for the valet parking option as now they could all wait patiently while the vehicle was delivered to the front door of the restaurant.

She saw the taxi approaching, but was surprised at the sudden and constant loud hooting. What on earth was wrong? Then she noticed that the vehicle was heading straight for them, the valet waving and screaming frantically inside. "Help! Run! No brakes! Get out of the way!"

Jamie leapt into action. "Shift everyone – keep away from the doorway. No, no –much, much further Pearl – get up to the far end of the car park. Kate – help them!" They got out of the way just in time as the taxi shot past and rammed straight into the entrance. "Stay over there, keep clear – Rose, you OK? Keep them all as far from the building as possible. I've got to get to the driver."

Rose was terrified the vehicle would burst into flames at any moment and, much as she admired Jamie's courage, she just wanted him to keep away from there. Terrified restaurant guests were screaming inside the building, and the management steered them all downstairs and out of the back door to assemble on a lower terrace.

The building housing the Monkey Beach restaurant was not intended to stand for hundreds of years. It had been inexpensively developed from a basic beach bar, well disguised with foliage and lights, decorations and a nicely presented entrance. The attractive double glazed doors that welcomed the guests were nailed onto very thin walls adorned with the gaily coloured awnings.

The combination of poor-quality building and a robust fast-moving minibus resulted in mayhem. At the point of impact, the walls collapsed, the doors smashed onto the floor and the awning sank down over the pile of debris. In keeping with a domino run, the entrance pulled down the front wall, the roof began to cave in and the side walls cracked and groaned.

Within a remarkably short time the sirens sounded and red fire trucks started arriving. There didn't appear to be any sign of fire but the steady collapse of the whole building meant help was needed to evacuate the guests from the lower terrace. Police cars followed soon after, white 4x4s with blue and yellow markings, disgorging a large number of officers. They talked into their phones and walkie-talkies, one summoning ambulances so they had paramedics on standby.

The group from The Summer House had a lucky escape. They had been in front of the building and the rescue crew could reach them, check for medical problems and take notes. The other guests, although safe, had a harder task to get clear of the almost totally destroyed building. Every few minutes there was another crash as more of the roof collapsed, or another window smashed.

The ambulances arrived and paramedics began to treat The Summer House party. The valet was bundled off to hospital as he was badly shocked. Pearl and Ted were Rose's main concern; she had slipped while running from the restaurant and needed slight bandaging, but she was concerned that her Mum or Dad might be traumatised. She knew that they might not be as resilient as the younger members of the party.

Chapter 12

Safely back in the bar at The Summer House, Pearl sat snuggled up in a warm blanket. Rose sat beside her and Kate stood beside the open window, breathing deeply to calm herself. The paramedics had given all members of their party a clean bill of health.

Ted brought round a small tray laden with glasses of brandy. "Come on girls, medicinal purposes only – let's all calm down and carry on regardless."

Pearl's characteristic resolve seemed to fail her. "It was definitely the brakes? Did they check?" she questioned falteringly.

Ted squeezed her arm. "Yes love they did – that young valet said there was nothing there when he pumped the brake, and the CCTV footage showed two men messing about under the car while we were at dinner."

Kate looked round. "Could they identify anyone from the footage?"

"No sadly not," said Jamie, appearing with cups of tea. "They were wearing black and had their heads covered, and all you could really tell was they seemed to be male."

Pearl took Rose's hand. "I'm trying hard love, I really am, but I do wonder if we have taken on more than we can manage."

"Mum, the police have promised me that they will pay McGuyver a visit tomorrow. Once he knows we're onto him maybe it'll deter him a bit. And think about it: if I give up, he's won."

"OK," said Pearl, looking up at Ted. "We're here for you – we always will be."

Jamie slumped down into a chair. "I wish I could see why McGuyver is dead set on hurting us."

Ted shook his head. "Jamie, lad, come on, it's called money: he was in on the deal with that land developer, wasn't he? Either there's more money to come or he'd already been paid his cut and couldn't afford to give it back. Who knows – but money is a strong enough motive for almost anything these days."

After another half an hour of going round and round in circles, Jamie said, "Kate – have a bed here tonight. They're all made up and ready – take your pick."

"Thank you – that would be nice. Perhaps I could write you a review at the same time!"

Bad news travels fast and when Rose got up at six-thirty the next morning and wandered down to the kitchen, Yvonne was already cooking – and worrying.

"I'm relieved to see you are all right. I heard from my neighbour about the trouble at Monkey Beach. The owners of the restaurant are devastated; they won't be able to rebuild in time for the high season. But most importantly, how are you and your dear mother and father? I was terrified someone might have been hurt?"

"We're all fine, Yvonne. Shaken up but yes, I think we're all fine. As I couldn't sleep any longer I've come down for a cup of coffee."

Pearl appeared at the kitchen door. "Us too – you OK, sweetheart?" She gave Rose a hug. "What about Jamie?"

"I'm fine, I think. I knocked on his door but no answer, so I thought it was best to let him sleep."

"Here's your coffee, and tea for you Ted – and I have something fresh out of the oven. The usual plan, Pearl? Sweet tea and sugar for shock, yes?"

"Quite right Yvonne – but with the amount we're eating I may have to rethink that plan!"

"I'll take my coffee back to bed if no one minds. I need to think about what to work on next." Rose desperately wanted to focus on positive ideas for the business in order to banish her underlying fears to the back of her mind.

* * * * *

A couple of hours later, heading towards the office, Rose bumped into Kate. "Kate! Morning, how do you feel today?"

"I'm fine. Can't say it was the best night's sleep ever, but that's no reflection on the wonderful comfy bed."

"Can you spare a few minutes to talk over a project with me?"

"Of course! Let me grab some coffee and then I'll come up into the office. Do you want a cup?"

"Please, if I could." Rose continued towards the office, deep in thought. Soon a somewhat perkier Kate arrived with a tray of coffee and biscuits. "So, what did you want to talk over?".

"I wondered if we could work something out with your great island crafts contacts. I don't want those ridiculous T-shirts with 'My Gran went to Barbados and all she brought me…' . I want real artisan beauty, souvenirs people will treasure as a reminder of their stay here."

"I understand; there are the most wonderful crafters on this island but yes, the tatty stuffy is much more prominent."

"What if we got a carpenter to create some beautiful cabinets to put in reception? We could offer them rent-free to start with, to the crafters of our choice. We could take a small percentage from each sale. What do you think?"

"Excellent idea! I wonder – once we're busy and booming…,"

she looked up at Rose for reassurance that would be the case one day, "when we have loads of guests we could give a talk or hold a class, with one of the crafters sharing their skills?"

"I hadn't thought of that, but you know what's around out there. Could we go and visit a few and get them signed up?"

"Sure. What sort of timescale could we give the crafters? I presume they would have to make extra stock…"

"I think if we could set a target of two weeks that would be perfect, but let's just chat and see if anyone is keen first. Half past ten here and we'll make a start?"

"Sounds fun. I'll see you later."

Jamie came bursting in. "Menus and brochures, they're great, look!" He carried two brown parcels, both of which had been ripped open. He put them down on his desk, pulled out a couple of samples and scrutinised them closely with Rose. The menus were printed on stiff card in the corporate colours – turquoise blue with gold around the edges. The breakfast options were laid out on one side, with light lunches and snacks on the other. The separate afternoon menu was still at the printers, and would offer a few delicious options, traditional scones with cream and jam and a selection of specialist teas.

"Look at the brochure!" Rose hopped from one foot to the other with excitement. "It's wonderful when you see those fantastic colour photos – it's a dream come true!"

"I do think we should feel proud of ourselves – and I'm sure your Dorothy would have been thrilled with these!"

"You're right – how I wish I could show them to her."

Jamie hugged her tightly, holding on for rather longer than she had expected. She broke away when the phone rang, taking a deep breath to steady herself and to make sure she sounded professional.

"The Summer House, Rose speaking, how may I help you?"

"That sounds good, Rose! Did you have to practise?"

"How rude, Mr McKay – I expect more from my lawyer! How are you and Kathleen? We do miss you."

"We're fine, but I had a call this morning from a friend and I'm worried about all of you."

Rose assumed he had heard about the events of the previous evening, "That was fast – how did they know?"

"It's not too mysterious. I made friends with the Chief of Police on the island years ago over many games of golf, and he's right on the problem you all had last night. How are Pearl and Ted – are you all coping?"

"Yes we are. Mum was particularly shaken up, but I think we'll be better in a day or two. No need to worry, over there in hot sunny England."

"Pfft! Hot sunny England indeed! It's raining cats and dogs here and Kathleen reckons her arthritis is playing up badly. We've been back close on a month now, and I believe she's pining."

"Do come and visit us soon, won't you? We all talk about you often, and my Mum misses Kathleen."

"Not me, only Kathleen?"

"*I* miss you, of course – but your wife seems to have the most fans."

"So we might be quite welcome if we happened to have some appropriate plane tickets around…?'

"How perfect John – we thought it would be ages before we saw you again."

"Usually it would, but as Kathleen was missing you all I checked out our frequent flyer miles. We have more than enough points to come over for close to no cost and I needn't use the holiday fund, assuming of course that we get free bed and breakfast somewhere…'

"Don't be daft! Of course you must stay here. And there's some exciting news: we have some 'real' guests coming this evening, and another couple tomorrow. Mum and Dad have a spare room in the bungalow, so if we ever got totally full you'd always have a bed."

"We'll see you tomorrow then. We're setting off for the airport now – good job you didn't turn us away!"

Rose was aware that this lightning visit had far more to do with the McKays' concern over the family's safety than any pretend arthritis story. "Tell us when the flight lands and Dad will come and… the taxi… no Dad can't come… yes he could… He can borrow my car. See you tomorrow."

Realising that her Dad's pride and joy was off the road reminded Rose how frightening certain aspects of owning this hotel were becoming. How Dorothy would have felt had she ever known didn't bear thinking about.

"That sounded like nice news?" said Jamie.

"Very nice, and just what Mum needs I reckon; Kathleen will be the best possible company for her and they'll both help buck us all up."

"So we all set?" Kate appeared at the office doorway. "Ten-thirty, you said?"

"Is that the time already? Give me two minutes. Jamie – Kate and I are going to scout out some good craft sellers with this idea we've had for displays in reception."

"Yeah sure, not sure this is something we've been through? Have I forgotten? Anyway, it sounds great."

"Sorry – I thought of it in the middle of the night when I couldn't sleep. I think it'll add interest and Kate is an expert on the classier craft side of the island."

"No problem – see you girls later."

Rose grabbed her bag and keys. "OK with my car?"

"Of course," replied Kate. "I've been phoning around and I've got several appointments for us."

"Great, Miss Efficient strikes again!"

"First stop is Westin and Coralie's home. It's not too far from here – fifteen to twenty minutes max – that should give us an excellent starting point."

Driving along in the warm sunshine, catching glimpses of blue sea and fabulous beaches, Rose felt some of the stress slipping away. Barbados was beautiful and she was, overall, much happier than she'd been when working at the Castle Hotel. But it was hard not to slip back into depression when she thought about the fact that someone was determined to destroy her project and hurt her family.

They drove past wonderfully colourful houses, the love and care taken in regularly painting them and planting the surrounding gardens obvious to all.

"Here, turn here, on the left."

Rose braked sharply. "Thanks for the warning, Kate – where now?"

"Sorry, I forgot that you don't know where we're going – it's that one, on the right down there – that gorgeous coral one with blue shutters."

The house was indeed a vibrant shade of coral, and the door and shutters were picked out in an equally dazzling blue. The overall effect was one of cheerfulness, and the house was flanked by beautiful shrubs and flowering plants in shades of coral, pink and white. The colour coordination was just stunning.

Westin was bending over in the front garden, weeding a flowerbed. He straightened up and flashed them one of his dazzling smiles. "If it isn't the two prettiest ladies on Barbados!"

"Westin, shall I repeat that to Coralie?" Kate grinned at him.

"The *three* prettiest ladies, then – my lovely wife would always be included."

Coralie came to the front door and Rose saw that he was indeed telling the truth: Coralie was stunning. She had close-cropped hair and enormous eyes, and Rose envied the colour of her skin, feeling very white and unexciting in comparison. Coralie was tall too, as was Westin, and towered over the two girls.

The temperature was on the rise, and they entered the cool house gratefully. Inside was just as charming. There were vintage trinkets and lamps, and pretty drapes. The overall effect was almost shabby chic, but with a lot more bling and drama.

"Westin, would you get us ladies some of your special lemonade, sweet one?" Coralie's eyes sparkled at him as she spoke and Rose suspected they had a very happy relationship.

"Are you ladies safe, being left with this big business talk?"

"Yes Westin I do believe we are. Perhaps you could impart some of your wisdom along with the lemonade in a moment..."

Chuckling to himself, Westin disappeared, presumably to the kitchen. Coralie gestured to the sofa and they sat down. "So tell me more, Kate, about this opportunity you wanted to share with me."

"I think Rose should tell you as it's her idea and her hotel."

"Hello Coralie! I love your home – it's every bit as gorgeous as your business card. My name is Rose Hill. I've recently inherited The Summer House and I want to make it as good as its former glory days."

"That would be wonderful. As a child I remember my Mama telling me stories about the royal parties that went on there – I truly believed it was full of princesses!"

"We've got a bit of an uphill job, but one of my ideas is to make the reception area interesting and beautiful by displaying island crafts. It could also make us all some money, too."

"So tell me more."

"I want some beautiful cabinets, glass-fronted and locked. I'm hoping to find a small selection of talented crafters who would like to display their work on a sale or return basis. We would ask for a ten percent cut on any sales, and if it works and people sell OK we'd ask for a small monthly rental. What d'you reckon?"

"I think it sounds a good idea. I'd have to make some more necklaces and bracelets, but I could do that over the coming weeks. When did you want the cabinets stocked?"

"I was hoping maybe two weeks? The sooner the better really. If we get good enough pieces, people might come to look at the crafts and then stay for a drink or coffee."

"Sounds good – but many of my pieces need a bit of explanation. I don't want some inexperienced receptionist selling without people understanding what they're buying."

Rose looked across at Kate. She didn't want to blow her chances of getting stock, but she couldn't think of an answer. "This is where I step in, Coralie. I'm having a tour desk in reception and will be helping people organise their stay in Barbados. I'll deal with all the craft sales and exhibitions, and you can train me before we start selling."

Rose silently thanked Kate a million times for saving the day. Coralie beamed. "In that case we would be delighted."

"We would be delighted to do what?" Westin returned with decorated glasses (no doubt Coralie's handiwork) and a matching pitcher, filled with home-made lemonade and ice. Ideas for similar sets for use in the bar or for serving drinks outside at the hotel flashed through Rose's mind.

"The ladies have suggested a most acceptable plan for our crafts bein' displayed in their hotel. I think it could be agreeable to all." Kate flashed a look, which Rose decided to interpret as 'trust me'. "So would you want to display some of your poems and love hearts, Westin?"

"If my Coralie will kindly agree to be my decorator, yes I would be amenable."

Rose hoped Kate knew what she was doing. Love poems and love hearts sounded a bit naff to her, but she trusted Kate. Westin poured lemonade for each of them and then produced a box of bits and pieces from behind the sofa.

"I don't get allocated as much room to work in as does my talented Coralie, but I have some samples here you might enjoy." He passed Rose a small but beautifully produced booklet with Barbadian flowers decorating the cover. Inside Coralie's art illustrated short poems. Rose flicked through, reading a few as she went. They were delightful, and definitely the kind of present a lover might buy a girlfriend or boyfriend. "These are sweet, Westin – I'm sure they would be popular."

Westin then handed Rose a collection of intricately carved wooden hearts. "Goodness! You make these?" They were wonderful; the engraved flowers and words were fabulous, and the overall effect was romantic and gorgeous.

"We would be delighted to stock these for you," said Kate. "Do you fancy a cabinet each, or one between the two of you?"

"I think we might share to start with. It's hard to make extra stock quickly and we only create enough pieces to make a happy life, not huge profits. We're not greedy."

"Thank you both," said Rose. "We'll look forward to seeing your gorgeous crafts in our reception area. I'm sure the visitors will adore them."

Kate interjected. "Now if you'll excuse us, we need to get moving. I have made Rose appointments all day to find more possible candidates! I'll be in touch over the next few days to discuss details, and we'll sign an agreement when both parties are happy."

"Anything that brings a beautiful young lady to my door

sounds agreeable to me," smiled Westin. Rose spotted a well-aimed nudge in the ribs from Coralie's elbow.

Back on the road again, Rose sighed with satisfaction. "They were all beautiful. I knew her jewellery was gorgeous, but I loved his hearts and poems too."

"Absolutely," agreed Kate. "So long as you put up with the smarmy chat, he's a sweetheart – and he worships the ground Coralie walks on."

"What's next?"

"I think the best place to go would be Geneva's shell jewellery. It's gorgeous – I was wearing a piece a few days ago, but you probably didn't notice it."

"If I'm honest I didn't – but the fact that you own some tells me a lot."

"It's real shells and sea glass mixed with silver chains, and I could buy every piece she makes if that wasn't a completely mad thing to do! I bet it'll be as big a hit as the beads."

"Have we got any other crafts? Not jewellery, I mean? Not that it really matters, but I was just wondering…"

"Yes we do have some: Mary Carey, this afternoon. She makes special cards and bookmarks using exotic petals."

"Pressed flowers, you mean?"

"Sort of, the medium is pressed flowers but she turns the petals into landscapes, set scenes and portraits, really clever. And the fourth suggestion I have is silk painting. Scarves and handkerchiefs all hand-painted by Bonny Louise. She paints beautiful stuff and I bet visitors would love taking scarves home with them."

"This is going to cost me a fortune – at least I'll have birthday presents for all my friends and family sorted!"

Kate and Rose returned to the hotel after a long day out, tired but happy with their achievements. Despite a room being offered,

Kate decided to go home, muttering about toothbrushes and clean clothes as she left Rose in the car park and drove off.

As Rose wandered through reception Jamie was behind the desk, smiling and chatting with two strangers. Of course – their first guests!

"Here she is! Rose – please meet Eva and Olly Johnson from Michigan."

"Please forgive how I look – I've been out around the island all day choosing wonderful crafts for our reception area."

"How exciting! My goodness Olly, you're going to have to put this on our regular list – it's turning out to be our sort of place."

"Thank you. I hope Jamie has taken care of you and explained how our breakfast and bar meals system works? As I'm sure Jamie will have told you, we have very recently reopened and you are our first guests!"

"I have indeed," smiled Jamie, "and we've even discovered that we have some favourite holiday destinations in common. Eva and Olly have been to the Lake District and stayed at the hotel I always look at and wonder if I'll be able to afford to stay in one day!"

"Oh! You are such a darling boy," said Eva. Olly, obviously used to nodding, did just that.

"I also offered Eva and Olly a special extra as our first guests: free breakfasts and any drinks in the bar for the duration of their stay."

A surprised Rose took a deep intake of breath, then instantly tried to disguise it by sneezing. Free drinks? They might drink us under the table – bang goes any profit we might have made. However, she needn't have worried, as Eva continued, "Wasn't that too precious of him? What a doll – mind you, we won't be costing you much in the bar. My Olly is a minister and we gave up the sin of alcohol many years ago. But those breakfast options on the menu look special, thank you – we'll enjoy that. Now if we could go to our room?"

"Of course. I'll be back in the office in a moment, Rose. I'll carry these suitcases up for the Johnsons. They're going to be staying in the Blue Lotus room."

"My oh my, Olly! Isn't that the darndest name for a room? Jus' beautiful – come along dear, you take this small bag."

Rose sank into her chair in the office. Their first real guests! Having installed the Johnsons in their room, Jamie soon reappeared.

"Sorry about that – but they were such nice people I felt it might pay to be especially kind to them – and once I realised alcohol was a thing of the past for them I reckoned the drinks offer was safe enough. And it was at the back of my mind that the couple coming tomorrow are getting fifteen percent discount, so it seemed fair?"

On hearing his reasoning Rose's earlier misgivings disappeared. "Sure – no problem with me – and isn't it exciting to have real guests! Did the room look good when you went in?"

"Oh believe me, your mother has been into that room a million times today. Beautiful flowers, a bowl of exotic fruit, fluffy towels and anything else she could think of. Tea-making bits and pieces, and fresh milk. She's forgotten nothing."

"Great! Moving onto other things – have you remembered that the night porter starts tonight? Are we happy he's a good choice?"

"Bobby? Yeah, safe as houses. Apart from anything else he's Edmund's nephew and bound to be on our side. He's been in hotels before and when I rang his last job for a reference they reckoned he was a pleasant enough man. Their only complaint was his tendency for laziness and they suggested management or a more taxing position might not be his forte."

"So maybe a night porter's job in a hotel with only a few guests might be right up his alley. He won't fall asleep on the job, will he?"

"Seems not – he loves cricket and watches it through the night on a sports channel on the computer. He should be OK, but we'll have to keep monitoring it. And coming from that family I'm sure he's going to be pretty honest."

"Good point. Just think Jamie: tomorrow we'll have four guests. It's all going to work, isn't it?"

"Yes, I think it just might." Jamie planted a fleeting kiss on her cheek.

* * * * *

On speaking to Eva and Olly Johnson the following morning she discovered that they had loved their breakfast, served on the balcony of their room. Yvonne had outdone herself and introduced dishes they'd never tried before, as well as the American pancakes and syrup that Olly had particularly requested.

"I can't imagine I'll be able to eat another thing all day," said Eva. "That is a talented chef you have there."

"I'm glad you're happy," replied Rose. "Now, do you have plans for today or do you need some suggestions?"

"We're fine for today, actually. I have a mind to go and explore Oistins and the department store there. Olly enjoys buying me trinkets." Looking at Olly's face it was difficult to tell if he enjoyed anything, but Rose took Eva's word for it.

The rest of the morning passed without mishap. Soon after lunch, however, the peace and quiet of the hotel was interrupted with the arrival of their next couple of guests. Rose heard them at the front door; they were loud and uncompromising (thought Rose, trying to remain professional as she heard them unfairly criticising the state of Ian's taxi). She noted quietly that their clothes, unlike the classy attire of the Johnsons, were cheap and brash.

She composed herself and put on her most charming smile. "Good afternoon Mr and Mrs Gately – how lovely to see you. You had a good trip, I hope?"

"Far from it – the plane was delayed several hours; we should have been here early this morning. However, now we're here we want your best room – and don't you go backing out of the twenty percent discount your clerk offered us."

"Of course we'll honour the fifteen percent discount stated in your confirmation email, Mr and Mrs Gately. Jamie, the manager, will be here to greet you shortly."

"You pop off and get back to cleaning the room, girl. Send the manager over now."

Rose paused. She was about to say who she was but thought better of it, and instead went into the office to fetch Jamie. "Quick Jamie – battle armour on! These two are horrors, we need to win them over. They've already tried to tell me you offered twenty percent, not fifteen – good job we talked."

"Right! Best behaviour here we come!"

About half an hour later she heard shouting from reception and, worrying for Jamie, she rushed out again. The Gatelys were back from their room, complaining loudly.

"Don't you think for one cotton-picking minute young man that you can short change us with some two-bit room because you're giving us a discount! We asked for a suite, and we're going to get one."

"May I help, Jamie?" asked Rose sweetly.

"Young lady – you disappear into that back office. We're sorting this with the manager – the last thing we need is some laundry maid poking her nose in."

Rose steadied her breath, hoping to goodness she would be able to sort this out professionally. "Please don't worry, Mr and Mrs

Gately. You aren't dealing with a 'two-bit' laundry maid, I'm the 'two-bit' owner of the hotel. I'm sure I can solve any problems you have?"

There was a silence. The Gatelys carried on undaunted. "Right – well you sort, this little lady. We're aware there is a good suite in this hotel and that was what we booked, and with a discount. Don't even try to hoodwink us."

"Tell me – what makes you think there might be a suite in the hotel? We only advertise en-suite bedrooms with king-sized beds. Could you perhaps have got confused between en suite and a suite?"

"Damn cheek young woman! We know an awful lot more about this island and this hotel than you suspect. We have friends who've stayed here before, and they assured us we should ask for a suite. Top floor, I believe it was."

"I'm sorry to disappoint you. The owner's accommodation is on the top floor, true, but my rooms are currently under renovation. If for some unknown reason I wanted to give up my bedroom I'm afraid there's no furniture or glass in the windows at the moment, which would make it horribly uncomfortable for you. How you knew about the top-floor suite I have no idea. I believe we have allocated you the Ginger Lily bedroom which is quite the loveliest guest room in the building. I hope that will be acceptable.

The Gatelys looked at each other and reluctantly gave in. "I see," said Mrs Gately rather stuffily. "Now I wish to be shown the breakfast menu. We'll have breakfast in our room early tomorrow, we have plans."

"Of course," Jamie nodded. "We would be delighted to deliver it to your room, and you'll be pleased to hear there is no charge for room service."

"Wouldn't damn pay it if there was!" muttered the husband.

Rose compared the two American couples and mused about how different folks could be. The Johnsons were delightful, and as a result all the staff would go out of their way to make their stay special. The Gatelys would be the cause of general celebration when they left!

Mrs Gately held up the menu and frowned. "This is all you offer at breakfast? Most of it's cheap Barbados rubbish. Who wants to eat damn flying fish at breakfast? Only fit for cats. Rainbow banana cake, oh my God – that sounds the same as the cheap rubbish you get on an island coach tour."

Jamie waded in, obviously as offended as Rose at the criticism of Yvonne's fabulous cooking. "No need to fear, Mr and Mrs Gately. We offer a full American breakfast with unlimited pancakes and syrup, eggs cooked as you like – there's plenty on the menu for a red-blooded American."

"Are you being rude, young man?" asked Mrs Gately.

"Me, certainly not Madam, I was hoping we could offer breakfast fare that will please you."

"We'll pre-order smoked salmon, cream cheese and warm bagels for my husband and I'll have an egg-white omelette with asparagus and rye toast. Decent American coffee, obviously." Saying that she flung the menu down on reception and they both stomped off to the lift.

"Jamie, we'd better make sure we're around early to see it goes smoothly – and where do we get asparagus or bagels? Neither of them is on the menu."

"I'll ring round some friends and any shops that are still open. I'm not going to let them beat us!"

* * * * *

At six-thirty the next morning Rose made her way down to the kitchen. Jamie turned up not long after. They were surprised to see Pearl looking flustered and wiping her eyes on her apron.

"Mum, what's the matter? And why are you here so early?"

"I had a text from Yvonne about an hour ago, woke me up. Apparently she has bad food poisoning and can't make it into work, and I'm panicking at having to produce all the breakfast stuff. The Johnsons are great people but they do eat a lot at breakfast, and then there's the Gatelys… having heard last night how unpleasant they are, I'm scared I'll mess it up for you."

"Don't worry, we'll help – Jamie, could you stay and help Mum? I'll go up to reception and take over from Bobby in case they appear or ring down. I'll contact Kate and see if she knows anyone who could cover in the kitchen for a day or so."

Bobby was predictably asleep in front of his cricket, and Rose once again pondered on the sense in employing someone so undynamic… but that could wait. Bobby protested that he had only just that second dozed off. Rose didn't waste time scolding him and told him to go home.

Using the desk phone she dialled Kate's number. "Kate – sorry – yes, I know it's the middle of the night. Look we have an emergency here – do you have anyone in your little black book who's a whizzo breakfast/lunch chef? We've got a problem with Yvonne…. Yeah… seems she has bad food poisoning and daren't come into work for a day or two and we have several guests… My Mum is doing her best but she feels a bit out of her depth… "

Rose tailed off as she saw a blur of red out of the corner of her eye. The Gatelys, clad in full running gear, were standing at the far end of the desk and must have overheard most, if not all, of her conversation.

"Food poisoning in your kitchen, indeed? I feel that local

Health and Safety and the press should hear about this. Cancel our breakfast immediately – we're not prepared to risk it… Ron, you do Trip Advisor and Twitter – I'll sort Facebook and the local authorities. Disgraceful state of affairs."

As she made her way back down to the kitchen, in need of comfort from her Mum, Rose wondered if this was an appropriate moment to break down or just sit and stare into the distance, praying it was all a bad dream.

Chapter 13

"Hello? Anybody in?" A voice came from upstairs in reception.

Jamie jumped up, breaking the rather morose atmosphere in the kitchen. "I'd better get up there. It might be the Johnsons, and the last thing I want is them leaving without paying as well as the Gatelys! Breakfast went OK, though?"

"Perfect, Mum was a star and they loved everything she cooked," said Rose. "Don't worry, I'll go and see who it is." As she neared the 'hello'-ing she recognised the voices. "John, Kathleen! You were going to ring – we could have fetched you. How lovely to see you." She hugged them both, then felt stupid as the tears started to fall.

"Oh come on my love, we can beat all of this. John, do you have a hanky?" Kathleen's maternal instincts came rushing to the fore.

"Oh but it's got worse," sobbed Rose. "This morning Yvonne rang in with food poisoning, and couldn't get to work. I was on the phone telling Kate, in the hopes she could find us a temporary fill-in, and two guests overheard the words 'food poisoning' and have left without paying their bill and threatening to tell the world via social media. It feels as though the bad stuff will never end."

"Let's sit down and have a cup of tea and see if we can put at least some of the world to rights. John – you were going to make a phone call?"

"Oh… oh right yes, I was." John disappeared with his mobile phone.

Rose and Kathleen made their way down to the kitchen to find that perfect British solution to all problems, a cup of tea. "Kathleen!" shrieked Pearl. "Surely Ted would have picked you up?"

"Oh we felt it would be much quicker to grab a taxi. I've missed you all and I'm worried about Yvonne; I'm fond of that young lady. Now fill me in on all the dramas since we left."

Just as Rose started on the sorry tale, Edmund the gardener arrived at the back door with his nephew Bobby in tow. "Bobby? You left hours ago." Rose got to her feet and looked at Edmund. "Edmund, what's wrong?"

"Bobby was talking to his mother and me and I felt you ought to hear what he said." Edmund looked fiercely at Bobby. Bobby seemed shy and stared at the floor. "Those American folks, those nasty ones?" he proffered, looking up slightly.

"Yes, what about them?" Rose said urgently.

"They wasn't running anywhere. They came down to reception dressed in that red running uniform about five-thirty this morning and stood outside the front door. They thought I couldn't see them but I was watching on the CCTV camera. I thought it was odd, wearing those clothes but not running. The man, he went up to his room I reckon and brought down their suitcases and put them into their car." Bobby looked more embarrassed. "I knows I should have offered to help but they seemed OK with them and there was a funny feeling, they were sneaking past me. And McDonald was out for eleven and it was a pretty tense match."

"Suitcases in the car?" Rose turned to Jamie, ignoring the fact that Bobby had been somewhat derelict in his duty as night porter. "But they hadn't heard about the food poisoning... why would they want to leave? They'd only been here a few hours."

Edmund looked grim. "Go on Bobby, tell them more."

Bobby's face was a picture of guilt and embarrassment. "I...

that is… I hadn't had no training, I was worried…" All eyes on him, he stumbled on, "I thought as they might need to pay with a credit card if they was putting cases in the car and I didn't know how."

"That would have been our fault Bobby because yes, we were going to show you the ropes today, go on…" encouraged Jamie.

"So I hides…" there was a pause and Rose thought she saw a single tear run down his cheek. She knew Bobby didn't have the highest IQ but she had been sure he would be suitable; maybe she was wrong. "I hides under the counter," continued Bobby. Rose pictured his large form crouching under the counter; certainly not the most successful hiding place for a man of his bulk. "Now tell them what you heard," prompted Edmund.

"I was hidden, they probably didn't see me and he got his phone out near the desk, there was only a small piece of wood between us, I was scared."

"I bet you were," said Kathleen in a comforting voice. "So what did this man say?"

"He was speaking to someone he called 'Boss'. He said everything was in place and that they were waiting for the cook woman to ring in and everything to kick off."

You could have heard a pin drop.

"Would you be prepared to tell this same story to the police, Bobby?" asked Rose.

Bobby's eyes widened and he glanced over at Edmund, who nodded firmly. "I yeah… no, yeah… I guess so… I's a bit scared of the police."

"Seems that might not be as helpful as we might have hoped." John's voice preceded him as he entered the kitchen. "What do you mean, dear?" questioned Kathleen.

"Speaking with Derek, Chief of Police – they followed up on our suspicion that it was McGuyver and went to his home to interview him. Long story short, McGuyver was attacked the day after we all last saw him but not fatally hurt. He and his daughter caught the ferry the following day and have been living on St Vincent, where they have family who are looking after him. Their opinion is that he probably has nothing to do with our problems whatsoever."

There was a gasp from the assembled company, then silence while they all tried to take on board the new facts. Jamie was the first to speak. "Thank you, Edmund, for bringing Bobby in. The Gatelys were obviously a plant, or at least intended to cause us harm. Bobby – we'll see you for work this evening. Remind us to show you how to work the credit card machine."

Bobby and Edmund made a hasty escape and John joined the others at the table. "So where does that leave us?"

"I don't know," said Rose, "I'm at a loss. McGuyver we knew and I could understand why he was mad at us, but if he's in the clear… what's happening?"

"I'm thinking out loud," said Kathleen. "John, what about that box of papers and photographs that Dorothy left with you? I wonder if we should look through them?"

"I agree," replied John, "nothing to lose. We might spot something and I think we would all enjoy a trip through the past. Pearl, we left them in your spare room, didn't we? Would you mind?"

"Of course, come on Ted, let's go and fetch them – I assume we could all look here in the kitchen?"

"You stay here," said Ted, "it's not that heavy."

While they were waiting for him to come back another visitor arrived in the kitchen. "Hi guys," said Kate, and Rose told her about everything that had been going on. "Has anyone checked on Yvonne?" Kate looked round the faces circling the table.

"I feel bad – how could I not have rung her again? I'll do it right now." Pearl took her phone out of her handbag and dialled Yvonne's number. "You poor dear, what…nothing? Oh my goodness… right, leave it to me, we'll be there in a few minutes… no I insist, yes Ted knows… no, I mean it, stay put, we'll be there."

Pearl replaced her phone. "We'll have to delay the history lesson. Poor Yvonne is struggling with all her children sick too, and she has no supplies in the house. I need to go and help."

"Can I come too?" added Kathleen. "Yvonne is a sweetheart, and I'd like to be able to help her."

With much huffing and puffing Ted returned with a large cardboard box and placed it triumphantly on the kitchen table. "Right Ted, look sharp! Poor Yvonne needs us. Supermarket and then her house – you remember where she lives? You took her home one night, didn't you?"

"Yes but, I thought, right… err… should I leave this here?"

"Ted, don't worry, I'll cope here," Jamie smiled at him. "When Pearl speaks we act: I've learnt that already!"

"Cheeky young man!" admonished Pearl fondly. "Come on, Ted. I just need to check Sparkle is following her schedule for the day." Ted shrugged and followed Kathleen and Pearl out of the kitchen on their mission of mercy.

Kate stood up and pushed her chair back under the table. "May I tell you about my plans? The Johnsons were anxious to have a look around the island and I explained that I could help. So we've booked Ian for the day and I'm taking them on a private tour around the island."

"Nice one Kate," said Rose, "that will give them a great day and should help deflect any negative publicity. Not that they seem Facebook and Twitter types, but you never know."

"They must have seen the initial social media stuff though, or how would they have booked?" said Jamie. "Anyway, that sounds perfect Kate – and might be a regular offering?"

"Let's see how today goes and build from there. I'll see you all later."

"And then there were three," John grinned. "Now I'm going to feel a tremendous gooseberry hanging around you two, so I think I might find the book I started on the plane and go and sit on the veranda – just the ticket."

"There's something really relaxing about doing nothing and staring at the beach with a cold beer and a good book," agreed Jamie.

"Too early in the day for a beer for me, but I'll grab a cold drink from the bar on the way out if that's OK?"

"Of course!" said Rose, "Shall I get a glass and a tray for you?"

"No, you two stay and have a good talk about what's been happening – it must be stressful for you both. I'll sort myself out."

As John left the kitchen, Jamie looked at Rose. "It all seems so unfair. No matter how hard we work someone is intent on sabotaging us. Will we beat them in the end?"

"Jamie, I have to admit I do feel intimidated, and I'm wondering if I can cope much longer. Despite Mum and Dad being here I feel alone, and like I'm failing on all counts."

"No, no one is failing – we'll win eventually."

Rose rested her head against his shoulder. She didn't want to weaken and look to him for comfort, but she felt as though her side was taking a really unfair beating. Jamie spoke again. "I'll repeat my offer. I could move in here permanently instead of just staying the odd night. It would help, maybe. To make you feel safer, I could be your personal guard dog?"

Rose paused, thinking. "I want to have you here permanently, truly I do, but it's too soon. It's placing all sorts of pressures on us that we shouldn't have to cope with yet. It takes time to learn to trust someone again."

"But I promise, I promise there's no way I'd walk out on you. Heck, I'm throwing myself into the hotel, working every bit as hard as you, managing without wages. I want this to work – I want *us* to work. Please trust me."

"I'll try, but be patient. As I said when we first bumped into each other again, the scars run deep and I need to make sure I'm properly healed. I can't cope with the hotel traumas at the same time as developing a relationship with you."

"But you do know how I feel, don't you? It's important to me that you realise how much you mean to me."

"Jamie, you know I like you a lot – but we need to take our time. The hotel drama is enough for now." Jamie sighed and left her to it.

Later in the day Pearl came upon Rose still working in the office. "Hi sweetheart! How's your day going?"

"Oh fine Mum – we have another two bookings from people who've seen us on Facebook. Perhaps everything will go smoothly for a while! How was Yvonne?"

"I'm sure she's on the mend. It was definitely food poisoning; violent sickness until your tummy is empty then it gradually goes away. Strange thing is she definitely can't have got it from work as her family all have it too, so it must have been at home."

"What – from whatever they had for supper last night, maybe?"

"That's what I suggested, but apparently they all ate different things. Her children are a bit fussy so she cooked a different meal for her and her husband, with pizza for the kids. She can't quite work out how it happened. The only suggestion her husband had was that they all had fruit punch to drink."

"But surely that would be in cans, or perhaps bottles?"

"We checked out their larder and apparently they buy fruit

punch in large plastic containers and get them refilled at the local grocery shop. They found a delivery waiting on the step last night, but Yvonne doesn't remember ordering any."

"Someone tampered with the fruit punch?"

"I suppose so. Neither Yvonne nor her husband wanted to think it could be connected with her work so I kept quiet; no need to rattle her. I've told her I'll cover breakfast for the next day or two; we only have the Johnsons and they seemed happy with my cooking this morning. Anyway, your Dad and I are going to have an early supper and watch a DVD."

"Good idea Mum. Thank you for being here for me; I dread to think how I'd cope without you and Dad to make me feel safe."

"We're all doing our best as a family. You have a nice evening with your Jamie too. I do like him, and I have great hopes for you two."

"Mum, don't you go planning your wedding outfit! It's early days – back off a bit, maybe?"

"That's me told! You have a good evening anyway," Pearl giggled.

* * * * *

The ringing of her mobile phone woke Rose the next morning. She felt loads better for a long night's sleep. "Hello?" Her eyes were too drowsy to see who it was.

"Rose, it's Kate – I'm down in reception. I think you'd better get down here."

"Oh God no – what's the time?" Rose checked her clock – half past eight! She had definitely overslept. "Kate, what's wrong, other than I should have been down an hour ago?"

"I think you should get down here now – see you in a minute."

Rose fumbled for her clothes and sloshed water over her face. She dialled Jamie's room number on the internal phone, feeling very grateful he had moved in but received very short shrift.

"Wassup?"

"Jamie, downstairs now, Kate needs us to see something." Rose hoped that the indecipherable mumble which followed meant 'yes Rose I'm on my way'.

She ran down the stairs, ignoring the lift as she wanted to find out what was going as soon as possible. In reception she saw her parents, John, Kathleen and Kate all circled around the desk, looking at something. "What's the matter, is anyone hurt?"

"No my love, but it's not good," replied her mother. She stood back and let Rose see the headline on the front page of the local paper: 'Food poisoning destroys local hotel, amateur cook runs amok in kitchens'.

Rose's mouth opened and closed again; for once she was speechless. "What do they mean?"

Ted smiled. "Sorry if it's inappropriate but I rather like the image of your mother running amok – not something I've seen before." Pearl slapped his arm, but managed to summon up a faint smile.

"This must be the Gatelys – this is what someone wanted to happen." The phone rang in the office and Rose went through to answer it. As she returned to the group she shook her head. "One of yesterday's bookings cancelled."

"I'm sorry, my dear," Kathleen put her arms round her. "We will win eventually. Good beats evil with hard work and enough people on your side."

Kate was fiddling with her mobile phone. "I'm afraid they've got to Trip Advisor too. There's a one-star review saying the place is filthy and they got food poisoning, which is a blatant lie."

Rose sank into one of the chairs and sobbed. "I'm sorry... I just don't have the strength to fight on any more."

"Come on, I'll get teas and coffees all round. You've only just woken up – a hot drink will do wonders." Kathleen gave Rose a hug.

The lift arrived with a ping and everyone scattered, trying to look busy. They assumed the Johnsons would emerge, and the last thing they wanted was to introduce them to yet another disaster. Right on cue Jamie and the Johnsons stepped out of the lift. "Morning all," Jamie seemed very chipper. "I think if that coffee is forthcoming you might make Eva and Olly a pot too. They have news that might call for celebration."

"I'm sorry Jamie, we're not in the mood right now. But of course we'd love to make you coffee, Mr and Mrs Johnson." Pearl remembered her manners and disappeared off to the kitchen, pleased to have something positive to do.

Olly spoke up, which unnerved Rose as she had never heard him comment before; Eva always seemed to jump in first. "I hope what we're planning will be good news for you all."

John moved away from the desk and Eva spotted the paper. "Oh my goodness, this is unfair – how has it happened?" Eva turned to Rose. "Please tell me." Rose related the story of the Gatelys, including what Bobby had overheard, and their definite suspicions that it was a deliberate attempt to sabotage the hotel.

"I reckon coffee and good old chat might be what's needed here," said Eva. "Gather round everyone; here comes Pearl with some goodies. I have to say Pearl, I'd be happy for you to run amok in my kitchen, those breakfasts are quite fantastic!" Pearl smiled, as did the others. It was hard to feel positive, but they were trying.

"So," said Jamie, "do you all want to hear what Olly and Eva have to say?" Rose took a long swig of coffee and decided that as things couldn't get any worse it had to be worth hearing. "Of course Eva – is there something we can help you with?"

"Stuff and nonsense girl, it's us helping *you* for once! I don't think you know that Olly and I are the managing partners of a Christian travel newsletter? No, I thought not."

Olly continued. "We send a monthly news-shot about world travel and places to visit for the more mature American Christian. We have the highest standards and the readership trusts our judgement implicitly. Eva and I have received outstanding service here and feel part of the family, and we plan to tell our friends and customers all about you."

Rose tried hard to feel upbeat and grateful. They were a lovely couple but telling a few friends at their church about the hotel wasn't going to save the world. She sighed heavily – and rather too loudly. "I'm sorry, does our news not please you?" said Eva sharply.

"Oh no, please forgive me! I'm endlessly grateful for the tiniest recommendation, and we have loved having you here. I'm so far down in dumps I think it would take a bomb to get me up and doing." Rose blew her nose on the tissue she kept permanently stuffed in her pocket.

"Hmm," said Olly. "We'll plan an inaugural trip, and we'll come too so we can ensure everything runs smoothly. I understand you have six en-suite rooms available at the present?" Rose looked up. "Why yes, there are several more under renovation but six that we're proud to share with our guests.

"That seems perfect to me," chipped in Eva. "A party of twelve is large enough to soak up any couples or singles that don't get on a hundred percent, but small enough to manage an exclusive tour. Kate – we would need to talk to you about that."

"Would you be able to find ten sets of friends able to take a holiday at the same time as yourselves?" asked John.

"Now I'm going to try real hard not to take offence at that remark, sir! But I'm going to take the blame as we may not have made ourselves too plain. Olly, do you have the cards and brochures?" From his small laptop bag Olly produced a couple of beautifully printed brochures and a handful of business cards.

Eva handed them round. "Christian Travel," she continued, "has been in business over thirty years and our email list goes out monthly to over 200,000 addresses. I would hope we could fix a trip here almost instantly. It's important to us that we accompany many of the tours personally, but we do have helpers that are equally qualified when we're not available. If it's acceptable to you, Olly and I'll stay another night and we'll have a business meeting about prices and what would be included. I could book out the entire hotel for several weeks of the year."

"Oh my goodness," said Pearl, flapping a brochure across her face to stop herself crying again, this time with happiness and relief. Ted looked across at Eva and grinned. "Apologies: if it's not her it's my daughter, you get used to it in my house. May I say how much I'll look forward to escorting you all to and from the airport."

"I think this will become a real favourite destination for our customers," continued Eva, "and you have to remember the accompanied tours would be no more than once a month." Rose and Jamie gazed at each other, mouthing 'once a month!'.

"Apart from the accompanied tours we offer special deals that include options other travel companies could not. Kate, we've been chatting about your idea for craft courses and demonstrations – those would go down a storm.

"My mind is reeling!" said Rose. "There are loads of ideas – cookery classes, crafts, private tours, perhaps special non-alcoholic cocktail demonstrations."

"Don't panic too much," laughed Olly. "Many of the customers do drink alcohol, so you won't lose all your profits there!"

"Could we reconvene later today when you've had a chance to crunch some numbers?" suggested Eva.

"Great idea – and thank you for this fantastic opportunity! We're all really excited," said Jamie. "In the meantime, folks, we'd better try and mend our bridges with the local paper and social media."

"Can I offer to speak with the paper?" said John. "The editor's another of my golfing buddies and I think he might be equally interested in a scoop on a sabotage effort and all the new attractions you are offering here. Strangely this could work to our advantage."

"We'll see you later," said Eva. "We're off to visit some of our favourite haunts from previous trips – would Ian be available?"

"I believe so," said Pearl. "I'll give him a ring."

Once everyone had gone their separate ways, Rose turned to Jamie, beaming, and hugged him hard.

"I can't believe this is happening – do you think things will work out OK?"

"I don't know – unless we beat whoever is trying to wreck our lives, it could go from bad to worse."

"But now there's so much to look forward to, and so many plans to make!"

"We'll see," said Jamie. "We'll see."

Chapter 14

"Yvonne! It's so good to have you back – how are you feeling?" Rose gave Yvonne a hug.

"Why I'm fine – I could've come back yesterday but these two ladies were enjoying themselves too much and wanted to keep me out of their kitchen, I reckon!" Yvonne gestured to Pearl and Kathleen, just taking some scones out of the oven.

Pearl wiped her hands on the tea towel she had tucked into the waistband of her apron. "I'm going to miss being in the kitchen, it's been fun – once I got over the shock of it all!"

"Never mind Pearl," laughed Kathleen. "Now we're dismissed maybe we should celebrate and go shopping."

"Good idea, Kath. Right – if nobody needs us, we're off to town for some retail therapy." Rose knew that Pearl would miss Kathleen when she went home, but at least there was another week or so to go before she and John left.

"Anything special you want me to do?" Yvonne asked Rose.

"Let me think. Nina's singing seems to have brought locals in each night this week… perhaps you could come up with some ideas for small bar snacks?"

"Sure, I'll get my cookbook out! It'll be nice to have some different dishes to make."

Rose could hear noises from upstairs, and thought she'd better check what Shane was up to. As she entered the bar there was a loud 'squawk' from one of the speakers at the back of the room and a puff of smoke.

"Damn," Rose instantly recognised the female voice. "Nina?" There was no sign of the singer, but then Nina appeared from under a nearby table. "I'm trying to fix my speakers. They're horribly antique but do the job. However, this one has decided to give up the ghost and I want to be able to sing tonight."

"Is it something my Dad might be able to sort out? He's quite handy with electrics."

"Happy to let him try – Shane is a liability with anything practical, and as you can see he wasn't sufficiently worried to meet me here this morning to at least give moral support. But I think I must apologise to you, I jumped to a very unfair conclusion and my behaviour was just plain wrong."

"I was wrong to hurt you too, it all happened on one of the worst days I have had since arriving here and you were just the last straw, I hope we can get past this. Despite our personal issues I'd hate to see you and Shane having problems. Is there anything I can do to help?"

"Not unless you fancy murdering Tilly and a few others in the neighbourhood… probably not. It's past helping."

"But Tilly is part of the group – aren't you all friends?"

"Friends! You're joking… she's just an outrageous flirt and thinks it's amusing to catch a guy, especially if he's attached to someone else in any sort of permanent arrangement! You can't trust her."

"Oh…" Rose wondered quite how to respond. "Let me go and find Dad and see if he can get your speaker working again."

She started her search for Ted in the kitchen. "Yvonne – have you seen Ted today? Any idea where he might be?"

"I have indeed – pleased as punch he was! Just picked up his replacement car… after that…" Yvonne tailed off and Rose hurried to reassure her. "Don't worry Yvonne – we all talk about it. And how stupid of me to forget – I suppose he'll be down by the garage playing new cars!"

Rose was right. Jamie, John and Ted were indeed talking cars. "Pretty hot you got the upgrade Ted, almost makes it all worthwhile."

"Hardly son, but yes – nice thing to happen. The garage had no basic models and they wanted to get rid of this one, so yup – a free upgrade. Look at those wheel rims – pimp my ride, eh? Isn't that what they say?"

John and Jamie were chortling at Ted's joke. Rose thought it was great to see the men she loved most laughing together. "Hiya! Sorry to break up the boys' club, but we have a minor electrical emergency in the bar – Dad, could you help? Nina's speaker has blown up and she isn't able to mend it. I don't have the faintest idea."

"Sure my love, I'll come and have a look. Not sure I know enough about speakers, but it can't be that difficult."

"I might be able to help," chimed in Jamie. "I was in a band for a while and we were always blowing them up – think it was a protest about our bad playing!"

"I'm no use at all, unless you want to sue someone for them blowing up!" John laughed, pleased with his own joke.

"While I've got you all here, how about a barbecue tonight and a browse through Dorothy's old photographs – would that be fun? Everyone up for it?" There were nods all round. "If any of you see Kathleen and Mum before I do, tell them too. They're off shopping at the moment."

"That'll be Kathleen's idea – she has some huge and important mission, apparently. Oh dear – maybe I shouldn't have said anything…" John faltered.

Ted raised his eyebrows. "I didn't hear anything – did you, Jamie?"

"Nah, nothing."

Ted and Jamie strode off towards the main building to sort Nina's speaker. John and Rose followed at a slower pace. "Dorothy would have been proud of the way you're slowly rebuilding the hotel. She knew what she was doing when she left it to you. If she'd left it to any of the vampires in her family…" John hesitated. "Sorry – that was rather unprofessional of me, but…"

"Only stating facts, Mister Solicitor. I often think back to the reading of the will. They were all beyond belief – I'm so glad we don't have to see any of them."

"I can't guarantee that. It used to amuse Dorothy that occasionally some of her relatives would stay at the smart hotel along the bay and have no idea that she either lived here or owned a property. Once she spotted them in town and had to hide in a shop doorway!"

"Please promise me I won't ever have to do that!"

Still laughing they arrived in reception to hear loud music coming from the bar. "That was fast – my Dad's good, but I'm not sure he's that good!"

They peered round the door to see Nina up at the microphone, singing along to her backing track: clearly everything was sorted. Ted and Jamie stood nearby, listening. "That was fast, Dad?"

"Heavens no, not down to me. That speaker went 'pop' and is probably dead unless the lass gets someone to put new circuitboards and Lord knows what else inside it. Seems Nina's made a useful discovery."

When Nina spotted Rose, she stopped singing and rushed over. "Look, look what we found!" She pointed to a collection of speakers and a couple of guitars sitting next to the stage. "We?

218

Where did you find them? What a stroke of luck."

"I just pointed the girl in the right direction," came a deep voice from behind her. There stood Soli, toolbox in hand. "Plenty stored away here that folks might not know was around."

"But that's a lot of money's worth of kit," said Jamie. "Indeed," replied Soli, "played by a lot of money's worth of people in the old days. We always kept stuff so they could play if they fancied."

"But who?" said Rose.

"A lot of bands and performers you've probably never heard of, but they were good. Now I must be on my way, just checking the last bits of the roof, making sure it's safe for you Rose." Soli smiled, but his eyes were sad as he walked away.

"Where were they, Nina?" asked Jamie. "There's a big storage space under the veranda at the back. It seemed dry and all these instruments were under there with a whole load more stuff. You should go and look."

"We certainly will," said Rose. Nina carried on practising her set and Rose thought how talented she was, even if she did have a bit of a fiery temper!

It was a good morning for everyone. Rose took a couple of bookings in the office. Jamie enjoyed playing with the Fender guitar they'd found. Rose didn't want to nag and get him back to work; he was clearly having fun, and was quite an able player. Ted wanted to wash his new car as there had been at least three specks of dirt on it and John had disappeared, no doubt to read on his balcony, which seemed to be a favourite pastime.

After lunch, Kathleen and Pearl came back loaded with boxes and carrier bags but refused to show anyone the contents until they were all gathered together. Rose rushed to meet them: she always liked surprises, and surprises that involved shopping sounded perfect! The others were all summoned in super-quick time, although Ted was reluctant to leave his beloved car in mid-wash.

"So come on, you two," said John, "let's see what you've bought!"

"You go first Kath, it was your idea."

Kathleen picked up one of the boxes and opened it. "One for you, one for you and one for you! I got one for everyone." She handed round some polo shirts, in aqua blue with a gold-embroidered "The Summer House" logo on the left breast.

"Oh how perfect!" said Rose.

"Stunning, stunning," said Jamie.

"One for everyone?" said Ted.

"Sweetheart, you get one for driving the taxi too."

"Now you show them the other bits." Kathleen giggled at Pearl. "While we were at it we thought we may as well get everything together from the same shop…" Pearl tailed off and opened more of the bags and boxes.

"Monogrammed pens for the bedrooms and reception. Aprons for the waitresses, monogrammed slippers for the guest bedrooms and – my indulgence, though I don't think they charged us for these… monogrammed mugs for you two, Jamie and Rose." She produced a pair of mugs, each displaying the hotel logo and their name.

John feigned displeasure. "And, young lady, how – may I ask – were these all paid for?" Kathleen would probably have ignored a real expression of displeasure, never mind a mock one. "I put it on your card, hope that was OK? I thought there was money left in the initial set-up fund?"

"Harumph," he answered (but with a smile). "Excellent idea I reckon."

Rose felt the barbecue would be fun. She invited Kate, Shane and Nina, and at Jamie's request they rang Tilly and Greta. She had asked Yvonne, too, but she needed to get home straight after work for the children.

Despite the lack of staying guests, the bar was full. Word of Nina's singing was spreading, and Yvonne's bar snacks enthusiastically received: maybe they could set some regular dates. Sparkle had been delighted to do overtime as a waitress tonight, but they would have to think about getting someone more permanent, pondered Rose.

It seemed strange to hear the hotel ringing with music, laughter and merriment. Usually the only sound in the place was the surf crashing on the beach below. Rose went out to the back patio where her mother and Kathleen were laying out cutlery and glasses, while Ted lined up bottles of beer and drinks. John sat at a nearby table. "I thought we could look through the box of photographs, just the few of us." He was clearly keen to get going.

"Come on!" Pearl agreed. "I'm dying to have a look." As she spoke Kate emerged from the hotel. "OK if I join in? I've been desperate to know what's in it ever since I first heard about it!"

Ted lifted the box onto the large table. "Here you go, folks." Everyone took a small handful of photographs or papers from inside and started to look through them.

"Oh my goodness! Look, LOOK!" shouted Rose, "Look who's in this picture!" There was a holiday snap of several women relaxing on this very patio area. "Who is it?" said Pearl. "I can't see properly in this light."

"Only Princess Margaret," said Kathleen. "I knew lots of celebrities had visited over the years… and John – you always said Dorothy never gossiped about the famous people who'd stayed here."

"Goodness me! Imagine having royalty staying here. I wonder which room she had."

"Looks like we might be able to find out." John fished an old registration book from the bottom of the box. "There seem to be decades of names and addresses listed in here."

Kate squealed with excitement. "Do you have any idea how valuable this is? I'd give anything to write a history of the hotel. Look… look here, this picture." She was hopping with excitement, making it difficult for the others to see the picture properly.

Looking over her shoulder Jamie's eyes widened. "Isn't that a famous pop group from back in the eighties? I don't remember their name."

John showed it to Ted. "I'm guessing many of these stars are more our era than theirs… look here, isn't that Eric Clapton? No wonder there are valuable guitars hanging around. Obviously Dorothy hosted several famous musicians."

"Look at this, though," Jamie was brandishing another photo, "if I remember my politics lessons correctly, that's the President of the United States sitting chatting with our Prime Minister a decade or so ago?"

"This is solid gold," said Kate. "You could have a bestselling book here."

"I'm not sure Dorothy would want to make money out of the reputations of her guests," said Rose, "but if we could find enough material to make an illustrated book about The Summer House, we could sell them in reception?"

Pleased with her idea, Rose turned her attention to a small photograph album that had been lurking at the bottom of the box. "John – you would recognise Dorothy when she was younger – this is her, isn't it?" She passed him the album.

Carefully turning the pages, he said, "Yes, certainly is. I'm not sure I recognise the man in the photos with her – these are real vintage pictures. And they don't seem related to The Summer House – it looks more like England, with those cliffs behind them."

"I wish I knew who the man was." The photo showed a young Dorothy enjoying a drink with someone. "They look so happy." The two seemed very much in love.

"Try taking the pictures out of the sleeves and see what's on the back," said Kate. "I've often found information that way before."

Everyone settled at the table while Rose fiddled with the photos. Most were blank on the back, until finally she found one with something written on it. The picture showed Dorothy with another couple; the same man from the other photographs, and a similarly aged woman.

"Got something!" Rose waved the photo at the assembled company. "It says 'On Eastbourne Beach with Eric and sister Julie Somerville 1970'."

"Jesus Christ!"

"John! Language, dear!"

"Apologies, but that has really shocked me."

"Why – who is he? What's the problem?" asked Jamie.

John answered, "This isn't any old profit motive – this seems to be personal. Eric Somerville is the land developer Rose turned down when she decided not to sell The Summer House. I know Dorothy was engaged once – maybe it was to this man?"

"Wow!" said Jamie. "That gives us an idea who might be behind all this trouble. Maybe we should go and talk to him?"

"Let me think about it," said John. "It's complicated."

"And about to get more so I fear." Kathleen held up a photograph taken from a large brown envelope, again separated from the main bulk of Summer House memories. "Look at this one."

In silence she passed the photo to Rose. It showed Dorothy sitting with Soli, clearly recognisable despite the passage of time. They were holding two babies, twins possibly, only a few months old. The focus was close enough to see that they were definitely mixed race. Kathleen was looking through the other pictures in the envelope. Dorothy with the twins in a flower garden, Soli with the twins sitting on the beach, Dorothy and Soli dressed up to go out and looking very much in love.

John sat quietly. "There has to be a sensitive story behind these photos – whether we want to pry and find out more is another matter. Dorothy never mentioned any children."

The lively atmosphere and happy laughter from earlier had evaporated. Rose spoke up. "Since Dorothy left me The Summer House I feel it's only right that I should find out the truth. After all, if there are children maybe I should share my inheritance with them?"

John patted her arm. "Well done for that generous thought, Rose – many people would have been straight on the defensive. We'll pay Soli a visit and ask if he wants to talk. Perhaps we should scan all these personal photos and take him a set – he might be pleased."

"That's been a bit of a shocker," said Jamie. "Not stating the obvious, of course…" said Rose sarcastically, for some reason irritated by his reaction. She felt completely thrown: not only had they discovered that someone they viewed as their enemy was – perhaps – a past beau of Dorothy's, but also that it looked as if she had children from her relationship with Soli.

"Come on everyone! Drinks and dancing, surely?" Shane came bouncing in, noticing too late the sombre mood of the party. "What's up folks? I expected a lot of happy faces – the bar takings have been through the roof!"

Rose looked up at him. "A few uncomfortable discoveries, Shane. You remember that box of Dorothy's old photos, the one we've talked about a lot?"

"Yes, anything juicy?"

"Cool it, Shane – a bit more sensitivity needed, I think." Jamie shot him a 'shut up' glance. "Sorry, have I put my foot in it?"

"We're a bit solemn, that's all. It seems that the land developer Eric Somerville may have been an old flame of Dorothy's, which would account for his over-enthusiasm for buying this plot. I think it makes him chief suspect as the saboteur, too."

Rose stood up. "Look everyone, let's not spoil tonight. Shane, that's great news about the bar takings. Let's have some food and cope with troubles tomorrow. Look, here come Tilly and Greta." She waved at the girls as they peered uncertainly out of the French doors. She walked over to John, and said quietly, "Perhaps we could pay a visit to Soli tomorrow together?"

"Absolutely," replied John.

They carefully tidied away the collection of pictures, and Ted took them to the office for safekeeping. Meanwhile Kathleen and Pearl brought marinated chicken skewers, sausages and burgers from the kitchen and started cooking. Everyone felt more relaxed, and gradually the cheerful spirit of the party returned.

"As we haven't got any guests in tonight, let's have some music," said Jamie.

"Good idea mate! Nina, could we borrow your iPod?" Shane looked at Nina.

"OK, but don't break it! Put the 'allsorts' list on, it's great for dancing as well as background."

Pearl, Ted, John and Kathleen sat together at the far end of the patio, where they could enjoy the music and still hear themselves talk. Rose felt tempted to join them but didn't want to be a spoilsport. Jamie had drunk several beers already, and was clearly having a good time. Ted valiantly tried to join in and dance, but first Pearl dragged him back to his seat, and Kathleen the second time.

Rose bopped and danced but it was a real struggle. Her head was bursting and she felt dizzy, yet she hadn't drunk a drop of alcohol. Eventually she knew the only sensible thing to do was retire to bed and hope everyone would forgive her. Jamie seemed disappointed, but Shane had started talking to him so he waved her goodnight and turned away. She went over to the older group and explained her headache.

"Just get to bed sweetheart."

"Absolutely, always another day," added Kathleen.

"We have a date for tomorrow?" queried John.

Rose nodded with huge relief and went indoors, taking the lift up to her room to make life easier. She took a couple of aspirin, pulled on a big T-shirt and collapsed onto her wonderfully comfortable bed. She was asleep as soon as her head hit the pillow.

* * * * *

A few hours later she was woken up by a very loud noise which seemed to be coming from downstairs. Still feeling remarkably fuzzy, she peered at the illuminated bedside clock and saw it was two-forty in the morning. The sound of music seemed to be coming from the patio... or perhaps the party had moved indoors to the bar? She wondered whether to go back to sleep or go and investigate.

Curiosity won and she got up, splashed her face with cold water, ran a brush through her hair and slung on a pair of jeans under her T-shirt. Walking downstairs the music was extremely loud. She could hear Eric Clapton's 'Wonderful Tonight', and it made her think about all the photos they had been looking at earlier. So many secrets... and a few in Dorothy's story still to be unravelled.

The party had indeed moved inside, but the numbers were depleted. Kate and Nina were nowhere to be seen; unsurprisingly nor were John, Kathleen, Ted or Pearl. The only person there was Shane who – despite the loud music – was fast asleep on the couch. Rose shook him, then shook him again, harder, receiving just a grunt in return.

"Shane, SHANE!" she shouted, but still no joy. She switched off the stereo. Oddly the ensuing silence seemed more effective at waking him up. "Where'sa… who'sa… wassup?" Rose tried hard not to smile at his groggy response. "Shane – where has everyone gone? And why is the music still playing? It's nearly three in the morning."

Shane frowned. He was obviously struggling to gather his thoughts, having drunk a huge amount and been deeply asleep. "Music still playing, they've gone, lucky him, no one ever suggested that to me."

"What do you mean?" Rose felt frustrated that she couldn't get more sense out of him, but persevered. "Where's Jamie and Tilly, Greta – all of them?"

"Tilly always did fancy him, seems she finally got her man." Shane was starting to doze off again. Rose shook him, and not very gently. "What are you talking about – has Jamie gone off with Tilly?"

"Tilly and Greta – off for a threesome I reckon – leave me out, see if I care. Didn't hear Jamie complaining. That's fine with me – Greta's OK but I don't fancy Tilly – he's welcome."

Chapter 15

Despite feeling it would be impossible, Rose did get back to sleep. As the sun rose she was aware of the rays streaking into her room and she smiled at the warmth for a second – but suddenly the memory of last night's events hit her and she squeezed her eyes shut again in the hopes that she could make it all go away. How *could* he go home with Tilly and Greta? She had thought that they were well on the way to rebuilding their relationship.

The question now was how she should handle it? Could she run the hotel alone? She felt like washing her hands of him, but then reminded herself that they had been working well as a partnership. Should she suggest continuing their business relationship despite his behaviour – could she manage that?

The hot shower was comforting and once she had washed her hair thoroughly and used every special body lotion and potion she could find to make herself feel good, Rose took a deep breath and ventured down to the kitchen.

"Morning love, you sleep OK? You look a bit peaky – maybe you should try and get some earlier nights?" Her mother looked at her with concern.

Yvonne bustled past. "Will you try my new banana loaf?" She was holding a tray of rainbow-coloured slices, garnished with a sprig of flowers and a sprinkling of fresh banana slices and walnuts."

"Fit for a king!" said Pearl. "It looks lovely," added Rose.

Although she didn't fancy eating the smallest morsel she tried some and declared it perfection.

"Rose?" Pearl peered at her. "You're not right – what's up, sweetheart?"

Her mother's kind words were the final straw and despite her prolonged shower, deep breathing, perfume and courage, Rose burst into tears. "Oh my goodness! I knew something was wrong… tell me, tell me?"

"It's Jamie. You know I went to bed early last night as I wasn't feeling well and Jamie stayed on with the others?"

"Yes, your father and I gave in around midnight – we were having such a great natter with John and Kathleen, but…" Pearl faltered. "So what happened?"

"I woke up at about half past two and could hear noises. I came downstairs to find Shane very drunk and fast asleep on the couch. He told me that Jamie had got together with Tilly. If he's to be believed, Jamie left with plans for both Tilly and Greta. I just didn't think he was that kind of person."

The tears became stronger and Pearl held her close. "Come on my love – we'll get past this."

"But how could he? We were mending the past – and we could have been so happy."

"I think we all felt that," said Pearl and Yvonne nodded in agreement.

"How do I think straight… what to do, how to react?"

There was a knock on the open kitchen door and there stood Greta, looking somewhat under the weather. "Rose, could I have a word with you – in private, please?"

"I suppose so," muttered Rose, somewhat unwillingly. She took Greta up to the office.

Rose sat at her desk and swivelled round to face Greta. She

indicated to her to sit in Jamie's chair. She had to try and think how life might be in future. Greta appeared to be struggling to speak but Rose felt very little compassion for her.

"So, your point is?"

"Rose, I have done wrong and I don't know how to make it better. I need your help."

"Need *my* help! Is that so…. That's rich, coming from you."

"It was Tilly's idea. She has this weird thing – she enjoys taking men away from the relationships they're in. I can't tell you how many married men she has seduced."

"Nice."

"Yesterday we were larking around at the bar at work. Anyway, we bet each other ten dollars that we couldn't get someone else's man to sleep with us last night."

"How sweet." Rose was disgusted that Greta and the boys had been such good friends.

"I knew Tilly and Jamie had always had a bit of a thing going and when you went to bed early she went into overdrive."

"You didn't do badly yourself!"

"Shane isn't loyal to anyone and Nina knows that, but Jamie… It wasn't his fault, Rose: she tricked him into stronger and stronger drinks, and she laced his beers with shots of spirits and deliberately got him off his head. At one point the only reason they were dancing is because she was propping him up. He barely knew where he was."

Rose felt worried now. "So why did he choose to go home with you both?"

"Tilly was laughing and teasing me. Shane had passed out – in fact I believe he's still in the bar asleep." Greta stopped for breath. "Tilly insisted that she wanted to take Jamie home with her, and when I pointed out he couldn't walk she bullied me into helping. We rang for a taxi and bundled him into the car. How we got him out the other end, I've no idea."

"But why did Shane make it sound as though Jamie was happy and planning to misbehave big time?"

"Probably because that's what Tilly told him. He was horribly drunk too."

"So what happened next?"

"We got him into Tilly's room. She was getting angry as it was obvious he wasn't going to be doing any of the things that she had in mind for him. He was snoring pretty loudly too, which bugged her."

Rose smiled to herself. Love him as she might she had to admit his snoring was horribly loud.

"Anyway, this morning I went into her room to check if he was OK. We've known the boys a long time and believe it or not I'm fond of Jamie – as a brother," she added hastily.

"And what did you find?"

"Seems Tilly pushed him onto the floor last night as she couldn't face him being in her bed making that noise. Anyway he was awake and he was crying – it broke my heart, Rose. Tilly was shouting at him, calling him a lightweight and pathetic and all that and all he could say was that his head hurt, he felt sick and where were you."

"Really?"

"I suspect that Tilly got him so drunk last night that he had no idea what was happening. Seriously Rose, Tilly's got some kind of kink in her character. She's often sweet and kind but she gets off on pinching other people's men."

"Obviously – but what does she intend to do now?"

"Probably nothing. She finished yelling at him, had a shower and walked out. I assume she's gone to work early. I decided I'd better come and see you as Jamie needs some help. He was given so much bad alcohol last night, I'm desperately worried about him."

As Greta spoke, Rose realised that she loved Jamie too much to turn her back on him now. It did seem as if he hadn't realised what he was doing. "Would you take me to your flat to see how he is? I'd like to bring him back here."

"Could we look in on Shane too?" asked Greta timidly. "I feel bad about that and it wasn't the fun game Tilly said it would be. Trouble is I've always had a bit of a thing for Shane, but I'm not sure he ever thinks of me as a female, only 'good old Greta.'"

John knocked on the office door. "Rose, are you free to go to Soli's?"

Rose opened the door. "Sorry John, could you rearrange? Something urgent has come up and I think I need to sort it out."

"Can I help?"

"No, no it's fine. Just something Greta and I need to do."

"I'll ring Soli and reschedule. You take care."

As he walked away Rose thanked fate for the millionth time that John and Kathleen had come into her life. They were such a special couple, almost like extra parents.

Greta buckled herself into the passenger seat in Rose's car. "Jamie does love you, you know. He's never happier than when he's with you. I've seen him a bit smitten before but with you it's the real thing. Don't let Tilly win. She may not have managed to get him to sleep with her last night, but if you two argue she'll be delighted."

Rose parked outside the block where Greta and Tilly lived, hoping very much that the latter wouldn't be there. When they reached the flat, Greta put her key in the door. There were no sounds from inside. "He's probably asleep."

Greta led her to Tilly's room. Jamie was on the bed, completely still, his T-shirt and jeans covered in fresh vomit. He was lying on his back, but – unusually – there were no loud snoring noises.

"Jamie, Jamie!" Rose rushed over to him. She tried to wake him, but it was no good – panic-stricken, she noticed his shallow breathing. She turned him onto his side in case he was sick again. "Greta. Get an ambulance." Rose held Jamie's hand and prayed. Please God, please – he doesn't deserve this; he's stupid, but nothing else.

Thankfully the ambulance arrived quickly and two paramedics rushed to Jamie's side. "Background?"

"Seems he drank too much last night and his drinks were spiked. I have no clue how much." The paramedics took vital signs and put him on a drip as they took him out to the ambulance.

Rose sat in the hospital waiting room for what seemed an eternity. She got on her mobile to her mother and explained what had happened. Pearl insisted that she and Ted should come down immediately. Rose felt too devastated to disagree but asked that someone should look after reception. Eventually her parents arrived, John and Kathleen staying behind at The Summer House.

After a tense wait of nearly four hours a doctor came into the waiting room and asked for next of kin. Rose stood up, wondering what was coming next. "I guess that's me – I'm a close friend and he has no family."

"I'm Doctor Royston. Your friend has severe alcohol poisoning. Fortunately he's young and his organs are strong. I think with some bed rest and constant fluids he'll pull through. Whether there will be any permanent damage to his liver or kidneys I can't tell you at the moment. I would add that playing around with spiked drinks is stupid in the extreme."

"You don't have to explain that to me." She hoped the serious stare she gave the doctor communicated how she fully understood the situation and had nothing to do with what had happened. "May I see him?"

"For a few minutes, one visitor only." The doctor glared at Pearl and Ted.

"Go on – you go in and I'll ring John."

Rose felt the corridor down to Jamie's room was a mile long. Everything seemed to be going in slow motion, yet she was desperate to see for herself that he was alive.

"Jamie?" Jamie turned his head towards her and winced in pain.

"Don't try and speak, I'm here – keep your eyes closed and rest. Let me sit here and hold your hand." Rose placed a chair quietly beside his bed and sat with him for about ten minutes. He couldn't speak, but their hands were tightly clasped.

A nurse popped her head around the door. "Time's up, I'm afraid – he needs to sleep."

"When can I come back?"

"Technically anytime. We don't have set visiting hours but I'd suggest this evening. Let him sleep through the day and we'll get some fluids in him. He should be much better this evening." Rose nodded, too choked to speak. She kissed Jamie's forehead and left.

* * * * *

Back at The Summer House, all was quiet. "Everything all right?" she asked John as she walked into reception.

"Absolutely fine my dear. More importantly, how is Jamie?"

"He'll be OK hopefully, just rest and some time needed."

"Thank goodness for that. Well, while you were out, Kathleen efficiently took two bookings. Not to be outdone, I talked to a company that wants to have a celebration here in the bar one evening, with Nina singing and some of those delicious snacks. Seemed a nice idea to me."

"We must leave reception to you more often!"

"Shane's still asleep in the bar. We didn't want to disturb him, although I noticed Kathleen determinedly vacuuming right outside the door for rather longer than was necessary."

"I wonder if he'll be fit to work tonight. Poor Jamie won't be working for quite a few days, I'm sure."

"So long as he's going to be all right – your mother did ring me."

As anticipated, Shane was still fast asleep. Rose shook him more gently than she felt like doing. "How do you feel?"

"Gerroff, sleep, grrroff…"

"Shane, you must wake up now, Shane…" Shane opened one bloodshot and seriously unhealthy-looking eye. "Bugger off, more sleep."

"Shane – you're asleep in the bar! What if a customer comes in for afternoon tea? You have to get up – NOW!"

Shane opened the other eye, peered around and shot up when he realised where he was. He winced at the rapid movement. "God almighty – what time is it?"

"Nearly half past two in the afternoon. You need to get up and washed at least."

Shane sat on the couch, running his hands through his hair. "Boy, what a night. Would be good if I could remember more of it…" Shane stared guiltily at Rose. "Jeez, what did happen, Rose?"

"Since I wasn't there, how am I meant to know?" Rose knew it was unkind to string him along but she didn't feel particularly nice at that moment.

"Is Jamie up and about?" Shane looked around warily. He realised something was wrong but was too hungover to work out what had happened. "No, Jamie isn't here and won't be for a while."

"Flippin' heck Rose – don't be mad at him! He was just letting off steam – nothing to get uptight about."

"Nothing at all I should be worried about?" Shane gave her a shifty glance. "Don't remember much, to be honest."

"I'd push you further but you probably can't remember. Friends should be there for each other, but you weren't there for Jamie last night, were you?"

"For God's sake woman quit bugging me! Jamie let down his hair a bit and you weren't there to supervise – so what? Give the guy a break."

"No Shane, you're the one I have to give a break to, because you didn't care enough to give a fig what was happening to Jamie. He's currently in hospital."

Shane rubbed his eyes and stared at her. "What? What happened?"

At that point Pearl came in with a bottle of water and a coffee. She dumped them down on the table near Shane, huffed loudly and left. "She mad at me?"

"We all are, Shane. If you hadn't been so drunk, Jamie wouldn't be where he is."

"What he do, fall over outside?"

"No, Shane: he has severe alcohol poisoning. He's been in hospital the last few hours on a drip and they're saying no visitors until tonight, and then only me. He could have died."

"No way, how much did he drink?" Shane was alternately gulping water and sipping hot coffee.

"Quite a bit, but nothing more than you did, the difference being that Greta is a nicer person than Tilly. As far as I'm concerned Tilly could have killed Jamie and I truly, truly, never want to see her again. She was spiking his drinks."

"Jamie is going to be all right?" Shane was looking down at the carpet.

"Yes I think so. He's still a bit rough but I hope there'll be a real improvement tonight. They can't tell yet if there'll be any permanent damage to his liver or kidneys."

"Jesus! I had no idea what Tilly was doing… daft cow, what was she thinking? I was stupid too. When Nina finds out it'll be curtains. She's wonderful, but I guess she deserves better than me."

"Maybe she does, but for now I'd appreciate some help. For starters we need a barman by about six tonight and you need to sort things out with Nina. She's on tonight, and judging by her recent success it might be quite busy. If you want food, Mum's down in the kitchen with Yvonne – they'll find you something."

Rose went back into the office and sat at her desk, her emotions running riot. Initially she had been uncontrollably angry, but now she realised how nasty Tilly had been she felt sorry for Jamie. She also felt a bit helpless and wondered how to cope with the anger and resentment she felt for someone who seemed to enjoy creating such chaos in other people's lives.

Kate knocked on the door. "Anybody home?"

"Oh hi Kate – come on in."

"So how's Jamie – and equally importantly, how are you?"

"Jamie will be all right I think. I hope to get better news this evening. How am I? Hard question… screwed up I think is the correct answer!"

"The saga continues, I'm afraid. Greta rang Tilly at work. Greta told her she'd rung you and that you'd had to call an ambulance. Tilly launched into an avalanche of abuse, said Greta had no loyalty, and Jamie would have been fine until she got home. Seems Tilly then lied to their boss and ten minutes later Greta didn't have a job anymore."

"Wow," was all Rose could summon.

"On top of that she told Greta to leave the flat and said their friendship was over. Anyway there's a happy ending to the story: I have a spare room and could do with the extra cash, so Greta's moving in with me. All we have to do now is find her a job."

"Not sure we should make any moves on that front. I need to find out how Nina feels first. The last thing I want is to give Greta a waitressing job and find out that Nina won't work with her because she's been playing around with Shane. Mind you, it depends how much Shane chooses to tell her…"

"I suspect Nina won't be surprised. I had a long chat with her last week and she mentioned that Shane was great but not her forever guy and felt it was right to cut him loose. I think she's had enough of 'the playboy' and would rather have no one than someone she couldn't trust to come home after work."

"Talk of the devil!" Rose spotted Nina walking towards the office doorway. "Nina – hi."

"Hello you two. I've just come from the bar – don't worry, but I've split up with Shane. I think the correct terminology is 'had enough already'!" She smiled, and the other two sighed with relief. "There's no animosity, no bad blood, but we won't be under the same roof at night again. There are plenty more fish in the sea… and less predatory ones at that."

"So are you all good to sing for us during the week?" asked Rose a little anxiously. "Of course, I love my job and I'll have no problem working with Shane – we can still have a laugh together."

"I'm hugely relieved! We were worried about you after what happened last night."

"So tell me – what did happen? I got some garbled thing from Shane about how I should feel glad he wasn't in hospital like Jamie and I shouldn't be unkind." Rose gave Nina a quick update. The singer was clearly shocked.

"No? Really? In hospital? How could Tilly do that? She and I have had a few run-ins, but I guessed she hated me being the centre of attention."

"Absolutely right," said Kate, "she needs to be the most important person in the room and apparently it was a laugh to catch men. I suspect that girl has issues, but we'll never find out! So Rose, big favour – could you see your way to giving Greta one of the new waitressing jobs in the bar?"

"I don't see why not – I can see you need to protect your new flatmate's share of the rent! OK with you, Nina?" Nina nodded and they all laughed.

The rest of the afternoon passed in a blur. Rose tried to get on with various tasks but her thoughts constantly strayed to the hospital and Jamie – and she realised they had left his belongings in Tilly's flat. She rang the hospital and asked if he'd had anything in his pockets and they said no wallet, no phone.

Rose sat for a few minutes and wondered what to do. She went down to the bar to see Shane. "Have you got a moment?"

"Sure," he replied. He was restocking bottles and, although moving much slower than usual, his giant hangover seemed to be on the wane.

"I have a problem. I've realised that Jamie's wallet and phone must be at Tilly's. Greta has been thrown out and I have no way of getting them back. I don't want Jamie to fret about them."

"No problem – that's one way I could redeem myself for last night." Shane winced. "I'll nip over right now as she'll probably be home between shifts."

Rose touched his arm. "Thanks Shane – I just want everything sorted out."

About twenty minutes later Shane reappeared, not looking at all happy. "Rose?" he peered round the office door. "Not good news – she wouldn't let me in and is refusing to speak to any of us."

"That girl has made me angrier than I've been in a long time – and that's saying something, remembering the nasty bloke I used to work for back in England. I'll have to fight fire with fire." Shane raised his eyebrows as though he wanted to ask what she was planning, but thought better of it and slunk back to the bar instead.

Rose picked up the phone and dialled an internal number. "John? Could you spare a minute?"

"Why sure, come on up."

Rose knocked on the door of John and Kathleen's bedroom. Kathleen opened it and welcomed her inside. "Do you want me to make myself scarce, dear?"

"No Kathleen, nothing you can't join in on too."

They sat on the balcony and Kathleen made tea. Rose opted for a bottle of water instead and let the sun warm her face in an attempt to calm herself down.

"Right, I have a situation with Tilly. She has basically blown a gasket, chucked Greta out of their flat, lost Greta her job and is now refusing to see Shane or anyone to return Jamie's wallet and phone."

"Goodness me! What a nasty piece of work," said Kathleen as she poured John's tea.

"I was wondering," said Rose, "if we should get really tough? Could Jamie bring a suit against Tilly for nearly poisoning him?"

"I suppose…"

Rose interrupted. "`Could speak to your friend the police chief? We could frighten her with a visit from the police and they could insist she hands over his belongings, and tell her not to leave town or some such?"

"I'll speak to him. I'm not sure they can stop her leaving town, but I might be able to arrange a visit."

"Thanks John. I don't want Jamie upset any further. I assume her game is to make Jamie go round there and beg for them back and that's not happening… ever."

John promised he would do what he could. Rose set off downstairs to the office, feeling a lot happier; she knew John would fix it.

The phone was ringing when she returned to her desk. It was the sister from the hospital ward querying whether she intended to visit this evening. Jamie had come round properly and had been asking for her, but another female had also been on the phone asking for visiting times, saying she was his sister. Rose told them not to let anyone else in as there was a police inquiry into the incident and Jamie had no sister, so it all sounded a bit suspicious.

She put the phone down, hoping she would be forgiven for telling a whopping lie about a fictitious inquiry. But stretching the truth, she told herself, might stop Tilly getting anywhere near him.

She couldn't concentrate on anything work-related, her mind too muddled, but somehow the afternoon passed and the time came to go back to the hospital. Thinking how little Jamie had eaten she wondered if fruit would go down a treat, so raided the kitchen for grapes and some peaches.

The hospital receptionist was friendly and Rose realised that her heart was thumping with a mix of anxiety for Jamie and general hospital fear. She reached his room and hesitated before knocking. There was no answer, but she opened the door and went in. Jamie was lying with his back to the door and seemed asleep. She walked around to the far side of the bed and saw to her consternation a few teardrops rolling down his cheeks.

Her heart went out to him. "Sweetie, are you OK? I have been so worried about you."

Jamie reached for her hand. "Come and sit with me. I've never felt this bad before – I thought I was going to die."

A nurse bustled in and overheard what he said. "Yes Mister

Jamie sir, I bet you do feel bad and if it hadn't been for your fairy princess here you might have died. Stupid man drinking that much, what were you a thinkin'? Trouble with all you men, drink first, think later." She checked his vital signs, entered a few notes on the chart at the end of his bed and nodded at Rose. "He'll be all right darlin' but yes he was bad, touch and go, it's gonna be a day or three. I wouldn't stay too many minutes."

Rose moved a chair close to the bed and sat down. Leaning forward she took Jamie's hand and stroked it gently. "You'll be OK – we'll soon be through this. They seem nice here, and the days will pass quickly. You probably feel sleepy most of the time anyway."

Rose realised she was prattling on out of anxiety and being in an unfamiliar situation. It probably didn't matter, as Jamie seemed unable to say much. "Everything and everyone back at home is fine. They all send their love. Especially Shane who is feeling stupid too today, I think. There have been lots of changes in the last twenty-four hours. Tilly has evicted Greta, who has gone to live with Kate, we have given Greta a waitress job and…" Kate stopped talking as Jamie was fast asleep and probably hadn't heard what she said. She kissed his forehead and slipped out of the room. The nurse at reception said tomorrow morning and evening might be best for visiting as what his body needed right now was sleep. Rose nodded and left.

Back at The Summer House there was quite a jolly atmosphere, which puzzled Rose a little. Everyone was sitting around in the bar, Nina was singing, beautifully as always, and there were a couple of locals listening. Kate and Greta were also there (a new friendship blossoming there, thought Rose). John and Kathleen were laughing heartily, and Rose frowned as she joined them.

"What's the joke?"

Pearl chortled, "Oh grab yourself a drink sweetheart, this is a story you have to hear!"

Shane beat her to it and brought over a sparkling mineral water with some slices of lime. Rose took a sip and closed her eyes. The cool liquid tasted sublime – who needs alcohol, she thought? "Let's hear the story."

John uncrossed his legs and leant forward. "I may have slightly crossed the line but I didn't do it alone, so I'm not taking all the blame… but I'm deeply sorry."

There were peals of laughter and Rose felt at a loss. "Sorry?"

"You asked me to ring my friend the chief inspector? So that bit's not my fault…"

As he trailed off Kathleen nudged him. "John, get on with it."

"He was rather taken with our plight and said it sounded as though the young lady needed taking down a peg or two. He organised a couple of officers he knows well to go round and ask for the return of the phone and wallet."

"And?" Kate was leaning forward now as well.

"Seems these officers did find Tilly at home. She opened the door to them but when they requested the return of Jamie's property she refused and tried to slam the door. This seems to have annoyed them somewhat so they told her she was under arrest for theft of one mobile phone and a wallet and proceeded to attempt to handcuff her."

"Wow," said Rose. "Anyway she went crazy and kicked both officers, stamped on the female officer's foot and gave them an absolute torrent of abuse."

"That seems an unwise move – what did they do?" Rose looked pleased at this turn of events

"As we speak, the young lady is behind bars at the local police station – for resisting arrest and assaulting a police officer. She'll be seen in court tomorrow."

"And the final touch?" said Kate, looking at Rose and Greta.

Greta spoke up. "I'm afraid I was angry. I rang her boss, my ex-boss, and returned the compliment she'd already paid me. I told him Tilly couldn't be at work for a day or two as she had been arrested for GBH and was currently in prison and going to court, and that he might need to find someone to fill her shifts for now."

"Mean," said Rose, "that's what we are – but it does feel good! Tilly will talk herself out of everything, no doubt, but at least she hasn't got away scot-free. Perhaps there is some justice in this world, after all."

Chapter 16

A week later (during which time Rose missed him terribly at the hotel) Jamie was back at work, happy to be behind the desk and chatting to guests. Rose suggested he did shorter days, until she was sure he was back to normal. His bout in hospital had shaken everyone, especially the younger members of staff, Greta, Yvonne and Kate. Despite Shane swearing he would never touch a drop again he only lasted a couple of days, but did seem to be taking it steady. Jamie too was saying he could never drink again and determinedly drinking mineral water or diluted orange juice. Rose wouldn't mind that being the case but she felt sure a small cold beer might lure him back before too long.

Tilly had been let off with a fine, but blamed everyone else for her problems and left the island to resume travelling. Rose was relieved they wouldn't have to deal her again.

A few days after his return, Rose was doing a shift on reception. She looked up to see two couples approaching the reception desk.

"Good morning!" she said brightly. "How can I help you?"

"Chalmers and Britehouse – we rang earlier. Two double rooms booked for this week."

"You have indeed, sir. Can I ask you both to fill in registration forms?" She produced two pens. "I hope your journey here was good?"

"We had an easy journey," one of the women began, "we only

had to drive along the coast. We were staying at…"

Her companion glared at her and interrupted, "Suffice it to say the other guests at the hotel were not to our liking. When one is staying at an expensive supposedly high-class hotel, the last thing one expects is nudity, unbridled sexual displays and drunken antics."

"Absolutely Madam, I do understand." Rose glanced at one of the men, wondering if the male members of the party may have been less outraged than their wives. "I hope you'll be happy here. We're quiet at the moment, and you should have nice peaceful evenings. Our talented singer appears in the bar several times a week, a not-to-be-missed event. Please note too that the gardens, veranda and patio are all at your disposal."

"No other guests?" asked one of the women.

"Not for tonight and tomorrow, but after that we have a party of four arriving. However we only have six bedrooms available so we're never overfull. We like to give our guests privacy, almost as a second home."

"See I told you! Eva and Olly always get it right – we should have listened to them in the first place."

"Ah, Eva and Olly – yes, they've got several bookings arranged and will be joining us again next week with a party of guests." It was interesting to hear how much clout the Christian Travel newsletter was having. They had taken dozens of bookings for the next few months. It was truly their lucky day when Eva and Olly discovered them! "I hope you have a wonderful vacation. Be sure to ask us if you want anything – we want to make your stay here perfect."

"See dear, that's how management should be – not the rude young man that virtually told me I was a prude. Their loss – we'll spread the word."

"Would you care to have a seat? We'll get you some

refreshments and take your cases up to your room?" Rose indicated the voluminous, comfy-looking sofas.

John came out of the lift and headed towards the desk. "Morning Rose, I'm off for a round of golf but I'll be back for our appointment with Soli this afternoon – OK Rose?"

"Yes, I'm all set for that too, I feel bad that we've had to delay, but hopefully he understood." Rose was looking forward to finding out more about the children in the picture and Dorothy's life on the island.

"Oh, no problem there. My golf game is a bit of a red herring, actually. I'm playing with Derek from the *Barbados Advocate* – it's a good local paper and should have a decent archive. I'm hoping there might be a chance of looking through them for information on Eric Somerville, see if there's any mention of him and Dorothy."

"It might give us a clue about why he seems dead set on scaring us off."

"I suspect that motive is purely financial, Rose. I may be wrong, but the prospect of gaining millions of pounds always brings out the worst in people. Right, I must make a move – I'll see you after lunch."

"Sure, have fun on the golf course!"

Yvonne came up with iced tea for their new guests and promised to bring some into the office too. Jamie took their cases up to the two rooms that Pearl had meticulously prepared. When he returned to reception Rose offered to take the guests up and show them their rooms.

"Oh I think we're rather enjoying sitting here, if that's all right with you It's wonderfully cool – I do hate the heat but it has to be borne. Simply all of my friends from the country club are coming to Barbados these days. My dear, these cookies are simply divine. You must ask your cook to give me the recipe – I could make some for the next bake sale."

"I'd be delighted, Mrs Chalmers. In the meantime I'll leave you to enjoy your tea and come back and take you upstairs in, say, ten minutes?"

"Perfect, my dear – now you go and chat to your young man," replied Mrs Britehouse. Drat, thought Rose – was it that obvious to everyone?

She passed Yvonne as she went back to the office. "They're raving about your new cookies! Could you write out the recipe for them? Would you mind?"

Jamie helped himself to his third cookie and Rose raised one eyebrow. "Do I get more than one, or am I on a diet?"

Jamie laughed. "Oops, sorry! I just keep eating." As he spoke he eyed the remaining cookie. "Go on then." Rose thought if she got desperate there were bound to be loads more in the kitchen.

"The rich and famous at their previous hotel obviously didn't go down well with Mrs Britehouse and Mrs Chalmers." Rose flicked through their emails, mostly spam again.

"All the better for us," replied Jamie. "I can't believe how brilliant the numbers of bookings are thanks to Christian Travel."

"I did wonder if we should, perhaps, allow Eva and Olly to stay here free as a thank you?"

"No Rose – that's a typically generous idea, but we've already struck a strong deal with them for their group visits and we always go the extra mile when they're here – I think that's enough. We do have our future to think about."

Rose reminded herself how often Jamie came up with a brilliant idea or guided them in a better direction than she might have chosen. They made a perfect team. She felt happy that they seemed to be talking about the future, too... but was he talking about the hotel, or their personal future together?

Once John had returned from his golf game Rose asked Jamie

if he wanted to come and see Soli. He declined, saying it was a personal visit and he was best staying behind holding the fort.

So Rose and John set off across the island to the parish of St John, on the eastern coast overlooking the Atlantic Ocean. They drew up beside a neatly kept hedgerow with swathes of bougainvillea clothing an entrance archway. The house was brilliant white, almost glittering in the hot sunshine. Before they'd knocked on the door, Soli opened it and greeted them with his beautiful smile.

"I'm honoured by your company. Please do come in. I have prepared some cold drinks for us."

"Hello Soli – thank you for inviting us." Rose stepped through, John behind her. "Come through, I have the fans switched on."

Moving through the house they saw much evidence of Dorothy's role in Soli's life. Pictures adorned the walls, and a particularly large framed black-and-white photograph of Soli, Dorothy and two children took pride of place over the mantelpiece. It seemed strange to Rose that Soli should have many reminders of their life together yet Dorothy hadn't talked about it to close friends like John and Kathleen or her mother.

They sat outside on the porch on wonderfully romantic rattan furniture with old-fashioned fans whirring above them. Soli had made a jug of iced lemonade and the whole scene was picture perfect.

"Thank you for seeing us. My apologies in advance if we're interfering or being curious when it's none of our business." John sipped his drink and made an appreciative face. "Nice lemonade, Soli – thank you."

Soli stretched out his legs. "There comes a time when it's good for stories to be told. Sometimes we leave it too long and then it's too late. I didn't get a chance to say goodbye or thank Dorothy for the good times and I'll regret that to my dying day. I only hope she's a'waiting up there for me and I get my fill of what to say to her."

"Did you know that she mentioned you in her will? She said to be sure to contact you first about any work that needed doing on the hotel. Do you think that was a message that she wanted us to meet you and talk?"

"I like to think it is. I ain't ashamed of the years we spent together, though she turned against me towards the end. I cherish every day I spent with her."

John replaced his glass on the table and leant forward. "Is it too much to ask what happened, Soli?"

"I don't rightly know where to start, but I guess startin' at the beginning works for most folks."

"That would be wonderful if you could." Rose smiled encouragingly at him.

"Well," Soli picked up his glass and took a contemplative sip. "It was back in the early days when Dorothy bought the hotel. It needed a fair bit of work and we got the contract to help out. We did roofing and carpentry, painting and so on, and turned our hands to anything that needed attention. Seemed I was there every day for a year. Every day this lovely lady would come out with drinks for us guys and I soon got to looking for her and our chats got longer each day. She was a beautiful lady and I fell in love with a bang, quite irresistible my Dorothy."

Soli fell silent again, obviously thinking back to those days, and Rose wondered if they should say something. But Soli continued. "So I talked to my friends and asked them what I should do, whether I should tell her how I felt and ask her out. Times were a bit different back in those days – Dorothy was the rich white owner of the hotel and I was a lowly black carpenter. It was a difficult match."

"So what did you do?" Rose felt saddened by the barriers that had no doubt affected many people at that time.

"I had a bit of rum for courage one afternoon, flask in my pocket. When she brought out our tea, I took that courage in both hands and asked her if she would care to go for a walk on the beach."

"How lovely!"

"I have to say it could have gone either way – I was scared. She might have been offended and thrown me out of work."

"No," said John, "not Dorothy."

"You are right; she said yes, and the next Sunday afternoon after church I turned up at the back door of the hotel and we went off to the beach. We talked and walked, we laughed and for me it was heaven come down on earth. I often think back on that day."

Rose worked out that it must have been thirty or forty years ago now that this first date had happened and yes, Dorothy must have been quite brave to defy convention and go out with a local carpenter.

"I could talk for days about sweet moments she and I had on walks and picnics. We never dared go into a restaurant, but had fun in our own way. We decided being together mattered more than what people would say, and at last Dorothy moved in with me. She worked at the hotel during the day but came home to me at night."

Rose loved the courage that Dorothy had shown in following her dream.

"I asked her to marry me, maybe a hundred times, but she never would. She felt we were happy enough as we were and she didn't need comments from my family or her friends to spoil a truly special relationship.

"Your family?" said John.

"Sadly my mother was a bit stuck in her ways and was angry that I didn't get together with a nice local girl and have loads of grandkids that she could show off to her friends. She pecked away at Dorothy, always a nasty comment or a put-down. It was mean."

"That's terribly sad." Rose felt one tear escaping and she wiped it away.

"Then one day the Lord decided it was time for a miracle. Dorothy had been feeling very unwell for some time so I persuaded her to go to the medical centre and they found she was pregnant. I can't tell you the joy and the celebrations that went on for so many months till our babies were born."

"Babies?" said Rose.

"Yes, the good Lord decided in his wisdom that we knew how to look after two babies at the same time and sent us twins!" Soli smiled and then was silent for a while, deep in thought.

Rose finished her lemonade and poured another glass for herself and John. They waited for Soli to go on.

"These pictures remind me of such happy times. The twins were called Joseph and Maria. The choice of names pleased my mother and Dorothy always did anything she could to keep the family peace."

Soli sipped his lemonade and then went to refill the jug. Settled in his chair once more, he continued the story. "She never gave up her glamorous hotel – it was different back then. All these big names in the films and royal people, it was like the stars in the heaven had come out to play every night. Dorothy managed that even with the children. She employed a nanny, Deborah she was, a good woman, and when Dorothy could she took time away from work to be with them. I worked most days of course, but there was always the weekends."

John shot Rose a glance and nodded towards Soli. The older man's eyes were filling with tears. "Soli – I feel bad bringing back these sad memories for you. Please say if you would rather stop."

"I'm fine. I think it's doing me good to talk – nobody much wants to listen to old Soli these days. The next part of the story is especially hard to tell. One day I was across the island working and Dorothy had organised a day with the twins. She made them such a beautiful picnic, I expect the cooks at work had helped with the food but it was always the thought that counted." Soli swallowed hard.

"They were all having fun in the garden. Joseph and Maria were eight years old and a real handful – they were always wilful but sweet with it, you always forgave them. Seems the telephone rang and of course there were none of these portable phones in those days. Dorothy ran into the house to take the call and it was the hotel with some problem or other and she was a bit longer than she meant to be. She always maintained she heard nothing… When she went back outside, Joseph and Maria were nowhere to be seen."

"No, my God, I can't bear it, were they OK?" Rose was making no headway with holding back the tears now and Soli wasn't far behind her. John passed her a clean white handkerchief, shaking his head sadly. "They weren't, were they, Soli?"

"No sir – they had squeezed under the front gate and she saw them playing in the road just on the bend. She shouted straight away but they just looked up at her – frightened of being punished, perhaps? Anyway, they ran further away. At the same time a petrol tanker came around the bend. The driver couldn't possibly have seen them. When the ambulance arrived, they were both pronounced dead."

"How devastating for you all. But for Dorothy having to watch… just a nightmare."

"The doctors had Dorothy on pills for a year but she wasn't sleeping right, nightmares every night. I tried to help her get over it and suggested we could adopt a little one or two; the good Lord knows orphaned children need love and a home. She blamed herself completely – if she hadn't been speaking to the hotel, if she had been five minutes quicker... We barely spoke – it was as if part of us had died. After trying to live on like that for several years we had a family dinner at my mother's house. Like I said my mother was not always a good person but I have to believe she was not evil. During the meal Dorothy left the table to use the bathroom and as she passed the kitchen she heard my mother telling my sister that it was all Dorothy's fault and if I'd married a good local girl and lived a normal life, someone as careless as Dorothy wouldn't have killed those children."

"No!" Rose couldn't hold back. "That's horrendous! Poor Dorothy – what happened next?"

"Dorothy took the car and ran away. I got my brother-in-law to take me home. I found out from my mother what had been said and I wish I could say she was repentant but I have my doubts… she's gone now, rest her soul."

"What did Dorothy do?" asked John.

"She took all her clothes from our house and moved into the top-floor suite at The Summer House. She barely spoke to me again. I tried often to talk with her, but she would shake her head and say it was all her fault. Gradually I gave up and finally I heard that she had gone back to England and wouldn't be coming back. That was a fair few years ago now."

"I'm guessing that would be about twelve years ago. Did you get the letter she left for you when she died?"

"I did," said Soli, lifting his head to look at John.

"I hope it gave some comfort?"

"It did sir – she apologised for the hundredth time which she had no need to, but she did say she had loved me. But felt she had ruined my life and that my mother was right, I should never have bothered with her. There was a cheque enclosed but I have never put it into the bank. I don't need her money."

"The money is sitting there waiting for you…" John hesitated.

"She wanted you to have it. She mentioned you had a project… if it's what I think it is, surely not taking the money is wrong?"

Soli gazed at John and Rose. "You're right – I never got past the fact that I couldn't take her money – I didn't stop to think what good that money could do. It's still waiting, you say?"

"It is, Soli. I opened a special account so no matter how long it took, the money would be there."

"Would it be rude of me to ask what the project might be?" Rose had an idea what it was, but didn't want to say the wrong thing. "Dorothy and I did discuss helping the orphanage and I think that's what she would have been talking about."

"It was. She wanted you to build an extension and renovate the existing building which would make many children's lives more comfortable."

"In that case sir, I'll take the money, for the orphanage, and we'll see what could be built. That's one big cheque and I reckon I could make a difference."

"That's the best news I've had in a while! If you need any help please do contact me in my office in England – and perhaps I could come and visit again when I'm out here? I seem to be coming rather regularly these days." John handed Soli a business card.

"We must be on our way, but please stop for tea when you're passing The Summer House," said Rose. "I think of you as family – it's important that we keep in touch."

Another fat tear escaped from Soli's sad eyes. "That's maybe the nicest thing anyone has said to old Soli in a long while, I appreciate it." He shook their hands repeatedly.

Back in the car, Rose buckled up her seat belt. "That was heart-wrenching."

"Strange – I had no idea about most of that. Dorothy gave me the bare bones of wanting to leave Soli money for an orphanage project and how I might have to encourage him to take it, but that was all. Poor Dorothy – what a burden to carry."

"I hope she had some happy days as well as the sad times we have heard about."

John snorted. "Oh yes, I think Dorothy had her fair share of gadding about and being alternative! Apart from her courage to defy convention and live with Soli she left a trail of glum suitors behind her. One of which I learned more about this morning!"

"Oh John! I forgot your golf game – come on – tell all!"

"No in-depth knowledge but apparently Eric was part of the 'in crowd' when Dorothy first came here and bought the hotel. They partied with the rich and famous and Derek wasn't sure, but he thinks maybe there are some pictures of an engagement party at The Summer House. Maybe Dorothy was engaged to Eric before she flitted off to live with Soli. Eric was considerably younger than her too which was unusual for those days. She was definitely a character. I don't think you should feel too sorry for her, but there were sad moments to be sure."

"Thanks for driving and coming with me, John."

"I wouldn't have missed it for the world, I'm surprised how much of Dorothy's life I don't know about!"

"What are you and Kathleen doing tonight? Jamie and I were planning a sandwich from the fish bar – care to join us?"

"That sounds wonderful – where and when?"

"I have some bits to catch up with, but how about seven o'clock in the bar? We can sit in a quiet corner and eat our takeaway and listen to Nina – I always enjoy that."

"Sounds a perfect evening to me." John waved at Kathleen, sitting with one of the guests on a bench in the flower garden in front of the hotel. "Seems Kathleen has made a new friend."

"Either that or she's doing some PR work for me!" laughed Rose.

Rose spent half an hour relating their tale to Jamie. She felt desperately sad about the accident. And poor Soli, losing the children as well as Dorothy – what a sad twist to his life.

At about six-thirty Jamie offered to go down and get fish sandwiches with all the extras, while Rose sorted out plates and napkins and cutlery. Nina took to the raised stage area about an hour later. They were all relishing their food and listening to the singing while discussing the afternoon's revelations. Kathleen and Jamie both agreed it must have been difficult to hear, but that maybe talking had helped to heal Soli's wounds.

There were quite a few non-residents in the bar, as had become the pattern any night that Nina was singing. Rose was grateful for the customers she was bringing in. Their evening take was quite respectable already and they hadn't expected any bar profits for months.

Nina broke into a song Rose had heard her sing before. After this afternoon's trauma she found it especially touching. 'Amazing Grace' was a time-honoured and much-loved ballad, but Nina gave it a new and intense poignancy. Rose peered round Jamie, sitting beside her. "Is that someone recording her on their mobile?"

"I think you're right," replied John. "Should I stop them? Is that a good thing or not?"

"Hopefully it might be a very good thing." Kathleen delicately mopped some mayonnaise from the corner of her mouth.

"Why?" asked Rose.

"Because that's the lady I was chatting to in the garden earlier on. Lovely lady, Pamela, I think her name was. Seems her husband's tennis partner lives in Nashville, not far from them, and he's something to do with music and records. She thought he might want to listen to Nina."

Chapter 17

"Left, left a bit… careful!" Kate peered over the teetering mountain of boxes she was carrying. "Please, let me take some of those – you'll hurt yourself." Rose took the top two and carried them through the door to reception.

The whole area was a bomb site. There were piles of boxes and tool bags and building materials all over the place. Soli was hammering away at an almost-finished showcase in the far corner, and two men (unknown to Rose) were completing an identical case further to the right.

"Goodness! It's a touch chaotic here – I hope the guests don't mind," laughed Kate.

"I spoke to them all first thing this morning before they went out on that rum tour you organised. I explained that it might be a bit disorganised when they got back, but we've still got a few hours to finish and get the stock displayed… and I see Soli has a couple of others working on them. It may be quicker than we think."

Coralie came over and asked which cabinet was hers. "I'm sure you'd prefer one with plenty of space around it so I've put you over there where Soli is working, and Westin's is going to be here." Kate pointed to an empty space. "I'm glad you agreed to have two showcases. It'll be another forty minutes or so before they're finished – I'd be happy to look after your stock?"

"No, truly – I feel much happier hanging around waiting – and anyway your Yvonne's iced coffee is just special!"

Kate spread her plan on the reception desk and examined it closely. "Soli, what sort of timescale are we on for the last two cases? I'm not nagging, just wondering."

"I'm not completely sure," replied Soli. "My nephew and another friend were due to come and help and they seem to have been delayed, but once they're here there will be three teams. I'm expecting to have the whole job finished inside another hour or so."

"That's fast," said Rose, overhearing. "But would that be a Caribbean hour or a standard hour?" She giggled at Soli.

"Oh, Miss Rose! Let's say a couple of hours."

Soli tested the electrics in the showcase he'd been working on. When the display lights were switched on inside the effect – enhanced by the inclusion of mirrors to show off the cabinet contents – was quite magical.

"That's bright – perfect!" said Kate. "Coralie – do you want to start moving your work in? Yours is ready."

Gradually all five cases came alive. Pearl and Ted came into reception to have a look and Pearl insisted on buying one of Coralie's bracelets (much to Rose's annoyance as she too had spotted it and had been sure her mother would love it for her birthday). Jamie came out of the office and exclaimed with delight. "Wow! That makes such a difference. It literally hits you between the eyes, but in a good way. Thanks Soli – beautiful job on the cabinets. Oh – phone's ringing…"

"It looks fantastic, doesn't it? Now Kate, have you got a sales system set up? The last thing I want is for everything to get muddled and make mistakes with everyone's takings."

"All under control, captain," Kate gave a mock salute. "Stop worrying – everything is going swimmingly. Find something else to worry about."

Rose knew that she was turning into a right old worrier, but events did seem to be running too smoothly and she constantly worried what might be round the next corner. The first of the Christian Travel tour groups was due to arrive after lunch. It would be fun to see Olly and Eva again, and they'd planned lots of interesting extras in the evenings, Nina had chosen several gospel songs to add to her normal repertoire. Yvonne had been practising new bar snacks and Shane had half a dozen non-alcoholic cocktails sorted out. He'd also been practising his juggling and smart repartee skills, which he maintained were a barman's stock in trade. Jamie wasn't sure, but she trusted Shane.

"Mum, are you happy that the rooms are ready and that you have enough help to cope with all our new guests? It's the first time we've been fully booked."

"Yes dear, no dear, three bags full dear! Haven't you got any jobs of your own to worry about? We're all fully prepared, we're on the ball and it'll go with a bang, you'll see."

Jamie reappeared, grinning from ear to ear. "I've got to tell you about that call! Mate of mine that I met on my travels – he's a journalist and has started with the *Sunday Times*. The editor showed him that email we sent weeks ago and has given him the article to write. It's a big deal for Simon and he wants it to be an impressive piece. I explained our history and about the team and the circumstances and he's well up for it."

"Yay!" said Kate.

"When does he want to come?" asked Rose.

"Ah yes… that's a bit of a drawback. He sort of assumed we're larger than we are and would have a room as we're newly opened… He wants to come tonight."

"Good God, what are we supposed to do about that?" said Pearl. "I can't magic up another room at this late stage – at any stage, actually."

"I was planning to be a bit cheeky, since I know what a nice guy he is… Pearl, Ted, would you mind putting him up in your spare room for a couple of nights?"

"Oh Jamie, we can't ask…" Rose was interrupted by her Dad. "Indeed you can, my lad, all hands on deck! Does he need picking up from the airport, though? I might be a bit pushed on that one."

"No, he's fine – he has some other appointment before coming here and said he'd grab a taxi."

"Right – all set!" said Ted. "Come along Pearl, don't forget your bracelet," he indicated the wrapped package on the reception desk. "Let's get cracking and spring clean the spare room, eh? And I'll get you breakfast supplies, or perhaps we should ask Yvonne to let us have some? I've got barely an hour before going to the airport for Olly and Eva's group."

Pearl managed a smile. "Yes, it'll all be fine. Rose. Jamie – you concentrate on the others arriving and we'll make sure the journalist is happy. What's his name, by the way?"

"Sorry, it's Simon, Simon Fullerton."

"Can't ever say it's boring working here! Right, I'm going to check the keys work in the cabinets and the stock sheets are correct," said Kate, smiling.

Jamie turned to Rose. "Why don't I grab some lunch bits from the kitchen and we could sit outside? It may get a bit busy over the next few days – maybe our last chance for some quiet time together for a while?"

"Jamie – that's kind but I'm not sure how much I could eat – I feel nervous… oh come on, why not? Get whatever Yvonne has spare and a couple of drinks and we'll sit on the veranda."

As they sat gazing at the view in companionable silence, Jamie – suddenly a little nervous, thought Rose – turned to face her.

"Would you mind if I talked about the past for a bit?"

"I'm not sure we want to go back over all that stuff." Rose felt disappointed that such a lovely lunch break might be spoilt by some painful memories.

"It's important to me," continued Jamie. "I've avoided telling you as it was never the right time or the right place, and it does matter to me that you know what really happened."

"If you must, then." Rose felt her appetite, what little she'd had, slipping away.

"I had a call to say my mother was in hospital and might not have long to live and was asking for me. It came right out of the blue and I was pole-axed; I had no idea she was ill, no idea what was the matter. I dumped everything and ran to her. As you know my Mum and I were on our own – I've never found out who my Dad was and have no brothers or sisters."

Rose felt guilty for resurrecting the hurt that was showing on Jamie's face, but quickly reminded herself that she had been hurt too.

"I got to the hospital and was told my mother had died twenty minutes earlier. I found it difficult to believe, to breathe, even to exist for a few hours. The nurse who'd been with her for the last couple of days gave me a letter that my mother had dictated to her. It was better than nothing, but a poor substitute."

"What did it say?" Rose could feel a lump in her throat and knew she would be in tears before long.

"Seems she had been suffering from ovarian cancer for a while – over two years in fact – but didn't share it with me because she knew I would put my university plans on hold and she didn't want that. I felt angry that I didn't get a chance to spend the last few months with her but was at uni living the good life."

Rose let the tears fall freely. She felt sad as she had been with him partying and yes, they had been having a great time. "But Jamie – why didn't you tell me once you knew?"

"Honestly, Rose? I went into a horribly dark place. I blamed myself for not being there – I was angry at my mother, myself, the world, God and anyone else I could drag into the scenario. I drank myself stupid, smoked a lot of weed, and was a complete idiot until one day my Mum's neighbour Janet came round and saved me. She looked after me, and cooked for me, and was just wonderful. I'll always be grateful to her for pulling me back from the brink."

"What did you do next?"

"Travel mainly, nothing to stay at home for, no one to care if I was alive or dead…" Jamie stopped as he saw the look of horror on Rose's face. "How can you say that? I was devastated and constantly worrying about you. I would have helped and supported you."

"Trouble was I was insanely angry with everyone and that included you. I hated the fact that we had been happy while Mum was dying. I cut you off to punish you – and myself."

"Oh…" Rose tailed off as she couldn't think what to say.

"I am very sorry I hurt you so badly. It's a poor excuse but I think I wanted the whole world to feel as sad as I did. I couldn't understand why the newspapers had no headlines about her… I half expected to hear her death mentioned on the television news, and of course there was nothing. Honestly Rose, I am beyond sorry for what I did – please believe me."

"Part of me wants to carry on being mad at you, Jamie. It's easier than understanding and rewriting how I feel, but I do feel sad for you. Although I only met your Mum a couple of times I remember how lovely she was. I'm so sorry that you had to handle all that grief alone. I wish you'd got in touch and let me help." Rose got up and went over to him, put her hands each side of his face and kissed him gently.

"Aren't we lucky that we have the chance to start over? I just can't believe we've found each other again. Thank you for being you, Rose," said Jamie, and kissed her back.

* * * * *

The group of twelve from Christian Travel had arrived safely and were clearly delighted when they saw their bedrooms. Olly and Eva smiled like proud parents as saw how happy their tour participants were.

"All right everyone: let's meet downstairs at seven for drinks. I am told there is substantial bar food on offer tonight so we won't need to go out for a meal. I don't know about all of you, but I never feel hungry after a long flight. Dress as you like, but Jack – that means you wear long pants! Barbados isn't ready for your knees yet!" A companionable ripple of laughter went around the group.

"Eva, you sure have made a darlin' choice here – it feels more like visiting family," commented Peggy, Jack's wife.

"Dun't feel nothin' like visiting your family, and that's the truth," muttered Jack. Peggy slapped him playfully. "That's quite enough, honey!"

"So any questions?" No response. "Good. Let's all go and get some rest. Feel free to explore the grounds – you're especially going to love the beach – and we'll see you all later!"

Olly and Eva peeled away to join Rose and Jamie for a drink. The foursome sat outside on the patio, sipping from tall glasses filled with home-made lemonade, ice and mint.

"Sorry we had to make the name change – Brett and Angela have traded places with a couple on next month's tour."

"Not the slightest problem," said Jamie.

"Now that you're all here, is there anything else we can help with? Anything we should watch out for?" asked Rose.

"There are a dozen things I could mention," replied Eva, "but nothing that really needs to be said. Gerry will make a fuss at breakfast if the eggs aren't done right, Charlene will ask for an egg-white omelette and then eat her husband's scrambled eggs, Carrie will take any spare bread rolls and stuff them into her bag as she seems to think we'll be starving them all day and she might save herself fifty cents. Nothing for you to worry about – we know how to handle them from years of experience."

"I'm sure you would like some time to relax – we'll see you in the bar at seven or so."

Once back in the office Rose and Jamie sat staring at each other in disbelief. "Can you believe it? We have a hotel full of guests, they all seem happy, the sun is shining, we have evening entertainment fixed for them – everything has worked out perfectly!"

"Hey hey – cut that out right now – talk about tempting fate! But yes, you're right – it's brilliant, and all down to you, Rose."

"I beg your pardon? I don't think so– without you, Mum and Dad, Kate, Yvonne and everyone it wouldn't have been possible."

"Maybe we're a family that works well together."

Long before seven o'clock the tour group were gathered in reception. Kate had decided to work late as she had anticipated a few sales, and she was quite right.

"Gerry, this would make the best present for our Nadia, and look – surely we must get this for Mrs Olofsson to say thank you for looking after little Pepsi?"

"Yes dear."

"Carrie, have you seen these darling bracelets?"

"Fine for those up to their armpits in dollars," came the huffy reply.

Rose felt thankful that Kate loved the sales side of her job.

Personally she found it hard to fix a smile and remain patient while customers tried to make up their minds.

Just then Nina arrived in reception, with a young man in tow, and waved at Rose. Rose, getting the wrong end of the stick, grinned back. Nina shook her head.

"Nina! Who's your friend?"

"Oh, it's nothing like that! I just wondered if you would let him play a couple of songs tonight? This is David, David Lawrence. David – this is Rose Hill, owner of The Summer House." They shook hands. "I met David down town in the music shop when I was looking for some new sheet music. David was trying out a new guitar… which he finally bought." She indicated the guitar case slung over her companion's shoulder.

"Tonight? OK – if he has your backing and you feel we would enjoy his singing…" Rose felt this was a bit difficult. It was hard to say no in front of the guy, yet she would have preferred to hear him perform before making up her mind.

"Knowing your taste in music you'll love him! Trust me on this one." Rose shrugged. "Sure let's give it a go – maybe halfway through your set?"

"Hope I won't disappoint," said David.

* * * * *

Despite her initial misgivings Rose felt quite excited about the evening. A whole audience in residence, locals arriving already (and it was still early) plus a new singer to entertain them. Simon, Jamie's journalist friend, had also arrived and had come straight to the bar before even seeing his room. He was happily sipping the local rum, clearly enjoying the music and jotting down notes.

Olly and Eva's group were sitting in a circle in the bar, Shane dispensing drinks as fast as he could. Since he had confirmed to Jamie that the non-alcoholic cocktails were every bit as profitable as the alcoholic ones, everything seemed to be perfect.

Jamie gave Nina a nod to indicate that everything was ready, and she stepped up onto the small stage.

"Good evening everyone" (enthusiastic clapping from the locals). "I hope you're going to have a fun evening. I have a whole selection of songs for you, old and new, and I'm happy to take requests – but I might need a day to practise them so do come back later in the week!" An understanding laugh went round the audience.

"I would also like to introduce a new performer to The Summer House, Mr David Lawrence. I only met David a day or two ago but I instantly fell in love with his music and I'm sure you will too! Now to start and get us all in the mood I'm going to sing one of my favourite songs – 'Amazing Grace'."

The soundtrack started. Nina's emotional singing ensured that not a word was uttered, and there were definitely a few tears around the room. She moved on to gospel tunes, pop and some country songs. Shane was working much harder than he was used to but he didn't seem to mind. The drinks were flowing, and Yvonne was rushing in and out with food and special orders. Everything is just right, thought Rose with a sigh of relief.

Suddenly she spotted Pearl and Ted at the door and waved them over. But oddly they didn't move; they looked tense, and she noticed with a start that their faces were pure white. Rose couldn't shout above the music, so she stood up to make her way across the room towards them, but Ted shook his head furiously.

Panic-stricken, she looked around frantically, trying to find Jamie. "Jamie, Jamie, what's wrong? There's something wrong with Mum and Dad." Jamie looked towards Rose's parents and it was then that they both noticed that Pearl was crying. Jamie ignored their frantic signals as he approached them.

"Sit down, or one of them dies."

Instantly the music stopped and silence fell across the room. You could have heard a pin drop.

Pearl and Ted moved apart slightly and the assembled company gasped as a man dressed all in black and wearing a balaclava was revealed, holding a gun to Pearl's back.

"Now if you'll come over here Rose Hill, I'll release your parents unharmed. They're not my intended target."

"No Rose, stay where you are!" Ted shouted. The gunman hit him across the head with his free hand and Ted crumpled to the floor. Jamie, focusing on the gunman, didn't see Rose race past him to reach her parents. The gunman grabbed her, twisting an arm behind her back, and shouted at Pearl. "Out of the way, old lady, or you'll get hurt!"

That provoked an instant reaction from Pearl and she kicked him fiercely on the shin. To everyone's horror there was a loud bang and the sound of gunshot ricocheted around the room. Pearl slid to the floor.

"Nobody move or you'll be next," said the gunman, but his voice was not as level as it had been. Rose was sobbing, and everyone in the room was in deep shock, when suddenly, from nowhere, there came a banshee scream. "Bloody COWARD!" A heavy thud was followed by a crash and the gunman fell to the floor. Standing behind him was Kathleen, her face an angry shade of puce. "I was so angry that he hurt my friend…"

John and Jamie leapt into action and rushed across the room to help Ted and Pearl. John got straight on to his phone to call the ambulance and police services. Rose sank to the floor and cradled her mother in her arms, hoping it wasn't going to be too late.

"Mum, Mum please look at me, tell me you are OK... Mum, I love you so much, please don't go, Mum..." Rose's sobbing made anything else she said inaudible. Ted, ignoring his own injuries, sat beside his wife, crying unashamedly. "Pearl my darling, Pearl, hang in there, we need you my darling, don't let go."

"Let me past," said Jack from the tour group. "I'm a doctor." The crowd parted. He knelt beside Pearl and felt for a pulse. "She's alive, it's a strong pulse – hold on lady, you're going to be fine, and I know it must hurt." He felt along her arm and down her body, checking for the bullet wound. With a gasp Rose noticed blood seeping onto the floor beneath her mother.

Pearls' eyes flickered open. "My darling Rose – far better a bullet got me than you. You know how much I will always love you."

With difficulty she turned towards Ted. "Don't worry darling – I'm a tough old boot. Hold my hand and I'll hang on for you. We have something special and I'm not ready for it to be over yet."

The ambulance crew soon arrived – luckily The Summer House wasn't far from town. "Excuse me, everyone move back please. Let us through to the patient." They found the bullet wound in Pearl's upper thigh. The bleeding was soon staunched and she was loaded onto a stretcher and carried out to the ambulance.

Shane had taken it upon himself to stand over the unconscious gunman, the latter's balaclava threaded with shards of broken glass. As the paramedics carefully cut it away they all recognised their enemy, Eric Somerville.

"How is any land deal worth someone's life? How could he do this?" Rose gulped between sobs.

Ted went in the ambulance with Pearl. A second ambulance took Eric, who was still unconscious. Kathleen and Rose had both been checked over and left in the good care of John and Jamie who recommended a small brandy while they waited for the police to question them.

John sat holding Kathleen close, and Jamie likewise with Rose. Shane yet again came up trumps dispensing 'medicinal' brandies to all and sundry, still sitting around the bar in stunned disbelief at what had happened. Yvonne offered hot sweet tea to those who couldn't stomach brandy.

John turned proudly to his wife. "Can you tell us how you did it?"

Kathleen paused. "I've heard about the 'red mist', and I suppose that's what happened. I saw that man with his gun to Pearl's back and I was so angry. I've grown to love Pearl as a good friend and I suppose the tiger came out in me."

'My little tiger," murmured John, hugging her even tighter.

"I'd noticed there were a couple of glass vases behind the reception desk, so I grabbed one and did an almighty overarm tennis swing towards his head." Kathleen rubbed her left arm. She suffered a bit with aches and pains in that arm on a good day, so this had no doubt aggravated it.

"And very effective it was too, my dear," said John calmly. "No it wasn't – if I'd been quicker he would never have shot Pearl. I blame myself entirely."

"Come on, stop that!" said Jamie. "You are the heroine of the hour, no matter what."

Rose's mobile, laid on the table to make sure she didn't miss a call, began to ring. "Quick, it's your Dad." Jamie passed her the phone. Rose snatched it and pressed the green button. "Dad, Dad – what's happening?"

"Good news, my dear – you can breathe again. Yes, your Mum is badly hurt but nowhere that will cause lasting damage. They're going to operate and remove the bullet. She'll be in hospital for a short while but will make a full recovery."

Rose felt the tears starting again and passed the phone to Jamie. "It's good news, but you'll have to speak."

"Ted, Ted – it's Jamie – Rose is crying too much to talk, you'll have to make do with me!"

"Happy tears I hope, son!"

"Oh yes, believe me, Now what news of you – is your head OK?"

"My head is 100 percent, thank you. But it seems I broke my wrist as I fell. They're going to get that plastered up a bit later – flippin' painful, but nothing like what my Pearl is going through."

"Oh Ted, I'm sorry." Jamie muttered to Rose out of the side of his mouth "Your Dad has broken his wrist." Turning back to the phone he asked, "What about the damned gun guy, Eric whatsisname?"

"He's in surgery as we speak. Tell Kathleen he'll be fine, but he got a hell of a lot of glass in his skull – it'll take a lot of needlework to stitch him up."

"I guess we should be glad Kathleen didn't kill him, but it's hard… Do you need picking up? Or shall I bring over some personal stuff for you and Pearl?"

"If you could bring some bits and pieces please. We're both being kept overnight, so some pyjamas, toothbrush, clothes?"

"We'll be down before long, Ted – and I'm happy you are both going to be OK. We've been so worried."

The other members of the hotel team were being quite brilliant, chatting to the guests and locals, administering free drinks, hot tea and snacks. And at long last Nina started singing quietly. She chose some gentle ballads and David picked up his guitar and they sang some simple duets, which worked well as calming background music.

The police interviewed Kathleen, Rose and all the major

players. As there were so many witnesses and it was getting late, they said they would continue in the morning once there was definite news from the hospital. They felt it was unlikely anyone would be charged except, of course, Eric Somerville.

Jamie asked Shane if he would stay in charge of everything until he got back from the hospital. "Can I say mate, despite earlier signs to the contrary, it seems to me you might be developing into a mega-deputy manager – just saying!" Jamie flashed Shane a smile and got Rose to finish her brandy. He had done his best to get her to stay at the hotel while he went to the hospital but she would have none of it. If there was a chance of seeing either her Mum or Dad she was taking it.

Once they had packed everything they felt might be needed into two small bags. they set off towards town. At the hospital everything was horribly cold and official. They weren't allowed to see either of the patients, but they talked to a doctor who repeated what Ted had told them about Pearl. She had a nasty flesh wound and would be operated on in the morning. It would take a while to heal completely.

Ted had glossed over his own problems. Jamie suggested they should have guessed when he told them he was being kept in too. Ted's wrist was a complicated break and he had banged his head when he fell. He was being checked for concussion and had a slightly irregular heart rhythm so would need observation overnight. Agreeing they would ring early in the morning, Jamie took Rose by the arm and led her back to the car. "I'm worried about Dad."

"Yes, me too, but we have to hope that he's tough enough. The hospital is good and I'm sure he'll be fine. Your Mum's prognosis is good too. But how are you feeling, Rose?"

"I feel a bit calmer now. I'm still shaken up and my heart keeps beating faster when I think about it. I hope I never have to live through anything like that again."

"Me too. When that gunman grabbed your arm I was so scared… I never want to feel like that again."

They drew up outside the hotel and Jamie reversed into his parking spot. He turned to face Rose and took her hand. "I thought for a brief moment that I was going to lose you. I can't tell you the horror I felt at the idea of life without you…." He looked intently at her. "My timing may be lousy, but I've got to ask you something now. Rose, will you marry me? I love you beyond anything – and I know now that my life is only worth living if it's with you."

Chapter 18

It took several weeks for life to get back to normal but both Pearl and Ted were overjoyed when she told them about the engagement. It was almost three months before Ted could drive safely and carry customer's cases, but Soli's nephew Georgie stepped into the gap and made a delightful driver. He insisted on wearing a uniformed jacket and peaked hat, but Rose felt if that was all he demanded it was bearable. He was a real showman, and the customers loved him. Once Ted was better, they decided it would be good to keep Georgie on. He became the baggage carrier on airport trips to save Ted's wrist – and the older man enjoyed the company too.

Pearl took longer than Ted to shake off the trauma. Rose was glad she could take time each day to spend with her mother. They advertised in the paper (the editor kindly didn't charge them) for extra housekeeping help. The new housekeeper Sally-Ann soon charmed everyone, and despite initial wariness over job security she and Pearl became firm friends. Pearl was more than happy to take a step back and become housekeeping consultant!

Eric Somerville had the longest stay in hospital. Many of the shards had penetrated his scalp deeply, and the healing process was slow, but three months on he was close to being released. Jamie took a phone call from the hospital with a request from Eric to have a meeting with Rose. She discussed the idea with her parents, John and Kathleen, and all agreed it might bring closure.

On the day of the meeting Jamie drove her to the hospital. She had agreed to allow him to stay by her side during the meeting. They parked outside the building that housed the long-term recovery patients. Jamie took Rose's hand.

"You don't have to go in and satisfy the old goat, you know – you could ignore him until the trial."

"I need to show some compassion Jamie – unless of course he starts spouting anything horrid at me, when you won't see me for dust!"

"Too true – come on, let's do this." Jamie touched the engagement ring on Rose's left hand gently. "Come on – we'll do this together, like everything."

They checked in with the ward sister and spotted Eric sitting up in bed. He was a sad sight, and horribly scarred. He looked up as they approached and stiffened visibly. "Thank you, thank you for coming Rose – I feared you wouldn't."

Rose realised how different he sounded from the bombastic property developer she had first encountered. They pulled chairs up to the side of his bed and sat down.

"I need to apologise," started Eric. "I'm extremely sorry for any harm I have caused your parents, you, and the hotel. I behaved appallingly, but I know now I was mentally unstable at the time."

Rose looked across at Jamie; this they hadn't expected. "Thank you for apologising. Yes, it's been a hard three months but luckily we have a strong family unit – and I include the staff in that." Rose felt pride rising within her as she spoke.

"I had a meeting with John McKay your solicitor – my assailant's husband I understand. Apparently he's told you all about Dorothy breaking off our engagement…" Eric stopped, rethinking his words. "Although that's all in the distant past I wanted to annihilate anything that reminded me of those years. I became fixated on destroying The Summer House. I apologise… and I'll certainly have enough opportunities to reflect on my actions, not to mention life-long physical reminders."

"I hope they begin to fade after a while, Eric. I'm sorry you were hurt by Dorothy but that's ancient history now. You must forgive us if we find it hard to understand how strongly you felt the rebuff." Rose was struggling a bit and flashed a 'help me' look at Jamie.

"Was there anything else you needed to say, Eric?" said Jamie, "I need to get Rose home."

"No, nothing – I needed you to understand that I realise I did wrong and that I'm sorry."

"Thank you Eric. I hope your scars heal soon and make life more comfortable for you."

"These make sure I can't forget what I have done," Eric lifted one arm awkwardly and they saw it was handcuffed to the metal bed. Rose flinched. "Goodbye Eric."

As they walked back to the car, Rose stared at the ground. "That was horrible, Jamie. I'm not sure whether he was sorry for the unhappiness he'd caused or sorry that he'd failed."

"John said that Eric's legal team plan to plead mental imbalance. I'm guessing he may get long-term care instead of prison. I felt a bit unsure about him, too – it just didn't come over sincerely. I felt a bit freaked out." Jamie took hold of her hand.

"Me too. But I suppose we've done our duty – if we had any. I need to put him out of my mind now."

"OK, let's do just that – we've got loads to do – are we going to get the wedding invitations out this month or not?"

"I've been so slow choosing everything! And I wonder how many we should invite? Probably only enough to fill the hotel, I guess. By the way, I've promised to go dress shopping with Mum tomorrow."

"Are you happy that we close the hotel to non-wedding guests for one week, or should we make it longer – it is Christmas after all?"

"Trouble is Christmas and New Year are such prime times for visitors – Olly and Eva wanted to book a New Year stay." Rose sometimes found it hard to put their needs above those of the business.

"That's it! Why don't we ask Olly to officiate?"

"Sounds good to me, but we can't have a whole Christian Travel group there the week of the wedding."

"True, but surely Olly and Eva could come a few days earlier and we could fit everyone in that way?"

"Good idea! You get onto Olly and see how he feels. Tread carefully, though, as Christmas Day will be precious to him and his flock."

Back at the hotel Rose nipped up to her room to have a quick shower, feeling that the unpleasantness of the hospital visit needed to be washed away. As she finished drying her hair, the internal phone rang and Yvonne asked if she could come down and take a call from some potential guests that she just couldn't handle (code, as far as Rose was concerned, for 'Help!'). She straightened her jacket and checked her reflection, determined to be the professional owner even if they were just being difficult on the other end of the phone.

Yvonne pushed a slip of paper towards Rose on which she had written the names of the callers: 'Wilson-Lawrence'. Rose's heart jumped as she realised that this must be Dorothy's niece and her husband. Did they know that this was the hotel Dorothy had left her?

"Good morning! Sorry for the delay – how can I help you?"

"I demand to talk to the owner or at least a senior manager.

That young girl is totally useless, she should be fired," came an unpleasant male voice.

"You have indeed been escalated to the owner. I'm Rose Hill, owner of this hotel. What seems to be the problem?"

"I'm trying to give you business, good business at that, and the only response I get is that you have a celebrity wedding pencilled in for the date we want to come. What sort of response is that? Surely decent business sense dictates better the bird in the hand than two in the bush? If you only have a pencilled-in booking surely our request for two rooms – a concrete booking with deposit – is the sane choice?"

Rose winked at Yvonne, noticing she looked worried. "I assume you wanted to come and stay over Christmas, sir?"

"You assume right – we want a family vacation of a decent standard without popstar idiots making a hotel completely unsuitable for children."

"Ah I see – you have had bad experiences at other hotels in the area."

"We have indeed. We require help with the children and do not expect to see semi-naked women cavorting in the public pool area."

Rose smiled to herself. What fun it was that he hadn't remembered her name! "I may be able to help, but sadly not with those exact dates. We do indeed have a celebrity wedding confirmed, and will be requiring the entire hotel. Unfortunately I'm not able to release their names – but I think you might understand if you heard who it was."

"Really?" came a woman's voice. They must be on speakerphone, thought Rose.

"Perhaps you would care for a break to look forward to after Christmas? We would be happy to organise interconnecting rooms for you, and maybe a full nanny or crèche facility."

"You would?" said the man. "That sounds a bit more like it. We're not paying through the nose for some teenager to come and play with her phone while the children run riot. Our Tarquin needs sensitive professional handling."

"It would be a qualified nanny, of course, and there would be no extra charge."

Yvonne gave a little squeak. "But…"

"Despite you sounding very young to be a senior member of staff, this is certainly a professional way to deal with good customers." He sounded very pleased with himself.

"Let me arrange the booking for you and take your credit card deposit, sir."

Once she had dealt with Amelia and Neil Wilson-Lawrence (and taken a pretty lucrative deposit from them), Rose went down to the kitchen. "What was all that about?" said Yvonne, quite fiercely.

"First the good news is that Jamie and I have definitely agreed to close the hotel to outsiders and have a wedding party for a week. We're planning to get married on Boxing Day."

"That's excellent news – I hoped that was the reason you said it wasn't pencilled in any more. But why were you nice to them and giving them free nanny services, what was all that about?"

"Amelia was Dorothy's niece. They were truly nasty to us and about us at the reading of the will and I felt it would be fun to show them how we have made good. They'll soon find out who I am when they get here! It may be a bit petty but it pleased me – but could you not mention it to Jamie for now?"

"Absolutely if that's what you want, but you puzzle me sometimes!"

"Rose, Rose – you down there? Come and see this!" Jamie was calling down the stairs from the office. She rushed up to see why he was so excited.

"Look! Look! Simon has emailed me the proof copy of his *Sunday Times* article. It was a real problem trying to make him ignore the whole trauma of that evening and judge the hotel on the rest of his stay… and if he included anything about the gunman they would turn down the article anyway, or pass it to the news desk … but I won him around in the end. And I threw in a free stay for him and his girlfriend next year, too."

Rose skimmed the article and her eyes widened. The whole tone was one of huge admiration and praise. He had turned their story of 'triumph over dilapidated hotel to dream vacation destination' into a fairy-tale review.

"If that doesn't bring in business I have no idea what will!"

There was a gentle knock on the office door. "Sorry – am I interrupting?" Nina stood there, looking uncomfortable. "What's up, Nina? Jamie pulled out a chair for her.

"I hope you aren't going to be too cross with me." Nina looked down at the floor. "Cross with you? Why ever should we be cross with you?" Rose felt anxious.

"Do you remember the guest who recorded my performance on her phone?" They both nodded.

"Remember the name switch you had to make on that first Christian Travel tour? It was for Brett Andersen, an important Nashville music agent. He wanted to get over to hear me the minute he could. Then 'that' night happened and he felt it was right to wait a while before approaching me."

"And?" said Rose excitedly.

"He rang me about a month ago and asked if it would be appropriate to talk. I explained we were all getting back to normal and we had a Skype call and have chatted several times since. The long and short of it is I have agreed to go to America to record some tracks to see what the record companies think – and he's sent me a two-year contract."

"Goodness, oh…! I don't know what to say – I'm so excited! You must be over the moon." Rose hugged her tightly. Jamie was smiling too, and patted Nina's arm.

"I am excited, of course, but I'm also worried about leaving you guys in the lurch. I don't know when I can promise to be back."

"I hope you are so successful you never come back, except perhaps on a starry holiday with your entourage!"

"But what will you do?"

Jamie spoke up. "I'd be happy if we could get David to sing full time for us rather than when you need a break – I love his music. Not as good as yours – obviously…"

Rose and Nina laughed at Jamie's embarrassment. "Funny you should say that – I've already spoken to David and he would jump at such an offer. Shall I get him to ring you?"

Jamie smiled. "We're beyond excited for you. When would you go? I don't suppose we could persuade you to stay till Christmas? Rose and I would love you to sing at our wedding?"

"Is it fixed?" Nina shrieked, and hugged Rose again. Jamie, clearly out of his comfort zone, stood back and waiting for hugging and shrieking to stop. "Yes, Boxing Day – all decided," said Rose.

"Done deal. My Mum's been begging me to stay for Christmas too. I'll ring Brett and tell him I'll be out at the beginning of January – I'm so happy for you guys!"

"If you could speak to David about ringing us to fix the New Year's slots?"

"Will do. Bye for now."

Rose turned to Jamie. "You're quite shy when it comes to women these days – could you not have hugged her?"

"Not really – I still occasionally think of her as Shane's girl."

"Shane is well and truly fixed with Greta these days. They seem to be pretty much permanently together – d'you think she could finally have tamed him?"

"Stranger things have happened," said Jamie, pulling her in for a long kiss.

* * * * *

The following morning Rose and Pearl headed into town to look for a wedding dress.

"Have you got the list of addresses, Mum?"

"Yes dear, I've rung them all and done my research. I think this one sounds best to start with but there are three or possibly four others if you don't mind driving a bit further."

"I'm sure the first one will be fine."

"Oh no, we're doing this properly! I only have one daughter to marry off – I want you to be perfectly happy with your dream dress."

"We don't have very long – it's only a month away, so I think we'll have to be content with what we get."

"You'll be fine – wait and see."

Rose tried on several dresses but none of them worked. Her mother wanted her to look tall and graceful, which Rose felt she could never achieve. She wanted a beautiful style that would also not look totally ridiculous on the beach, as they planned to get married by the ocean and walk back to the hotel for the reception.

Maisie, the assistant in the first shop, was endlessly helpful and enthusiastic.

"I have an easy test: if the bride and her mother cry when she puts the dress on, that's the one. If I have a particularly tough bride, I manage with only the mother crying as a fall-back. Let me show you some more."

She brought out an ivory gown, a colour that would enhance Rose's natural skin tone. It had a sweetheart neckline and layer upon layer of tuile under a beautifully embroidered skirt. "Made here on the island – it's the start of a new range for a small business that puts its heart and soul into every dress."

Rose looked at her Mum, and they both nodded. As Rose stepped out of the changing room Maisie was studying Pearl, and nodded sagely as Rose's Mum began to well up. "Passes my test for sure."

"Oh Rose! You look like a princess – and that embroidery is beautiful."

"I love this one! I'd not planned anything this intricate but this stitching is gorgeous –and I love the fact that it was made here on the island."

Pearl turned to Maisie. "It doesn't need a single alteration – it could have been made for her! May we have this one?"

"Actually this is meant to be the model and it's a three-month wait for a dress at the moment… Sorry – I didn't say that, did I?"

Rose felt wildly disappointed. "I adore that dress – would there be any way I could persuade the person who makes them to let me buy this one?"

Maisie took a deep breath. "Trouble is without a model they won't make any sales until she has the time to make a new one."

"I see," Rose tried not to show how upset she felt.

"But," Maisie smiled at Rose and Pearl's hopeful faces, "the main wedding season isn't until after Christmas… and considering most people plan up to a year in advance, I guess I might not miss too many dresses."

"You made the dress? The new company is yours?" Maisie looked embarrassed and nodded.

Rose clapped her hands with glee. "We're planning to extend our services at The Summer House to weddings next year – I don't suppose you would want to be involved? We could offer dresses unique to the bride and perhaps display one at the hotel?"

"I'd adore that! I didn't know you worked at The Summer House – my friend used to work there but the manager was truly nasty. But I heard that a new lady owns it now, so if you think she might be interested…"

"I think the lady who owns it would be thrilled if you would agree to work with her and her mother on this new venture."

Maisie stuttered and tried to hide her discomfort. "Oh my! I mean… do you mean?"

"Yes, I'm Rose Hill, the owner, and my mother Pearl will be helping me with this new idea. We haven't got far with the planning yet as we have my own wedding to work on for now, but after Christmas – would you help us?"

"I… oh… yes! Yes, it would be a dream come true."

"Seems two dreams are going to come true!" smiled Pearl. "Now off with your dress – we need shoes and all sorts."

Maisie opened a cupboard to reveal several shelves full of wedding shoes. "I'll ring Julie my florist friend – she could bring round some flowers and help you choose what you would like for the big day?"

"You are a real one-stop shop! Thank you – we would love that!"

* * * * *

As the big day got closer Pearl seemed to be even more agitated than Rose. Lists had been written and rewritten. Jamie had been tasked with organising the marriage licence and guests' flights, transport had been sorted with Ted on hand for airport collection, and all Maisie's contacts had helped with plans for flowers. Yvonne took charge of the reception food.

Suddenly it was here. Olly and Eva were flying in on Christmas Eve, despite church commitments. They had no family and felt that over this special Christmas with their Barbados friends they could leave the church at home in the care of other ministers and preachers. The majority of the guests were local, as both Jamie and Rose had made such strong bonds with their staff and friends on the island.

The morning of the wedding dawned bright and sunny as so often in this paradise. Jamie had been sent to Shane's for the night as Pearl insisted that it was bad luck to see the bride on the day of the wedding. They all knew it was daft, but Jamie went along with it anyway.

When they were all ready, Rose sent the four bridesmaids downstairs before her. Their dresses were palest pink: 'rose' had been the colour Pearl wanted, and Rose saw no point in dissuading her. It really suited all four girls: Nina, Greta, Yvonne and Kate.

"I'll tell your Dad you're on your way," said Nina.

Rose got into the lift and gazed at her reflection in the mirrored walls. She was delighted with what she saw and could see a real glow of happiness in her face. So much had happened in this last year. Who could have guessed how her life would change!

The doors sprang open and her father stood waiting for her. He held out his arms, biting his lip in a vain attempt to hold back his emotions. "Come on Dad, don't you get me started! Let's get going." Ted sniffed, and gently took her arm.

The happy, smiling guests were already sitting on pretty white chairs set out in rows on the beach, gentle music filling the air. Then the wedding march started and everyone stood up as Rose, Ted and the bridesmaids stepped down the beach in a measured fashion.

Olly took the service beautifully, and everyone could feel the love and emotional atmosphere surrounding the ceremony. Once vows were given and promises made, they all decamped to the gardens of the hotel, resplendent with arches of bougainvillea and ropes of tropical flowers. Maisie was taking pictures madly for the new wedding business portfolio and the official photographer was snapping left, right and centre.

The tables were placed in the shape of a horseshoe, so that everyone could see and be seen. Yvonne and an army of friendly helpers had outdone themselves, and Rose was aware that Yvonne was fretting at having to sit at the table and not be serving herself.

The speeches were sweet and not overlong. The best man, Shane, took the mickey out of Jamie as always and reprised some of their worst shenanigans when they were travelling together. As the speeches were coming to an end, Rose leant towards Jamie and whispered something.

Jamie stood up. "Would you all excuse us for a few seconds?" He seemed puzzled, and shrugged at Shane. "Poor self-control I'd say!" Shane quipped.

They walked away from the tables and disappeared through one of the floral arches. No more than a couple of minutes later they returned. Jamie had a huge smile on his face.

"Sorry to delay proceedings. Seems my wife felt she needed to tell me something privately and ask my permission to add a speech of her own."

There were huge guffaws all round as Rose stood up. "I want to add to the thank you messages Jamie has already given. We owe you all too much to even begin to thank you properly. But you have all turned my life around, and I want to thank you all from the bottom of my heart. Mum and Dad particularly, you have been superstars."

She coughed, and hesitated before continuing. "Unknowingly, Yvonne was first to almost be in on my secret. I offered extra services to a couple with difficult children, with a free nanny option when they come and stay with us next month. I was thinking that it would be good to have a permanent nanny on the staff. Mum, Dad, you are about to add another role to your portfolio – Granny and Grandpa."

Predictably Pearl cried; Ted tried hard to keep a stiff upper lip, but as the congratulations got more and more enthusiastic he failed. The marriage celebrations were long and happy, and as the afternoon wore on the Barbadian sunset made a beautiful backdrop for pictures. Maisie took the perfect shot of Jamie and Rose holding each other for the first dance, exchanging a genuine look of wedded bliss.